LIFE CHANGER

BJ HARVEY

Life Changer

Copyright © 2021 by BJ Harvey

Ebook ISBN: 978-0-6487638-5-7

Print ISBN: 978-0-6451075-0-0

Edited by Creating Ink

Cover Designed by BJ Harvey

Photo sourced from Shutterstock

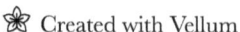 Created with Vellum

Chicago Rom Com World
Reading Order

The Bliss Series
Temporary Bliss (Bliss #1)—Mac and Daniel
True Bliss (Bliss #2)—Kate and Zander
Blissful Surrender (Bliss #3)—Sean and Sam
Permanent Bliss (Bliss #4)—Mac and Daniel Wedding Novella
Finding Bliss (Bliss #5)—Noah and Zoe

The Game Series (Bliss Series Spin Off)
Game Player (Game #1)—Matt and Mia
Game Maker (Game #2)—Zack and Danika
Game Saver (Game #3)—Cade and Abi
Game Ender (Game #4)—Thomas and Amy
Game Breaker (Game #5)—Cameron and Sarah
Game Planner (Game #6)—Jase and Natalie

Cook Brothers Series (Game Series Spin Off)
Work in Progress—Jamie and April
Work Violation—Jax and Ronnie

Working Back—Bry and Faith
Hard Work—Cohen and Skye
Working For It—Ezra and Gilly

Chicago First Responders (Cook Brothers Spin Off)
Show Stopper – Marco and Renee
Life Changer – Rhodes and Dee

Chapter 1

Rhodes

I have a problem. I'm dreaming about a woman I've never even met before. I know who she is. I know where she is. It would just be creepy to meet her—or even initiate contact. But if I don't get this little fixation of mine under control soon, I'm going to end up doing something stupid—more stupid than not paying attention as I turn the corner, about to walk past the object of my obsession's restaurant.

But thank god I am, because one minute I'm frozen mid-step as Dee Duncan stops on the sidewalk outside Delish—she's talking animatedly into her phone before hanging up and sliding it into her purse—the next, a tall, lanky guy in a black hoodie and jeans launches into a run straight at her. At first it looks like she's just going to be knocked over, not that the piece of crap is going to yank her purse off her shoulder and sprint away with it in a middle-of-the-day mugging.

I've closed half the distance between us before I realize I'm moving. When she falls to the ground, grabbing her arm with a cry as she hits the pavement, I'm torn between going to her aid or hunting down the SOB and beating him to a pulp—and I'm not a violent man.

My body decides for me, and I'm bending down beside her, the world grinding to a halt the moment her crystal-green wide eyes meet mine.

"Are you okay?"

"Ye . . . yeah. My purse! It's got my keys and everything in it."

I hand her my phone. My fingers brush hers as I dump the device in her hand, but I don't let myself dwell on how smooth her skin feels—later I will, but right now, I'm on a mission. "Code to unlock it is one, nine, eight, one. Call the cops. I'll be back," I say before I'm on my feet and running after the mugger.

"Wait. No!" Dee yells from behind me, but I don't stop. I round the corner I saw the mugger take and spot his hooded head already halfway down the block. *He probably thought he was home and free. Have I got news for him?*

I'm almost close enough to ambush him, but he glances over his shoulder, his eyes widening before he darts down an alley and takes off. But being a city firefighter means I'm no slouch in the speed department, and lucky for me, I'm a shit-ton faster than he is. And by the time he's halfway along, I'm close enough to swing my arm out and hook my hand in the strap of Dee's purse, jerking the kid to a stop.

I grab his shirt and pull him around to face me. I'm ready to teach him a lesson.

"What the hell, man?" he spits out, his voice full of hot air and bluster that doesn't match the wariness I see in his eyes. His gaze roams my face and perhaps wisely reading my angry expression, he changes tack. "Look, man, no harm, no foul, right? I'm just . . ." He lets out a big sigh, and for the first time, I really take him in. Old worn clothes, a smell not worth mentioning, and a downtrodden demeanor that hints he's more resigned and tired than scared. It occurs to me that he's probably around the same age as my sixteen-year-old son, Jake.

"Right," I say, letting him go and standing to my full six-foot-three height. "This can go one of two ways. You going to drop the macho bullshit and listen to someone willing to give you a break?"

The boy living in a man's world far too soon tilts his chin, but when his shoulders slump, it's clear he's a product of circumstance.

"You stay around here?"

He grunts and averts his eyes. "All around," he mumbles. "You going to call the cops?"

I don't miss the edge to his voice. "Depends if you plan on stealing a hardworking woman's purse again?"

"I—"

I spear him a scathing look, and he crumbles under it. I actually feel sorry for him.

"Nah. I saw her standing there and figured she wouldn't miss it."

"Do you miss having a bed to sleep in?"

"Every fucking day, man."

"It doesn't matter what it is—whether it's a bed, a roof, a hot home-cooked meal, or even a purse, usually, they all mean something to someone."

"I'm just so damn hungry and desperate, and—"

"Over the hard life?"

"Yes!" he spits out, and his anger clearly isn't at me.

"Right. So, how about this." I reach into my pocket and grab my wallet before unfolding a couple of twenties and holding them out for him. He goes to snatch them off me, but my fingers hold firm until his gaze jerks to mine. "You use this to get some food into you, and you let me make a call for you so you have a warm, *safe* bed to sleep in for a few days."

His eyes jump wide. "Whoa. You'd do that?"

"Wouldn't say it if I didn't mean it, bud."

Skepticism hardens his expression, and he arches a brow. "Why should I believe you?"

"Honestly, you're right to question me. But I'm legit. My name is Rhodes, and I work for the CFD. I've got nothing to gain from lying, dude. I've got a son your age, and you're far too young to be living on the street—whatever the circumstance. So instead of calling the cops, I'll cut you some slack. 'Cause something tells me you haven't had much of that lately. Am I right?"

He nods, the relief shining back at me tugging at my heart-strings. If I hadn't already decided to help him, that look would've secured it.

"Good. So, take this." I let go of the bills, feeling verified when he doesn't move to snatch it this time. Instead, he's looking at the money in his hand like it's a lifeline.

"You sure you don't expect anything for this?" he asks.

I shake my head, hating the fact he even has to ask that question. Kids should have time to be kids, not worrying about people's intentions. "What's your name?"

"Pete."

"Well, Pete. Life may not have been good to you yet, but it will. This is me just offering you a break."

His look of relief is all the thanks I need.

"I will ask you to do one thing though. I want you to think of a way to apologize to the woman who owns this purse, because she didn't deserve what you just did to her at all."

"But . . . the cops?"

"Pete, I'll take care of that. I said I would, and I meant it. Now, you know the shelter by Grant Park?"

He bites his lip, and his eyes go up as if he's wracking his brain. "Yep. Three-story brick building. Kinda old, but clean."

I grin. "Yeah. Go in and tell the manager Rhodes sent you. I'll clear it with them, as long as you turn up, Don will look after you."

Pete looks at me with such wide-eyed wonder, I can almost see the carefree teenager he *should* be. *God, Lily would be smiling so big if she could see me right now.*

"You sure?" he asks, his voice turning defensive.

"Yeah. Don's my dad. I'm gonna call him and he'll be expecting you." I lock eyes with the kid once more. "You'll go there?"

Pete nods. "I will. I'll go and talk to Don and say you sent me. And the lady, I'll think of a way to say sorry. Without, like, scaring her. Okay?"

"See that you do," I say, putting my dad hat back on. Pete waves and walks backward before turning around and hurrying away. "And don't eat crap. Get a salad or something!" I yell out to him.

When he disappears from sight, I shake my head, hoping my gut feeling was right.

It hits me that I'm standing alone in a dirty alley, in the middle of the Loop, holding a handbag. *Shit, Dee!*

I make quick work of retracing my steps, and I'm soon rounding the corner near Delish.

"There he is!" Dee says, pointing me out to the cop standing next to her—a cop who looks right at me. His eyes widen before he shakes his head and smirks at me while Dee runs toward me.

"Oh my god, you got it back," she hurries out, taking her purse from my outstretched hand.

"Are you okay? 'Cause that's more important."

She freezes and blinks as if I've surprised her. It's cute as hell. *I may be a big man, but that doesn't make me a Neanderthal.*

"Yeah, thanks. Officer Rossi wanted me to go get checked out at the ER, but I'm fine."

I arch a brow, and her eyes widen.

She holds her hand in the air as if to give me a scout's honor salute. "I promise. I'm okay. My arm is a bit tender, but otherwise, I'm more embarrassed than anything. I should've been paying attention instead of talking on the phone."

I rest my hand on her forearm. "You did nothing wrong . . ." *Dee,* I just manage to stop myself from saying.

She blushes, and I think *that* may be my favorite look on her. Then I mentally kick myself, because it's way too weird to have a favorite *anything* about this woman I've just met in person but already feel like I know after watching her videos. *Am I a stalker now?*

We stand there staring at each other, her purse now hanging over her shoulder, my fingers still on her arm, and if I'm not mistaken, it's almost as if we're having a moment. *God, I've been out of the game so long I can't even be sure anymore.*

"Miss Duncan?" Gio Rossi calls out, walking toward us. I jerk my hand away like I've been caught breaking the law. He nods my way. "Rhodes," he says, his lips twitching.

"G."

"Wait, you know each other?" Dee says, her head shifting between us. "I know Chicago can be a small world sometimes, but what are the odds?"

"Indeed." Gio muses. "Your vigilante here is our family's best friend—well, my brothers and I, anyway."

I open my mouth to explain further, but Dee beats me to it. "Oh, wow. So, it's serendipity, of sorts."

"Something like that," Gio replies. I give him a death glare that *thankfully* he reads before changing the subject. He looks down at Dee's purse. "I take it you caught up with the offender?"

"I recovered the bag and came straight back to return it to its rightful owner. How about we leave it at that."

Gio arches a brow, his expression full of understanding. It's not the first time I've stepped in to try and change the direction of a delinquent teen's life. "You send him to your dad?"

I nod. "Yeah. Whether he turns up there or not is another question."

"Wait," Dee says, speaking up. "You let the mugger go?" Her tone isn't angry. It's . . . curious.

"Yeah. I'm sorry if that's not what you expected. I kind of threw my phone at you, barked out orders, then took off like a bat out of hell. But when I caught up to him, he was just a desperate kid living on a wish and a prayer. He just needed someone to give him a chance."

"Oh wow," she whispers. While in the alley with Pete, I hadn't really thought about how Dee might react to me letting him go, but I didn't expect her to be looking at me with wonder.

"I'll check in with Don and keep my finger on the pulse. Ms. Duncan—"

"Dee, Officer. Call me Dee."

Gio smiles. "Okay, *Dee*. Are you wanting to press charges?"

"Oh god, no. I'm just grateful Rhodes, here, was able to get it back for me. My keys and phone are in there. It would've been a pain in the butt to get the locks changed at the restaurant *and* home."

"And is everything still in there?" Gio asks.

"Damn, I didn't even check. I was too busy thanking my Good Samaritan here." Dee opens her purse and rummages through the contents inside.

"Rhodes is *good* like that," Gio murmurs, and I narrow my eyes at him, which just makes his smirk deepen.

Dee lets out a sigh of relief. "Phew. It's all here."

"Okay, Ms.—*Dee*." Gio catches himself. "If that's everything, I'll leave you both to it."

I don't miss his intimation but choose to ignore it. *Because Lord knows the Rossi brothers won't let me live this situation down anytime soon.*

"Thank you, Officer. Sorry to waste your time," Dee says, holding out her hand to Gio and shaking his. "And I meant what I said. Make sure you come down for a meal. I know I can't give it to you on the house, but that doesn't mean I can't give a heavy discount," she adds with a wink.

"I might just do that, Dee." He turns to me. "Later, hero," he says. I'm tempted to flip him the bird, but since Dee is standing next to me, I'm thankfully able to refrain.

Gio and his partner get into their patrol car and soon drive away.

"I should let you—" I say, as Dee holds out her hand, "Here's your phone back."

Both our eyes widen before she blushes, and a wry grin curves her plush, pink lips. She pulls my cell out from her back pocket.

"Thanks. I'd kind of forgotten about that in all the drama."

"I am truly grateful, Rhodes. Not many people would jump in to help a stranger like that."

I'm suddenly struck with a bit of guilt. *Probably not the best time to admit I know who she is, right?* "I'm a firefighter. Helping people is my job."

Her eyes grow soft and warm. "Oh. Well then, I guess I was lucky that one of the CFD's finest was walking by in my time of need then." *Wait. Is she flirting with me now?*

"It's no trouble, honestly."

"Handsome, honest, *and* humble. That's a dangerous combination, Rhodes."

Yep. Definitely flirting. "Not sure about the humble part."

Her hazel eyes crinkle at the sides. "Ah, gotta be impressed by a man who *knows* his best attributes."

My cheeks burn hot. *What the hell, Rhodes? Man up already.* "I'm just glad it turned out for the best."

"Definitely. Well, I'll let you go, but you *have* to come back for a meal on the house. I can't be seen to be bribing police officers, but since you're not on duty, I can show my gratitude without getting you in trouble."

"It's not necessary—"

"Nope," she says, shooting me a beaming smile. "Bring the family. Make it a big night out."

"That'd be me and my son, Jake. He'd probably eat you out of house and home." I tilt my head toward the building. "Or your restaurant, as the case may be."

"Oh, bring it on. My ten-year-old hasn't managed to do that, and I swear he was born with hollow legs."

I chuckle. "Boys. They keep us on our toes."

"And at the grocery store, it seems," she says with a laugh.

"That too. I'll let you go. I'm sure you're busy."

A flash of disappointment crosses her gaze. "Yes. I have to get home in time for hockey practice, then back here for the dinner rush. But please, Rhodes. Do come back, try the food. I'm a bit biased, but I promise it's good. And it'll fill even the most ravenous growing teenage boy. Make sure to call ahead and I'll tell my maître d' to put you at my table."

"I'll pay my way though, Dee."

She opens her mouth to protest but shuts it when I continue.

"But you *can* repay me by joining *me* for a meal." *I put myself out there. That's progress.*

Dee bites her lip and studies me, as if weighing up her options. For a moment, my heart lodges itself in my throat. Maybe I misread the signs—or she's just not that into me.

Then she rolls her eyes. "Oh, I *suppose* I could be persuaded," she says, a gorgeous, cheeky grin transforming her already beautiful face. "But you better be as charming at dinner as you are now, Mr. Hero. Otherwise, I'll have gotten my hopes up for nothing."

I wouldn't be able to fight my smile even if I wanted to. Flirting with Dee might be my new nighttime dream fodder. "I'll try my best, Ms. Duncan."

She smiles and starts walking toward the restaurant. "I look forward to seeing you again, Rhodes. Hopefully, next time, there'll be no police officers involved." She shoots me a wink then disappears inside the building, leaving me standing on the sidewalk playing back the last thirty minutes to make sure that really just happened.

When my cell starts vibrating with my best friend Marco's name on the screen. I bring the phone to my ear and walk along the sidewalk. Marco is going to have a field day with this since Jake has already told him I watch Dee's cooking videos and going by how soon he's calling me, it looks like Gio is already spreading the word. "Hello. Look, it's not what you—"

"You saved Dee Duncan from a mugging? Damn, Rhodes. You sure know how to make an impression on a girl, don't ya?"

Kill me now.

Chapter 2

Dee

I'm about to leave for dinner with my brother, his wife, and my two nephews when Flynn—my ex-husband and still roommate—walks into the kitchen, having just arrived home.

"Hey," I say, slinging my purse over my shoulder. "How was work?"

"Busy, but good."

Flynn used to work crazy hours, but after experiencing burnout at thirty-five, we did some traveling with Harvey while he took a much-needed hiatus. The bonus being that we got to experience different cultures, and I was able to learn from a ton of top international chefs, expanding my food knowledge and my palate. The downside was that it made us realize we were better friends and parents than partners and lovers. But to keep a steady ship for Harvey, we decided we'd still live together, and life has kept moving on. In many ways, we're better now without the relationship and sex stuff between us than we were when we were married. That's not to say I don't miss dating, lust, and that butterflies-in-the-tummy feeling. Oh, and sex.

"You're home early . . ." I add, turning my ear to the second floor and frowning when I *don't* hear our ten-year-old bounding down the stairs.

"Yeah. My last two appointments canceled, so I decided to come home and see Harvs before you guys left." It's then that Harvey bursts into the room, stopping midway to me before turning toward Flynn and changing direction.

"Dad!"

"Hey, buddy," Flynn says, bracing himself before the boy tackles his waist.

"You said I wouldn't see you tonight."

Flynn ruffles our son's hair. "I thought I'd surprise you before you two go to Uncle E's. How was school?"

"*Sooo* good. We started to plan our science fair projects."

"Oh yeah? And what are we doing this year?"

Harvey shifts and looks around the room for his backpack before running over to it, rummaging inside, and pulling out his science folder.

"Baby, have you brushed your teeth?" I ask.

"Yeah, Mom," he replies, totally distracted by the task at hand. "Here it is." He bounds over to his dad. "See? I'm going to test the friction of shoe soles on different textured surfaces."

"Ah," Flynn replies, glancing up at me. "A physicist, then."

Harvey's brows bunch together. "What's that?"

"Well, your mom's cooking is like chemistry, right? Mixing lots of things together to create something else."

Harvey nods.

"And I'm more a biologist, except I work with kids who I need to make better."

"Yep," our son replies, accentuating the *P*.

"So, you can be the family's physicist. They look at energy and forces and structures and how they affect the world."

Harvey tilts his head, making me smile because that's a mannerism he only has me to thank for. "So, energy is like power?"

"Yep. And speed. Then there's force. The friction of shoes on different surfaces for example."

Harvey's eyes go wide before he grins and fist pumps the air. "Awesome. Billy Nelson can kiss my butt, 'cause I'm *totally* gonna beat him now. He's just doing a boring old volcano." Harvey rolls his eyes like that's the most dull project ever.

"Hey. Don't knock a good volcano creation. You seem to love my lava cake. That's like an eruption, isn't it?" I say, leaning a hip into the kitchen counter and narrowing my eyes at him in mock annoyance.

"Nah, Mom. That's a *food* explosion. That could never be lame."

I glance over at Flynn, who's struggling not to laugh at our son's logic.

"Thanks, Harvs. All I'm gonna think about tonight is your mom's lava cake. And since you two are out for dinner, I'll have to make do with . . .?" He quirks a hopeful brow my way.

I sigh dramatically, but it's all for show. "I brought some spaghetti Alfredo home for you from the restaurant. I'll even let you steal a glass of the Syrah in the pantry to have with it."

"*Nice*. I knew I lived here for a reason," he muses.

I push off the counter with my arm and huff out a breath when I tweak the bruise coming up on my arm.

"What's wrong?" Flynn asks. I have the attention of both father and son now.

"She was rubbing her arm when she picked me up from school too."

I wave them off. "It's nothing."

"Didn't sound like nothing. Want me to check you out?"

Rolling my eyes, I try distraction. "I just knocked it."

Flynn turns to Harvey. "Hey, champ, I've got a book for Uncle Ezra in my room. Can you go grab it? It's the one about European architecture."

Harvey looks to me and then his dad. His gaze is skeptical before he shrugs and runs to the kitchen doorway. "For the record, *A*, I know you're about to talk about something I don't need to hear. I'm ten, not an idiot. And *B*, this is totally the *last* time I run up those stairs. Sheesh." Then he spins around, and all that can be heard are his heavy steps up the stairs .

"Right," Flynn says, all business now. *Damn doctor.* "What happened?"

I sigh as I undo a few buttons of my shirt and push it over my shoulder, revealing not only my bra strap—which is nothing Flynn hasn't seen many times—but a purple bruised line across my bicep from where my bag strap caught before I let it go.

Flynn probes the muscle with trained fingers before pinning me with a stern stare. "Wanna tell me what this is about? Or should I just assume it's something to do with your new video posted today: 'Food to Make a Bad Day Go Away?'"

I start straightening my shirt, making sure it looks the same as it was before since Harvey is due back any minute. I try to stare Flynn down, hoping he'll let the issue go. Unfortunately, he's as stubborn as I am. "Kid grabbed my bag on the sidewalk. It got caught on my arm before I let him take it," I say with a sigh.

"Shit, Dee. Are you okay otherwise?"

"Yeah. I was a bit shook up. I mean, I didn't expect to get mugged outside my own restaurant in the middle of the day. But it worked out in the end." *Even better if Rhodes comes back to see me.* "Honestly, Flynn. My bag and phone were recovered, and by then, the cops had arrived."

"So, you've made a report?"

I avert my eyes, my teeth digging into my lip as I look to the door, willing my son to suddenly appear.

"Dee," Flynn growls. "Damn, I forgot how nice you are."

Harvey runs back into the room, a big coffee-table book under his arm, saving me from answering any more questions. "Got it, Dad."

Thank god for my kid.

"Right, you ready to go, Harvs? I know for a *fact* Aunty Gilly has made a big pot of chili for dinner."

"And ice cream for dessert?"

I smirk at him. "Since when do we *not* have ice cream at Uncle Ezra's house?"

"Yay!" He turns to his father and hugs his waist. "Bye, Dad. See you when we get home."

"Bye, champ. Say hi to everyone for me." Flynn's gaze shifts to me. "Take some Advil. It'll help."

"Yes, Doctor." I smirk.

Flynn shakes his head. "Always a smartass. If I'm not here later, I'm at Sophie's." Sophie is Flynn's girlfriend of six months. She never stays at the house, but she's lovely and she dotes on Harvey, so that's a plus.

"All good. I'm working tomorrow night though. Can you be home for Harvey?"

"Always. Now go. Our son needs his chili and ice cream."

I step in and kiss his cheek. "Have fun, and don't do anything I wouldn't do."

Flynn chuckles. "That doesn't leave much, does it?"

"Shh," I stage-whisper, catching Harvey's smirk. "Can't have our kid getting any ideas."

"You know I can hear you, Mom, right?" Harvey giggles.

"I think we've got our hands full with this tweenager. What do you think, Dad?"

Flynn chuckles. "Have fun, guys. Harvs, look after your mother."

"Will do."

And with that, our son takes my hand in his and leads me to the door, like the mini protector-in-training he is.

IT'S after dinner that my brother brings up the elephant in the room. I didn't feel the need to tell anyone about today's incident because it all worked out, and it's just the embarrassment that I was caught unawares that I'm left with. But then again, I also met a charming, intriguing, incredibly sexy man who flirted with me. I flirted back, and now he may—or may not—come to have dinner at the restaurant sometime in the future. *God, I hope he does.*

"So, I may have heard you had a little fun today?" Ezra says when Gilly, Harvey, and my nephew, Hudson, leave the room in search of ice cream. Ezra and Gilly's daughter, Olivia, is already in bed, having fallen asleep in her high chair during dinner.

My brows go up as I rest my hands on the table. "Is that so? Which little birdie in a police uniform told you that?"

My brother's lips twitch, his eyes alight with amusement. "I don't reveal my sources."

"Bullshit," I say with a laugh. "Gio has a big mouth."

Ezra lifts his wine glass to his mouth. "I would have hoped my little sister would have told me."

"Not so little anymore, big brother."

His eyes turn soft. "You'll always be little to me."

My heart swells. "Stop being sweet."

"I can't help what comes naturally," he says as his eyes turn concerned. "You're okay though?"

I nod. "Yeah. I kind of had a knight in shining armor come to my rescue." *And boy, what a good-looking knight he was.* Well-kept light brown hair, the perfect amount of stubble covering a square jaw, kind blue eyes, and a smile that made me forget all about being mugged.

"Oh?"

I can't help the wry smile that curves my lips at the memory of Rhodes apologizing for letting the kid go. That show of compassion hit my soft spot, well and truly. A man who jumps in to help not one, but two strangers like that is definitely a man I want to get to know better. The fact that he's hot as Hades is just a bonus.

"That smile says there's a story there . . ." Ezra muses.

"Maybe. Maybe not."

"Okay, Dee. I'll let you keep your secrets this time," he says with a wink. "Now what are you doing next weekend?"

I scan my brain. "Nothing much. Flynn is going fishing for the weekend and the restaurant is covered, so it's a mom and son weekend."

"So, movies, baking, and PlayStation then?"

"Pretty much," I say with a laugh. "Why do you ask?"

Ezra is an open book—always has been, always will be. But there's a semi-cautious edge to his expression that piques my curiosity.

"The firehouse is having a barbecue. It's at Skye and Cohen's house this time and we're using it as an excuse to have a final get-together before the baby comes. Everyone you know is going to be there, including Mom and Dad, so it would be cool if you and Harvey could come."

"Aww, that sounds good. Will give us a chance to catch up with

Faith and Bry too." Our youngest sister, Faith, and her childhood sweetheart, Bryant, both work full time. And with two kids under five, a house that they are forever renovating, and my unsociable hours at the restaurant on top of that, we don't get to catch up as often as we'd like.

Ezra shifts in his seat and clears his throat. "I might have an ulterior motive as well . . ."

"Mmm hmm." I take a sip of my wine and rest my glass on the table.

"We've got a friend who we'd like you to meet. But apparently you already did that today…"

My mouthful gets stuck halfway down my throat, and I start spluttering. "*What?*"

"Yeah . . . look, another little birdie—"

"Not the police officer birdie?" Then something occurs to me. "Wait . . . the friend isn't Gio, is it?"

He smirks. "*No,* a different friend this time. Gio is a good guy, but I'm not sure he could keep up with you. He's more of a stay-at-home-and-chill kind of person."

That gets my attention. Because Gio is Skye's brother, and she works with her husband Cohen at a fire station. *Surely the world isn't that small . . .*

"Rhodes Anderson. The man who stepped in to help you today."

Yep. This world is completely too small. What are the odds? "Okay."

Ezra's head jerks back and I know I've surprised the hell out of him. "*Really?*"

"Yeah. It's just a casual meeting amongst friends and family. He seems like a good guy."

"He's a fucking great guy, Dee."

I kind of got that impression, but I'm not going to admit that to you, brother.

"So, tell me about him. I wanna be prepared for this blind date setup."

"It's not a—"

I level my brother with a stare, seeing right through him before throwing my head back and barking out a laugh. "You're so full of shit, Ez. This is totally a setup, and I'm up for it. Does this mean Rhodes knows I'm your sister?"

Ezra's grin widens. "Nope."

I quirk a brow. "You don't think you should tell him?"

"Nope," he replies, just as sure of himself.

"What about the YouTube account?"

"Apparently he already watches the videos."

My body jerks at that. "Wait . . . if he knows about the vlogging, does that mean he knew who I was *before* today? Was he outside the restaurant to check me out?" *There goes my thoughts of serendipity . . .*

"Now that I *can* clear up. He'd just been to see his parents at a homeless shelter downtown and happened to be walking by when you were attacked."

"Okay. That seems like a bit of a weird coincidence." I tilt my head and bite my lip. "Are you *sure* he's on the up and up?" *Surely I haven't been out of the dating game for that long that I can't trust my gut instinct about a guy.*

"Stop thinking so hard and looking for a problem where there isn't one. If it helps, he's a widower with a sixteen-year-old son. He's also a career firefighter who works with Marco Rossi—Gio's brother, by the way, and little birdie number two—which is the same firehouse where Skye and Cohen work."

It makes sense and seems like a logical explanation. But it's a little close to home. What if we don't get along outside of 'just been mugged and checking I'm okay' situations? "Do you ever think this entire friendship/family group is *way* too incestuous?"

Ez leans back in his chair and shoots me a shit-eating grin. "Yep. But there's no pressure here. If you don't want to be set up with Rhodes, he doesn't even need to know. No harm, no foul. But if you do, then a BBQ where mutual friends are there to make it a little less awkward than a straight blind date is a safe bet."

Harvey walks back into the room with Gilly and Hudson, both of the boys carrying bowls of ice cream.

"Did you ask her?" Gilly says before turning to me, not giving Ezra a chance to answer. "Did he ask you?"

I giggle and nod. "Yes, he did, and yes, I will."

"Yay. He's *such* a nice guy. And *hot*," she whispers. "Right, Ez?"

My brother sputters around his mouthful of wine, glaring at his wife. "Hot, baby mama? Really?"

"Hey. I'm married, not *dead*," she says, rolling her eyes.

"I know he's hot. He was the one to help me today when I was mu—" I stop, feeling Harvey's gaze boring into me.

"When you were what, Mom?" he asks.

I look his way. "When I was outside my work."

"Who helped you?" he presses, his ice cream no longer his main focus.

"A nice man. A very good-looking man. And one who seems to think your mom here is all that and a bag of potato chips." Gilly winks at me, and I groan at the impending rapid-fire questions my son will no doubt have.

"Really, Gilly?" Ezra says, chuckling under his breath. "Should I leave you two alone for this conversation?"

"You should do it, Mom. You need more friends. I mean . . ." Harvey shrugs. "You don't go out and meet people. You're always at work or with me. And Dad has a girlfriend, so why can't you?"

"You want me to get a girlfriend?" I tease.

Harvey rolls his eyes and sighs. "You know what I mean, Mom. But I have to like him before you accept a date. Okay?"

My brows shoot up, totally taken aback by this unexpected turn of events. I didn't expect Harvey to be so on board with this but also want to *approve* any man I date.

"Is that right, Uncle Ez? Do I get to approve the guy she dates?" Harvey asks my brother, who nods, his eyes shining with pride.

Ezra ruffles my son's hair. "I think that's fair. We're the two most important men in her life. Well, your dad, too, but that might be a bit weird, right?"

I grimace, because Flynn and I are in a good place. He's moved on and Sophie is awesome. But that's not to say I'm itching to add someone else to the mix. The joys of not dating two years after an amicable divorce. I can only imagine how that would go down. 'Hey, by the way, I live with my ex-husband, and he's my best friend. Wanna meet him?'

Harvey nods and turns to me, his shoulders pulled back, his little man chest puffed out, and a determined glint in his gaze. "Right. You can meet Uncle Ez's friend, but I want to as well."

I hold my arm out, and Harvey comes around the table, stopping right in front of me. "Okay, how about this. I meet the guy, feel him out—" Ezra and Gilly start laughing under their breaths, earning narrowed eyes from me. My son frowns adorably. "I'll get to know him, but before I agree to go out on a date with him, if it even gets that far, then I'll ask your permission."

"You've got my permission, Mom. If you're dating someone, that means he could end up being my other dad, like my friend Jesse has, and any guy that might be my other dad has to treat you right, like my real dad does."

My heart melts. My boy feels deep and he feels hard, and the look in his eyes and the sincerity of his words tells me this is important to him. *God, I love my kid!* "Come here, kiddo. I love you, you know that?" I ask him, jerking him into my arms for a huge bear hug.

"Mmm hmm," he mumbles against my chest.

"So, you'll do it?" Gilly asks, wiping happy tears away from her smiling face.

I nod, looking between my sister-in-law and brother. "Yes. But don't tell him. Let's go for the element of surprise."

Ezra's lips curve into a wicked grin as he rubs his hands together. "I'm looking forward to this BBQ now. Something tells me this one is going to be interesting."

Chapter 3

Rhodes

"Dad! Marco and Renee are here," Jake says from my bedroom doorway.

Looking at him in the mirror's reflection, I frown in confusion when he scans me from head to toe.

"You sure you don't want to wear a nice shirt or something?"

Turning around to him, I quirk a brow. "Sorry, kid. Didn't think the firehouse BBQ was a fashion show."

'It's not," he answers quickly. "But considering you're a lieutenant and all, shouldn't you put some effort in?"

I then realize he's also not wearing just any old clothes he's found on his floor as per usual. "Why are *you* dressed up?"

Jake looks himself over. "I wanted to wear a shirt with my jeans. You should try it sometime," he adds with a smirk. My spidey senses are pinging, but I'm not exactly going to complain about my teenage son putting in some effort. He's a good kid, but he's also a sixteen-year-old boy who's all about girls, sports, social media, and gaming. Pretty much the same as I was at his age, except I already had the girl, I played varsity baseball, and social media consisted of Myspace, not all the different sites available now.

Almost twenty-three years later, I'm a widowed single dad who's contemplating taking up Dee Duncan's offer to one day go into her restaurant for a thank-you dinner. Of course, she probably doesn't see it as anything more than that, but the woman fascinates me even more after the scene outside her building last week. She flirted, I flirted back, and then I had to go, but the chemistry was there. I'm not *so* out of the game that I don't remember what it's like to feel a spark with a woman. I just haven't wanted to have it ignite with anyone in the five years since my wife, Lily, lost her battle with ovarian cancer.

Jake walks over to my closet and rummages through the hangers before pulling out a black short-sleeved button-up and holding it out my way. It's the exact shirt I had been thinking of wearing to Dee's restaurant when I next had a clear night with no work, obligations, or when I wasn't a walking zombie because of said work and obligations.

"Put this on. And do something with *that*." He points to my hair.

"Jake, wanna clue me in on what's going on? Is this more than just a normal firehouse catch up?"

"No. Nope. Not at all," he replies cautiously. "You just never know who might turn up. You said you were open to dating and putting yourself out there. Why not practice tonight? Then we can work on getting you into speed dating or making an online profile for you or something."

"You really are team dating now, aren't you?" I smirk and take the shirt from him. Moving over to the bed, I reach behind my shoulders and tug off my CFD tee before replacing it with the shirt.

It was only recently that I decided I should put myself out there and consider dating again. That just happened to coincide with my

growing fascination with everything Dee Duncan after Jake intro-
duced me to her videos months earlier. At first I thought it was just
another foodie with a god complex spouting their unqualified
dribble about an amazing hamburger they'd bought, but I couldn't
have been more wrong. Dee captivated me from her first smile to
the camera and the following tirade about plant-based products that
did *not* taste the same as the real thing. Then she'd covered non-
animal product ones that—when done right—*can* taste okay. I've
been a meat-eater since conception—all Andersons are—but the
video had even me considering trying something different next time
I was at the grocery store.

"Don't forget the hair," Jake says, walking out of the room. "Oh,
and that cologne I got you for your birthday."

That kid is something else. He's awesome, and I'm proud of the
man he's becoming, but he never fails to give me glimpses of 'what
the fuck' now and then.

After putting some putty in my hair and styling it, and giving
myself a spritz of Bvlgari Man, I slide on my boots and walk into
the newly renovated kitchen and living area to find Marco and his
girlfriend, Renee, standing in a huddle with Jake, the conversation
ending abruptly when they see me.

"Don't stop on my account," I murmur, giving them a suspicious
side-eye as I grab my keys and wallet from the dining table.

"We're just talking about school," Jake says at the same time
Marco says, "Thinking of going to a Bears game."

I look between my son and his godfather with raised brows,
while Renee struggles not to burst out laughing, her eyes sparkling
with amusement before she hides her face behind Marco's
shoulder.

"So . . . school *and* the Bears. That's the best you can come up
with? Really?" I catch sight of Marco's top and shoot Jake a glare.
"Why does Marco get to wear a CFD T-shirt and not me?"

Renee sighs, putting her hands on her hips and glaring at the two. "Jesus, guys. Just tell the poor man."

"And let him stress about it the whole way over there? Were *you* calm before your first date with Uncle Marco?"

Marco smirks at Renee, who looks a little flustered. "Hmm, princess, when was our first date?"

Renee's cheeks turn pink, but she still manages to scowl at her boyfriend while she does it.

To his credit, Jake shakes his head at Marco, tut-tutting in disappointment. "Marco, have you learned *nothing* from me? You don't embarrass your woman in front of company."

"Or at all," Renee mutters.

Jake nods. "Or at all. But Renee knows I'm right. If we tell Dad now, he'll build it up in his head, and just his luck, he'll get nervous and shit."

"Jake . . ." I warn. "Language around a lady."

My son rolls his eyes. "It's Renee. She's hardly a—" He wisely clamps his mouth shut at the shocked expression on said lady's face. Marco just chuckles and hooks an arm around Jake's shoulders. "Hey, bud. Welcome to the doghouse. Get comfortable. It might be a while."

That makes me laugh under my breath—well out of angry-woman-death-stare range.

"Right. As fun as it is to be the only one in the room without a clue, it's not my birthday, I haven't got a new job, and there sure as fuck isn't anything else in my life exciting enough to be celebrated with a surprise party. So put me out of my misery, and just tell me already."

Marco's amused eyes turn to mine. "Rhodes, language around a lady."

"Oh, fuck off, Marky Mark. Unless you're going to tell me what the hell scheme you've cooked up with my son."

Renee's gaze switches between Jake and Marco before she sighs and moves my way. "Okay," she says, stopping in front of me and reaching out to straighten my collar. "Hmm, nice touch with the cologne."

"See, Dad? Told you!"

"Rhodes, stop charming my girlfriend," Marco adds with a sigh.

I roll my eyes, meeting Renee's amused ones. "Okay. You're being set up with a woman tonight, and I don't want you to freak out. Because then Jake and Marco would be right and I'd be wrong, and you *really* don't want them to gloat the whole drive to Cohen and Skye's. *Believe* me. Jake beat us at pool last week and he still texts Marco every day to toot his own horn. So just smile and nod, take a deep breath, and act like there's absolutely nothing to freak out about. Can you do that?" Her eyes bore into mine but it takes a while for her words to register.

"Wait . . . you think I'll freak out? What, is she someone awful or something? I mean . . . did *Scotty* pick her?" Scotty is the equivalent of our station's class clown. He's a good guy, and I trust him with my life every shift. He's just . . . *Scotty.*

"*No.* She's lovely. I just need you to be cool about this, because Marco arranged it, and since Jake found out, he's become kinda invested in 'Operation Get Dad Dating,' which is sweet, but—"

"Potentially setting himself up for disappointment?" I say under my breath.

"Yeah. How *do* you feel about it?"

My lips quirk up. "Haven't met her yet, have I?"

"Oh my god, I can totally see why you and Marco are friends," she says with a laugh. I hook an arm around her shoulder and pull her into my side, catching Marco's narrowed eyes and Jake's cautious expression. "I've already got my date right here, boys. So you two can relax. I've got all the woman I need with Renee."

"Hands off my woman, Anderson."

"Aww, sorry, Lieutenant. Rhodes has got that helpless bachelor thing going for him. And then there's Jake. That makes father and son the whole package," Renee says, rubbing my chest while arching a brow at her man.

Jake is looking at the ground, his shoulders shaking with laughter, and Marco, the possessive idiot, is already halfway across the room to reclaim his girlfriend, making the rest of us chuckle.

"Now, we better hit the road so I can meet this woman you're setting me up with. Who knows, Jake, you might've got it right the first try?"

His head jerks back. "Really?"

"No, ya knucklehead. But I appreciate the positivity."

"Just don't freak out, Dad. Okay? Be yourself, and she's bound to like you. At least enough for a proper date, right?"

"Wow. Great pep talk, kid. And what kind of loser am I when my son feels the need to give me dating advice?"

"You're not a loser, Dad. A little lame, but not a loser."

"Quit while you're ahead, Jake. *Especially* if you don't want me to 'freak out,' as you put it."

Thankfully, I'm not worried. I'm more curious as to who Marco might've set me up with, and why he thought the firehouse BBQ would be the best situation for what is for all intents and purposes a blind date.

I guess I'm about to find out.

Chapter 4

Dee

Skye and Cohen's backyard is full of people, but in the hour since Harvey and I arrived, I haven't been able to relax. I'm nervous—with actual butterflies in my tummy. Thankfully, Mom and Dad and their best friends and lifelong neighbors, Marcy and Rick, are here too, which means that all of the grandkids from the Baker and Cook families are being spoiled rotten, entertained, and well-fed by the oldies. Everyone else is kicking back, talking shit, and enjoying a few drinks. Everyone except me, that is, because I'm a chef, and I can never sit idle when there's food to prep, snacks to make, and dishes to serve. It's just not in my DNA. Yet doing it all while constantly watching the back door and the side gate in anticipation of seeing the man you've agreed to be set up with does not a cool, laid-back, carefree Dee make.

To make matters worse, the gorgeous white shirt I was wearing when I arrived—one I'd chosen because it perfectly showcases everything my mama gave me—is now covered in what looks like a combination of blue cheese sauce, buffalo wing grease, and potentially a side of guac. None of which can be fixed with a quick dab job in the bathroom.

I'm standing by the kitchen sink, busying myself with the accumulated dishes, when a round-bellied Skye walks in, carrying a tray now devoid of the wings. "You need to come to *every* BBQ, Dee. Seriously, your food is *amazing*. If I had any room in this tummy, I'd be begging you to make some more."

I fold the kitchen towel over the rail of her beautiful freestanding oven range and grin over my shoulder. "With a kitchen like this, you'll be able to whip up gourmet feasts yourself soon." I nod at her belly. "After you've mastered the whole new-mum thing, of course."

"Yeah. That'll be a while I think. I've still got a few months to go," she says with a laugh. She walks around the huge kitchen island and stops in front of me. "So, I'm gonna be blunt, 'cause that's who I am, but also, you know I want to see my friends happy, right?"

I hold my breath, her expression unreadable as I brace myself for a 'don't hurt Rhodes's speech.

Her eyes drop to my shirt. "You need to come with me so we can raid my pre-pregnancy closet and fix up this mess. 'Cause I have it on good authority that Marco, Renee, Jake, *and* Rhodes are ten minutes away, and as much as that mess you've made is adorable, it's *not* saying 'Date me. I'm a catch.' Besides, I know the Lieutenant well and I'm sure we can find something *clean* that will get his firehose pumping—so to speak."

My mouth drops open at her candor, but I'm thankful, because I may have looked well put together when I arrived, but my passion for cooking means I'm now more of a hot mess than a hot blind date.

A few minutes later, we're shut behind Skye and Cohen's guest room door and standing in front of a wide double closet filled to the brim with clothes. Skye waves her arm out. "My closet is your closet. It's not like I'll be wearing any of this stuff anytime soon. By the way, your video today was hilarious."

I jut a hip and paint on my best TV presenter smile. "You mean 'What Not to Eat Before a Date?' I was going for funny, entertaining, *and* informative."

"Well, you definitely succeeded there. Cohen wondered what the hell I was cackling about."

I give a fake bow. "Pleased to be of service. And holy smokes. This closet is amazing." I look over my shoulder at Skye. "Do you want to be my sister-wife? Seriously, I'd take a walk on the polyamory side for your wardrobe."

Skye steps forward and starts flicking through her hangers. "Something tells me your living situation is complicated enough without adding wife-sharing to the mix."

"Probably true. But I wouldn't say it's *complicated* . . . Maybe just a little different and unexpected."

She pulls out a white low-cut shirt in one hand and a bright red sleeveless one in the other, her eyes switching between it and me before she shakes her head and puts it back, replacing it with an almost sheer black shirt and nodding to herself. "Unexpected is right. But I respect you and your ex-husband so much for it. I've never met him, but Ezra speaks highly of him."

"Ezra speaks highly of Rhodes too." I wasn't planning to garner information from Skye, but now that she's opened the door, I'm damn well walking inside.

Skye shoots me a wry grin. "Finally! I was starting to think you'd never ask. We've only got five minutes, so we'll have to go with as many questions as possible, rapid-fire style. If I know it, I'll answer. And while we're doing that, I'm going to take my growing cankles and sit down on this bed while you choose between prim and proper and a hint of saucy minx underneath," she says, handing me a white shirt. "Or hot-blooded single woman who's confident, sexy, and putting myself out there with this black one."

I shake my head and look between the two tops, knowing exactly which one is more my style, as Skye crosses the room and gets comfortable on the mattress.

I hang the white one back on the rail and start working the buttons of my ruined shirt. "Okay. Is he a serial killer?"

Skye's head jerks back, a smirk curving her lips. "Unexpected opener. I like it, but nope. Not to my knowledge."

"Is he a stalker?"

Skye's brows bunch together. "He's rather enamored with a certain YouTube food vlogger, but nope. No stalking in his history. He's new to this dating thing—as in, a newborn."

That's surprising. His flirting the other day was far from rusty.

"But the important thing of note is that you're the first person to capture his interest in the past few years."

"Good to know we're on a level playing field then." I slip the black shirt over my shoulders and turn to face the mirror as I do it up.

"You really are. He's a single dad, and you're a single mom, who just happens to live with her ex-husband and have a weirdly healthy, productive, and *civil* relationship with him."

"Flynn and I didn't end our marriage because we didn't love each other."

"You just weren't *in* love, right? I get it."

"Is that weird? Will Rhodes have a problem with that?"

"Rhodes Anderson can be like a bull in a china shop if he's pissed off. He can be quiet and withdrawn if we have a bad outcome at a callout. He's staunchly loyal, will do anything for anyone, has a heart of gold, and a soft spot for those close to him. But I can tell you without a shadow of a doubt that he is *not* close-minded. He lost his wife five years ago and has raised possibly the best teenager I've ever known. So, no, Dee, you have absolutely nothing to worry about when it comes to whether Rhodes is a good man—a *hot* man."

I nod at that assessment before I can stop myself.

"And he may be shocked as hell that you're his blind date, but he will *not* be even one little bit disappointed."

A knock at the door stops me from asking anything else, but after Skye's ringing endorsement, I think I know enough. Skye pushes herself to her feet, shooting me a wry smile before looking me up and down and nodding with approval. "Come in..."

"Y'all better be decent," Ezra says, making me laugh.

"Yes, Dad," Skye replies sarcastically, just as my brother pops his head in.

"Always a smartass, aren't you, Skye?" He glances my way and does a double take. "Looking good, Dee. And right on time, because they're here."

My chest gets tight and those butterflies aren't just fluttering—they're damn near causing a tornado in my stomach. "This is weird. You're all being weird. A setup. At a firehouse BBQ. Who does that?"

"We do," Skye and Ezra reply in unison.

"Take a deep breath. Be your charming self and get down there before your son subjects Rhodes to a Spanish Inquisition, the ten-year-old edition." Ezra's smirk broadens as my eyes widen and my mouth drops open.

Then my brother is jumping out of the way, and I leave a laughing Skye and chuckling Ezra in my dust as I rush out of the room and make a beeline for the backyard.

Unfortunately, I'm too late. As I burst through the French doors leading outside, Harvey's mini-alpha-in-training voice reaches my ears as he looks up at an amused-looking Rhodes, a look-alike teenager who could only be his son, and another couple next to them. What's equally amusing and surprising is that my son seems to have recruited Jamie Cook's son, Axel, to have his back and join his little welcoming committee. And everyone else in the backyard have all fallen quiet, all attention now on the show that's playing out in front of them.

I jerk to a halt and brace myself for whatever Harvey is about to say, because Flynn and I don't filter ourselves around our son, and Harvey is just as protective of his mom as my ex-husband, brother, *and* the Cook brothers. I can never predict what is going to come out of his mouth so this could go either way.

"Hello. I'm Harvey. I'd like to know what your intentions are with my mom."

I'd be shocked if I wasn't slightly mortified, given that he hasn't addressed the question to Rhodes. He's asking the guy who could only be Marco, and it's probably because he's wearing a CFD T-shirt and Harvey knows Rhodes is a firefighter. The *actual* man I've been looking forward to seeing all week is wearing a nice button-up shirt and jeans that hug his hips—and likely his nice butt I couldn't help but ogle the other day. His hair is messy in a styled way, and there's a light smattering of stubble covering his jaw that makes him look all the more handsome.

Marco chuckles and holds out his hand to my son. "Sorry to say, bud. But the man you're looking for is this guy." He claps Rhodes on the shoulder. "But definitely grill him. A man should always look out for the women in his life, right?"

"Yeah, sir. My dad says it's my job to keep my mom happy and make sure everyone else in her life makes her happy too."

Then my not-so-blind date for the evening steps forward and leans down to hold his hand out to dwarf my son's one. But my little man stands his ground and looks Rhodes straight in the eye.

"Hey, Harvey, I'm Rhodes. I'm not sure I've met your mom yet, but you've certainly made me want to if she raised a fine, protective son like you. This is my son, Jake. The man wearing the CFD T-shirt here is Marco, and that's his girlfriend, Renee."

Holy swoon, Batman. All my nerves evaporate, because without knowing I'm here, Rhodes has just proven he's as genuine as the man who stepped in to help me the first time we met.

"Oh," Harvey murmurs, his little head switching between the four adults standing in front of him. Axel puts his hand on my son's shoulder and says something I can't hear before Harvey looks back at his new best friend and nods. "So, Mr. Rhodes, please make my mom happy. She's the very best mom and my favorite person in the entire world—apart from my dad . . . and maybe my uncle . . . oh, and my dog—and she cooks yummy food, and she's always looking after me, and I need to make sure you're not gonna make her sad or cry, because then I'd have to do what my mom and dad say I shouldn't do."

Rhodes's lips twist to one side as he quirks a brow. That sexy, half-puzzled, half-amused look on a man should never be under-rated. "And what's that, Harvey?"

"Kick you in the balls," he deadpans. And suddenly the back-yard erupts into laughter as my mouth curves up with pride. *God, I love my kid.*

To his credit, Rhodes doesn't dismiss Harvey's words or not take them seriously. Instead, he holds out his hand and shakes my son's hand again, meeting his gaze. "Okay, Harvey. I love my mom too, so I appreciate you looking out for your mom and making sure she is treated well. Is she here? I think I'd like to meet her now to tell her what a fine man she's raising."

Before Harvey can reply, Jake's eyes lift and inadvertently meet mine. He stills, his mouth agape as he closes his eyes and shakes his head before opening them and staring back at me. He flashes me what can only be described as a shit-eating grin, teenager style. Then he's elbowing his father in the side and whispering in his ear.

Rhodes's head jerks my way, his blue eyes boring into mine before they snap to a grinning Marco and his beaming girlfriend and a smirking Jake. I bite my lip, focusing on breathing in and out in the mere moments it takes for Rhodes's shock to morph into a dazzling smile. He shines it my way, and it has my knees knocking and my thighs clenching together.

For my first ever setup—my first *date* since my divorce—I think all the little birdies involved have done well. I can only hope it keeps getting better.

Chapter 5

Rhodes

Of all the women I imagined I was being set up with, Dee Duncan would've been at the bottom of the list.

But here she is in the flesh, looking gorgeous and smiling at me, which makes me think she was expecting me.

The idea that this could be a prank flits through my mind, mainly because I'm all too aware that everyone is watching.

Jake is first to move, walking over to her. "Hi. I'm Jake. I'm a huge fan of your channel and food . . . and, uh . . . My dad and I watch your videos. I got him hooked on them. I've even caught him watching them without me. Okay, now I'll shut up, because I'm being a starstruck idiot."

Dee laughs and shakes her head, holding out her hand for my rambling son. "Nice to meet you, Jake," she says, glancing over his shoulder and mouthing *"hi"* at me.

"Did you know?" I murmur to Marco beside me.

"I'm the one who set it up with Ezra."

I jerk my eyes to my best friend, my brows furrowed. "What's Ezra got to do with it?"

Marco's grin widens. "Dee Duncan is her married name. Dee *Baker* is Ezra's sister."

Color me surprised.

"You'd think you'd know that with all your low-key stalking."

"I haven't been stalking her."

He holds his hands in the air. "Oh right, just watching her videos and googling her. Sorry, my bad."

I turn back and see Jake and Dee talking, wishing I could hear what they're saying. Dee nods at my son before throwing her head back as she bursts out laughing.

Marco elbows my ribs, jolting me out of my daze. "Are you just going to stand there staring at the woman or are you going to go up and introduce yourself—again?" he muses. "Because if you don't, Scotty is gonna try his luck a second time, and Ezra already said he's warned him off once. Not sure I like his chances though."

My eyes snap to my coworker in question—a man far too cocky for his own good—as he gets up out of his chair as if to head this way.

Ezra stands, blocking Scotty's path to Dee.

"Shit." When I turn back to Dee, she's leaning against the back deck railing, brow raised, her lips twitching as she looks me up and down as if waiting for me to make a move—literally.

I close the distance between us until I'm standing in front of her and loving the way she doesn't even try to hide that she's checking me out, "Fancy seeing you here, Ms. Duncan."

She tilts her head to the side. "We did say we'd share a meal together, didn't we?"

I chuckle. "Yeah, just not with such a curious audience."

Dee leans in, and a hint of Jasmine hits my senses. "You also said no police officers would be involved, but here we are." She glances toward Gio, who meets my eyes and lifts his beer bottle in the air, sending me a smirk.

If I wasn't standing in front of a beautiful woman I want to get to know, I'd flip him the bird for being a smartass. "In my defense, this was a blind setup. For me, anyway."

"That's an interesting way to ask whether I knew it was going to be you, Rhodes." Her lips curve up as she shoots me a wink.

"Want to come inside and I can get you a drink?" I ask, feeling the weight of everyone's eyes on us

"Absolutely," she says. She must also be aware we're providing entertainment to our family and friends.

I follow her lead and walk beside her into the kitchen. A relieved sigh escapes my lips once we're out of sight. "Thank god for that."

"Not much of an exhibitionist there, Rhodes?"

"Not with that crowd. Do you know how much crap I'll get from Scotty on our next shift? He's like a dog with a bone, that guy."

"He seems harmless. He was asking me all about my restaurant and whether I do private dining."

I groan and shake my head. "I bet he did. And what did you advise him?"

Her eyes dance with humor. "That I'm here to meet a lieutenant and only *he* would get the pleasure of a private dining experience with me . . ."

Wow. Nice. "You don't play games, do you?"

"Nope. Do you?"

I shake my head. It's been so damn long since I've actually *dated* a woman—or been interested in dating one—that now I'm putting all this pressure on myself to perform. *A whole new kind of performance anxiety right here.* "What are you drinking?" I turn toward the refrigerator to see what our options are.

"Hey, Rhodes?" I stop and meet her gaze. When she gifts me a soft, sweet, fucking gorgeous smile, I'm stunned for a moment. "Jake told me to go easy on you."

My brows shoot up, not sure whether that's a good thing or a bad thing. "Did he now?" I reply cautiously.

"Hey, my son told you he'd kick you in the nuts. Yours said you might be a bit rusty with the whole flirting and dating thing, but not to worry because you're a good guy with a huge . . ."

I stare at her, mouth agape.

She giggles. "*Heart*, Rhodes. A huge heart . . . And to give you a chance, even if you're a bit awkward to start with."

"Not sure whether he helped me or not."

"Oh, he totally scored points." She tilts her head. "But it also means he doesn't know we already met, does he?"

I shake my head, my cheeks burning. "Nah. Marco knew because Gio called him as soon as he could, then Marco was in my ear the minute I left the restaurant the other day."

"I swear you men can be as bad as gossiping women."

"You have *no* idea. Especially those Rossi boys."

"I grew up with Ezra and the Cook brothers next door. They didn't let us girls get away with *anything*," she says, snickering.

"So, my son threw me under the bus in terms of being nervous, possibly awkward, and totally out of practice with this whole dating thing. Good to know."

"Rhodes, if it helps, I'm in the same boat. I just hide it well."

I nod and turn to go to the refrigerator before opening the door and checking inside, hiding the pleased—and relieved—smile on my face.

"I'll have a white wine if there's any in there. I've been kind of wired and a little nervous, so I didn't want to drink too much before you arrived."

Not finding any drinks, I close the door and look her way. "You're refreshingly honest, you know that?"

Dee shrugs. "There's no other way to be. If you're always upfront, then no one can ever question your integrity. I'm honest in life, in business, in relationships—all of it."

"Wow," I say, impressed at how down-to-earth and open she is. She scrunches her nose and bites her lip, which of course has my eyes dropping to her mouth and my body getting ideas it definitely shouldn't for a . . . Is it even a blind date if we know each other already?

"Is that a good wow or a 'shit, she's a space cadet—abort mission immediately' kind of wow?"

I nod. "Definitely a good wow. It's an impressed wow."

She preens a little at that, and that small show of vulnerability warms my chest and eases my nerves. Dee doesn't seem to be a woman who fades into the background, and it's that self-confidence and backbone that draws me to her. But any guy will see a glimpse of a soft spot and want to protect it. It calls to the alpha male in me. "The whole way here I've been worried about what kind of woman Marco—and probably the crew, too—would set me up with."

"Then you saw me."

I make a point of looking down her body from her face to her toes and back again, memorizing every single curve as I go. My grin deepens when her breath hitches. "Yep. They get an A-plus for setups. I can relax now."

"Good," she replies. "Because in the interest of full disclosure, Ezra did ask if he could set me up, and it just happened to be the same day that I'd met you."

My brows jump. "Did he now?" I ponder that for a second before moving across the room to Cohen's big icebox, popping the lid open, and looking inside. "And did you know *I* was the friend?" I ask, my voice echoing a little. When Dee doesn't answer, I straighten and look over my shoulder. I'm more than pleased to find Dee's eyes aimed at my ass, and I laugh to myself when her body jolts as she realizes she's been sprung. "Should I stand up so you can get a good look?" I say with a chuckle.

Thankfully, Dee doesn't miss a beat, not even acknowledging the red blush tinging her cheeks. She holds her hands in the air, palms out. "Hey, any red-blooded woman would be a fool not to check out a handsome man's butt." She shoots me a cheeky smirk. "And to answer your question, Ez said your name, and I agreed straight away."

My head jerks. *Fuck, I like hearing that.* "So, you're a woman who knows what she wants?" I walk over to the island where she stands and pour her a white wine before handing it to her.

As luck would have it, Scotty bellows, "Dinner's ready," from the backyard, calling a much earlier end to our stolen time together than I'd have liked.

"Catch up later?" I ask, knowing I'll track her down regardless. All of my worries about who I was being set up with vanished the moment I realized it was Dee. I just want to take the opportunity to spend more time with her.

She lifts her drink in the air and holds it there until I touch the neck of my beer bottle to her wineglass. "To not-so-blind dates," she toasts. "And Good Samaritans who look *really* good in jeans."

That last comment has me laughing when Jake and Harvey walk into the kitchen looking for us.

"IT'S A SMALL WORLD, isn't it?" Dee takes Jake's empty seat. It's the first chance since dinner and speeches that we've had to chat.

"It is. I had no idea that you were a Baker."

I catch a hint of amusement in her eyes. "To be fair, my professional name is different. And it's not like you *know* me as Dee Baker, is it?"

I scrub my face with a groan. "Need I ask what you've been told about me?"

"Nothing bad. I do know you've watched my videos though. It's good to know you're a fan."

"Blame Jake for that. He showed me a few months ago, and I became a fan."

She tilts her head. "Fan of my content or . . ."

I laugh. "Does it make me a creep to say it's the videos *and* the host?"

A knowing smile appears. "It tells me you have good taste. But it does raise another question . . ."

I arch a brow. "And that is?"

"How *did* you come to be near my restaurant when that kid swiped my bag?"

I lift my beer to my lips before taking a long drink to cover my embarrassment. There's no way I can tell her I just happened to be there. She'll run for the hills, and this has been a whole lot less awkward than it could've been.

"I mean, as far as stalkers go, you're more nice than creepy. At least you're not digging through my garbage for mementos or sending me underwear and asking me to wear them and return them in the mail."

My mouthful gets stuck in my throat, and I start choking, my eyes bugging out of my head as I gape at her. "You're kidding, right? That didn't happen."

"Only once, thank god."

I shake my head in disbelief. "So, to answer your question, I was in town to catch up with my parents and without thinking, ended up taking a wrong turn."

"Couldn't get me out of your head?"

"No. I mean . . . *Shit.*"

"It's okay. I mean, if you *were* to stalk me, I don't think I'd complain." She lifts her wine to her mouth, smirking against the glass.

"And I definitely don't want your panties." My words don't register until her eyes widen and her lips twitch. "Oh, shit. I mean—"

She pushes up to get out of the chair, and for a second, I panic.

"Stop. I—"

Leaning forward, she rests her hand on my arm, sending a jolt of heat through me. "I'm fucking with you, Rhodes. But since we said we're being honest . . ." She moves in closer and drops her voice to a whisper. "I'd at least *consider* the request if it came from you." Then she snickers and leans back in her seat, leaving me sitting there stunned speechless.

Marco, Renee, and Jake return, my son taking the seat on the other side of me, looking between Dee and myself.

"Sooooo . . . how's it going . . .?" His singsong voice has me torn between shoving him off his chair and cracking up laughing. Jake trying to be a love guru when it was Marco and Renee was funny. When it involves me—not so much. To make it worse, he's going to want a debrief on the way home, and knowing Marco, he'll love being a bystander this time.

Dee's shoulders shake with silent laughter, whereas I just roll my eyes at my son. "How are *you* doing, Jake?" I ask.

"Good, Daddio. Really good. Although"—he lifts his chin in Dee's direction—"not as good as you, I bet."

"God, you two. You're doing that weird conversation thing without having an actual conversation," Renee says.

"Is this what I have to look forward to when Harvey gets older?" Dee asks.

"Probably," I say with a nod. "Kids. Fun to live with, can't live without them."

She giggles. "And they steal a little bit of your sanity as each day passes?"

I point my finger at her. "Yes! Which means you've got time to protect your mind while you still can."

"Hey. I'm sitting right here, you know?" Jake says, pretending to sound offended.

I roll my eyes at him. "Yeah, Jacob Dylan Anderson. I hear you."

"Damn, Jakey boy. Your Dad is on fire tonight." Marco messes up Jake's hair, earning him a teenage-boy grunt. "So, Dee. Renee and I were wondering if you'd like to join us for ax-throwing next week."

"Put the woman on the spot, why don't you," Jake mutters, earning a death stare from me. In return, he shoots me a smirk, telling me he's having way too much fun with this.

Dee grins. "Said woman *is* sitting right here."

Our eyes lock and she quirks a single brow.

"What do you say, Rhodes? Want to make it a double date? I mean, Marco *did* bring us together, not knowing I'd already kind of asked you out."

"What?" Marco says. "You didn't tell me that?"

"In my defense, I thought Dee was being nice and offering me a meal to say thanks. It was me that made it a condition that she join me."

Jake stands, looking first at Dee and then me before throwing his hands in the air with a loud, "Ugh. I give up. I tried. I really did. Adults these days!" Then with a muttered, "I'll be in the car," he walks away, still shaking his head, leaving the rest of us to laugh at my son's antics.

"We're heading off. Do you want to come with us?" Marco asks. "Or do you want us to take Jake and you'll find your own way home?"

Smooth, Marky Mark. Real smooth.

"Actually, I'd better be heading home anyway. I've got a staff meeting and ordering in the morning, and since Mom and Dad took Harvey home with them, I now don't have a ten-year-old to manage. So I'm thinking I'll go relax and enjoy the serenity and have an early night." Dee downs the last mouthful of wine and stands.

"Yeah. We've got an early start too," I say, not wanting the night to end but knowing my twenty-four-hour shift will drag if I don't get a good sleep.

"We'll meet you in the car." Renee hooks her arm in Marco's elbow. "Nice to meet you, Dee."

The two women grin at each other. "You too. I'll get Rhodes to let you know about next week."

Renee's smile widens before she waves and walks away.

"So . . ." I say, turning to face my not-so-blind date.

"So . . ."

"You sure you want to come on a double date?"

"Well, it will be a hardship, but Marco and Renee seem nice enough," she says, unable to keep a straight face.

"You're one of a kind, aren't you?"

She sighs dramatically. "It's hard to be this awesome, but I try."

"You do it well."

Her gaze softens, and she smiles. "Nice to know I made a good impression."

"You made that the other day. Tonight just confirmed I wasn't wrong."

She scrunches her nose in what is a quirk of hers that I really fucking like. The only problem is every time she does it, I want to kiss the confusion away. *Slowly does it, Rhodes.*

Dee reaches out and grabs my phone off the table before pressing the home button and holding the screen up to my face to

46

unlock it. She enters her contact details into my phone—even going as far as to take a photo of herself blowing a kiss and adding it to her info—before reaching around and sliding said phone into my back pocket. The blood in my body diverts south, and central, other parts of me threaten to get their hopes up.

Then she puts a hand on my shoulder, lifting on her toes and brushing her lips against my cheek. "Call me, Rhodes, and we can arrange our winning ax-throwing strategy in person." After shooting me a smile so dazzling it reaches inside and rocks my world, Dee turns and walks into the house, leaving me standing there, eyes on her ass in those tight jeans..

You'd like her, Lily, I think, closing my eyes and imagining her watching with a smirk from heaven.

And in my head, I hear her replying, . *I already do, Ro. I already do.*

Chapter 6

Dee

I'm sitting in my office at the restaurant, buried under a mountain of supplier invoices on Wednesday afternoon, when my cell rings. "Hello, this is Dee."

"Hey, it's Rhodes." Just the sound of his deep, raspy voice in my ear provides an instant cure to my mid-week monotony.

"Well, you certainly took your time, mister," I muse, earning an even more arousing chuckle.

"A man can't seem too eager. Apparently there's a specified timeframe in which a man must wait before calling a woman. Well, according to Firehouse 101's self-appointed love guru. Supposedly, I'm his new pet project."

I lean back in my chair and lift my ankles to rest on my desk. "Is that so?"

"So I'm told. In fact, didn't your video today ask the same question of your subscribers?"

I giggle at that. At the end of my vlog about best first-date foods, I asked people to comment on the current dating rules surrounding time to wait before calling. Or if the girl is allowed to call if she doesn't *want* to wait for the guy. I thought for sure I would get trolled for having non-food related content but was pleasantly surprised at the varied and mostly positive responses I received. "And is the person sharing this wisdom with you single or attached?"

"He's *very* single . . . No, Scotty, you *can't* talk to her. Yes, I'm dating her. No, you can't talk me up. Goodbye," he says, and I bite my lip, trying not to laugh. "Sorry. That man is like a dog with a bone."

"So tell me, how did you decide on the right moment then?"

He huffs out a laugh. "To be honest, I couldn't wait any longer."

"Right. Well, you just scraped in there before the deadline."

The phone falls silent. "Wait . . . there's a deadline?" He sounds genuinely surprised.

I take pity on him. "Nah. Although, Harvey *does* keep asking if the firefighter has called me."

"Funny that. Jake has been hounding me to call as well."

"Smart boy, that son of yours."

"Too much so sometimes."

"I don't know. He seems to have a good head on his shoulders."

"Yeah, he does," Rhodes's voice softens with obvious pride. "I can't take all the credit. His mom was the intelligent one. He got it from her." Then there's rustling down the line before there's a faint "shit" in my ear. "Sorry, I guess it's not good dating practice to mention my late wife when calling to ask another woman out."

By god that thoughtfulness makes me swoon. "Hey. I won't hold it against you as long as you don't hold Flynn against me."

"Flynn?"

"Ex-husband, baby daddy, best friend . . ."

"Oh right. I'm messing this up, aren't I?"

"What could you mess up when you haven't even asked the question yet?" I tease.

"I'm a bit out of practice with this stuff."

"That makes two of us then."

Rhodes's relieved sigh makes me smile.

"Let's make a deal. You don't censor yourself around me, and I'll do the same. Then, neither of us has to mull over what is right or wrong to say. We haven't had a date yet, and I'm really looking forward to doing that, so how about we wait to agonize over mentioning important people in our past, or better still, don't agonize over it at all."

"You're a smart woman."

"I like to think so. Now, if you've called to compliment me, I'm not going to stop you, but I'm *hoping* you're calling to organize the much-anticipated double date."

He chuckles, and that's just as endearing as his admission he's rusty at dating. "Anticipated?"

"Of course. You see, there's this hot firefighter I want to get to know better, and I'm up for a bit of ax-throwing in order to achieve that."

"Is that right?" he replies, sounding amused. "What a coincidence. There's this gorgeous chef I've met that I want to get to know too."

"That *is* a coincidence. Maybe we should do something about that?" I cannot wipe the smile off my face. One might almost say I'm a little giddy at the prospect of spending more time with Rhodes. *There's those butterflies again.*

"Marco and Renee were thinking Sunday afternoon since our next twenty-four starts Monday morning."

"Twenty-four? As in, twenty-four-hour shift?"

"That's the one."

"Damn. You need an early night then."

He laughs, and I vow to keep him laughing whenever we're together.

"Hopefully not *too* early."

"Well, I wasn't going to say it, but I was thinking the same thing."

"Aww, are you going to play hard to get for me?"

"A woman has to keep a couple of tricks up her sleeve."

"I wouldn't know. That's not to say I don't want to see what you're hiding."

A surprised laugh escapes me and a few moments later Rhodes joins me.

"Damn, sorry. I didn't mean it like that."

"So you *don't* want to see me naked? That's disappointing, because I've definitely been thinking about *you* that way."

"What?" he says with a snicker. "You weren't joking about being honest, were you?"

"Nope," I say, accentuating the *P*. "Ask and you shall receive."

"I'll file that away for future."

"As long as you use it to your advantage, have at it."

"You're a surprise, Dee. A good one."

"That makes me happy, 'cause when you haven't dated in over a decade, it's hard to know whether you're doing it right."

"Oh, you're doing it right." His voice takes on a rough edge that I *really* freaking like.

"Okay. So, as much as I'd love to keep talking all day—and I mean that—I'm drowning in paperwork, and I have to dash home to see Harvs before I'm due back here at six."

"Ah, the busy life of a famous chef."

"And mom. It's hard, but so damn worth it."

"I hear you. I'll let you go. The bells could ring at any moment and then I'd have to jump anyway. Does three on Sunday suit? Can you get a sitter?"

Oh, yeah. I guess we'll have to cross the whole 'I live with my ex-husband' conversation at some point. "Yeah, Flynn and Harvey have a standing Sunday dad/son date, so that's covered."

"That's good. I'm lucky that Jake takes care of himself whether I'm there or not."

"Joys of having a teenager."

"Yep. So, would you be okay with me picking you up? I may be rusty, but I'm still a gentleman."

Swoon! Damn, if this man is not careful, he'll ruin me before the first date. "I'd like that, Rhodes. I'll text you my address."

"Sounds good, Dee.."

"We've still got our dinner at the chef's table to organize too."

He laughs quietly. "And you're planning another date before we even have our first."

"Hey, I've been wanting to feed you *before* my brother and your best friend decided to play matchmaker."

"So, you're saying we'd be here regardless of the setup?"

"I definitely hoped so."

"Me too, if I'm being honest."

"It's the only way to be."

"For sure," he says, as bells sound in the background. "Duty calls. But, Dee?"

"Yeah?"

"I'm looking forward to Sunday."

"Me too. Until then, take care and stay safe."

"Will do, chef. You too."

Then I'm left sitting there, staring at a pile of admin that has far less appeal than thinking about Sunday. I feel like a teenager again. Now I'm counting down the days to my first—albeit double—date with Rhodes.

Before I can start daydreaming like a mooning girl with a crush, my office phone rings with a situation in the kitchen. *Duty calls.*

IT'S NOT until after Harvey's bedtime on Thursday night that I get a chance to speak to Flynn in person and without our curious ten-year-old hanging around.

"You wanna watch *Iron Chef* or *Law & Order* tonight?" he asks, remote pointed at the television as I sit down and stretch out at the other end of the couch. I'm in pajama pants and a hoodie, a glass of red in my hand, and I'm still trying to work out how exactly to broach the subject of Rhodes with the man who knows me better than anyone.

"Penny for your thoughts? 'Cause that wine in your hand might distract you for a while, but it definitely won't give you any answers," he says, grabbing my attention. My eyes snap to find his amused ones looking my way.

I frown at him. "It's annoying when you do that. Get out of my head."

"Sweetheart, you've been a bundle of nerves since I got home."

I sigh. Sometimes getting along with your ex-husband isn't as great as it sounds—like, say, *now*.

It didn't even take us long to get to this point. We were always good at the best-friends part. It was the being in love and passion stuff that fell by the wayside.

I turn to face him, crossing a leg under me and cradling my glass in my hands. "Okay, so I'll just preface this by saying I know I don't *have* to tell you, but I also want to. And this was bound to happen. I didn't see it coming though, and it's weird to talk about this with you, because it's new—newborn baby new—and I—"

"Breathe, Dee."

I slowly inhale then exhale and my tense muscles relax. Right . . . I can do this. I don't know why I'm nervous. I mean, he's dated.

"You've met someone," he says, like the damn infuriating mind reader he is.

My eyes jump wide, narrowing as his shoulders shake with laughter. "You're such a jerk, you know that?" A disbelieving snort escapes me. "Seriously, you *always* do that."

Flynn shrugs, lifting his tumbler of whiskey to his smirking lips. "So, I'm right. *That's* what has you so wound up? You were nervous to tell me you're interested in someone?" He reaches over and gently squeezes my knee. "Dee, this is a good thing."

"Wait . . . what?"

He pulls his arm back and furrows his brows. "It's not a good thing?"

"I mean, yes. It is. A good thing, I mean. But I'm. . ." *Losing my god damn mind,* I tilt my head. "Were you worried when you first told me about Sophie.?"

"A little bit, but I also knew that you'd only want the best for me and you have always wanted me to be happy."

"I have. I do."

"So, my question to you now is why would you think that I don't want the same for you?"

"I know you do. It's just—"

"Weird, strange, new territory?"

A dry laugh bubbles out of me. "All of the above."

"Exactly. But you and I aren't exactly normal exes, are we?"

"Thank fuck for that."

His eyes crinkle. "So, there's nothing I want more than for you to actually get out there and *live* your life alongside everything else you've achieved. There's never been a doubt that we love each other, Dee. It just ran its course. But I know more than anyone that you're a good woman with a lot to give, and any decent man will see that."

"Probably indecent ones too."

"Only if you're really lucky," he retorts.

I bark out a laugh and shake my head.

"But seriously, I'm not going to go all jealous ex on you. Might screw with his head a bit, to keep him on his toes, but I want you happy, and I want to see you with someone who *makes* you happy."

"Wow. So, it's not hard?"

"Wouldn't go that far. I was shitting myself before you met Sophie."

"Yeah, and she *knew* about me."

"To be fair, your vlog was blowing up, and you'd finished that local media tour, so I didn't want to throw her in the deep end when she turned up to see you were in fact *that* Dee Duncan."

"Probably a good plan there. But you had nothing to worry about. I knew you wouldn't sleep around just because we weren't together like that anymore."

His lips twitch. "Probably should've while I had the chance."

I snicker. "You're as likely to do that as I am. We saved ourselves for our wedding night, for god's sake. We missed our whoring around days."

"Man, why didn't we listen to everyone when they said to try before you buy?"

"Because we both wanted the lifelong guarantee?"

"Probably," he says with a smile. "So, wait, does this mean you haven't explained our somewhat peculiar living arrangements with him?"

I avert my gaze, earning a *tut-tut* from Flynn. "I didn't think it was exactly a first-meeting-worthy conversation starter."

"Probably a good plan there," he replies, repeating my words back to me. "And now?"

I can't stop the smile that tugs at my lips. "We've got a double date with his best friend and girlfriend on Sunday."

"Nice. No pressure. An easy casual get together without the risk

of awkward lulls in conversation, which means you won't psychoan-
alyze everything that happens and everything that's said and start
worrying about how it's going."

"*So* fucking annoying how you do that," I mutter, taking a sip of
my wine.

The smartass smirks. "It's true though."

I roll my eyes. "Maybe. Doesn't mean you have to point it out."

He laughs to himself. "I figure if you know that I know, maybe
you'll be more aware of it. Or better still, not do it, and therefore
you can relax and be your gorgeous, charming self and have him
eating out of your hand by the time the night's out."

"It's not my *hand* I'd want him eating."

"Damn," he says with a dry laugh. "I may be fine with you
dating and all, but let's not share bedtime stories just yet, deal?"

I giggle and hold out my arm, shaking his hand in mine. "Deal.
And he won't stay over or anything . . . I mean, if it gets to that
point."

Flynn nods. "Never thought you would. Well, not without us
sitting down and talking about it first. Not sure we're ready for
sleepovers and passing each other in the hallway. And what about
Harvey?"

"So, um . . . about that . . ."

His amused eyes turn curious.

"He, ah . . . right. Okay. So, Ezra asked if he could introduce
me to Rhodes—that's the guy—and Harvey overheard, so when we
went to the BBQ on Saturday, he picked out who he thought
Rhodes was and stated in no uncertain terms that he loves his
mama and what he'd do if I got hurt."

Flynn's brows shoot up. "That's my boy. So, what did he say he'd
do?" There's no mistaking the pride and amusement in his tone.

"Essentially, that he'd kick him in the nuts. Although I wonder if
that suggestion came from Axel."

"Damn. I *really* like our kid."

I grin. "Me too."

"Well, then, whatever happens with Rhodes, tell him Harvey's warning goes for me too."

I laugh at that but also sigh. "Yeah, sure. *That'll* have him coming back for more."

Flynn shrugs. "He'll want to regardless, Dee. Trust me. You could wear a burlap sack and talk his ear off, and he'd *still* want to date you."

"You haven't even met the guy."

"Don't need to. I *will*, but I don't need to. I already know you wouldn't waste your time on a man who isn't worthy. You've got good taste in men. I mean, look at me." His shit-eating smirk so big I'm surprised he can breathe.

"You're *such* a dork."

"A good quality dork though. A *doctor* dork."

I down my wine and hold out my glass for him. "Okay, then, *doctor* dork, you can prove how good you are by topping up my wine."

"What the lady wants, the lady gets," he says, moving to his feet and taking a bow as he divulges me of my glass.

"I've trained you well."

"Now *that* is something I should warn this Rhodes about," he mutters as he walks out of the room.

I gasp. "Heard that!"

"Meant you to!"

I laugh, glad that Flynn and I made sure we worked toward the respectful, loving, and successful co-parenting friendship we have now. Life would be a hell of a lot harder without it.

And for all I know, my date with Rhodes on Sunday could be the start of the next significant relationship in my life. Bring it on.

Chapter 7

Rhodes

"I'm leaving," I call out as I grab my wallet and keys from the counter.

"Wait." Jake appears in the doorway. "Hang on. I just have to make sure you're respectable."

I roll my eyes, but to pass inspection, I hold out my arms and do a 360 turn before meeting his gaze and raising an eyebrow. "What's the verdict?"

He twists his mouth and sways his head from side to side. "You'll do. I mean, I probably would've worn loafers instead of sneakers with those jeans since you're going to a bar."

"An *ax-throwing* bar, and it's a Sunday afternoon, not a Friday night. I'm going for smart casual."

"Emphasis on casual," he retorts.

"Yep. Stop trying to make me nervous. I'm hitting my stride in the confidence stakes with Dee. Don't need you derailing my progress," I say jokingly.

"Okay, yeah. I get that." He crosses the room until he's in front of me, his expression turning serious. "Is it weird? For you, I mean?"

I think on that for a moment. "Is it bad if it feels natural? I *was* nervous, but something about Dee makes me feel at ease. It's like I already know her, which doesn't make sense at all. It just feels *right*."

"Good," he says with a firm nod. "Be yourself. She'll either like you or run for miles. And hey, if this works out, you might end up on one of her videos."

I reach out and cup his shoulder. "I can tell you right now that it will never happen, whatever the outcome. But it certainly helps that you're being so okay with all of this."

Jake rolls his eyes. "Dad. Mom passed away, and that sucks—it'll always suck—but she didn't want us to put our lives on hold and not be happy. Of all people, you know that."

That I do. "Love ya, kid."

"Love you too. Now go. You never leave a lady waiting. Don't you know that?"

"Your grandmothers have taught you well."

Jake's lips curl into a smirk. "That one came from Pop actually. He said he wooed Nana Nora from the first day he met her."

I laugh and shake my head. "Yep. That's definitely my dad. You staying home?"

"Well, since I'm not sitting my license for a few more weeks, I figure I'll hang out here and catch up on homework."

"Be good then. I left money on the counter for you to order in."

"Nice. Now hurry before you really are late."

I hold my hands up in surrender. "Okay, okay. I'm going."

"Remember to woo, Dad. And open doors for her. Chicks love that," he calls out as I walk along the hall.

I snort. "Says the *single* kid."

60

"I *choose* to be single. I'm waiting for a showstopper, like Uncle Marco."

"Bye, Jake."

"Woo, Dad. And don't scare her off."

Good to know my kid has confidence in me. But as far as supporting me in this new stage in my life—*dating*—he's a cheerleader, life coach, and wingman all wrapped in one. I thought he fluked it with giving advice to Marco when he first met Renee, but now he's moved his good intentions on to me. He'll probably make sure all of us guys are hooked up and settled down before he starts college. *Heaven help us all!*

Thirty minutes later, I pull my SUV into a parking space outside a renovated two-story home. It's not so different from my own house. Mine is still a work in progress though. It's the same house Lily and I bought when she was pregnant with Jake. Jake and I made a deal after we lost Lils that we'd finish it by the time he left for college.

Not that I'd ever sell it. There's too much history and far too many memories. I often think about how good it would be for Jake to raise his own family in the house one day.

Now it's time to potentially make new memories. With that in the forefront of my mind, I lock the car and walk up the path to the porch. I'm about to knock when the door swings open and a man looking strikingly similar to Harvey appears.

"Hey, you must be Rhodes. I'm Flynn," he says, holding out his hand.

I shake it and smile, relieved he's not making this weirder than it has to be. It makes sense he'd be here since Dee said he had a standing date with Harvey on Sundays. "Yep. That's me."

Silence stretches between us. We both stand there, looking at each other.

"Oh, shit, sorry. Do you wanna come in? Dee's in the bedroom finishing getting ready."

I laugh and rub the back of my neck, stepping inside behind my date's ex-husband. "It's okay. We both know this is kind of awkward, right?"

Flynn snorts. "Honestly, yeah, it's the first time I've had to deal with meeting the guy dating Dee, but that's to be expected when we share a house, right?"

I open my mouth to reply but freeze at his revelation. Thank fuck I cover quickly. "Right. I guess that makes sense with Harvey and all."

Flynn's gaze narrows slightly before widening. "Oh fuck. You didn't know, did you?" He scrubs his mouth. "Damn. I dumped her in it. Look, sorry, but it is just a living arrangement. It works for us, it works for Harvey, and I've got a girlfriend that I'm kinda crazy about. So please don't feel threatened or go all alpha dog on me," he says, his lips twitching.

How can I hate this guy now? "Thanks for explaining it. I'm surprised, but I'm sure Dee meant to tell me."

"To be fair, Harvs and I should've left by now. You've kinda been blindsided, but it was completely unintentional."

"You know, you're making it hard for me not to like you?" I say, making him laugh.

"Good. Because you're the first guy Dee has gone out on a date with in two years, so I'm glad you're not a dick either."

Footsteps grab my attention, and when I look up I meet Dee's slow-growing smile as she walks down the staircase toward us, her eyes going from soft and warm to wide and worried when her gaze shifts to a grinning Flynn leaning against the wall. "Oh fuck."

"That's what I said,' Flynn said.

"Um . . . I mean . . ." Dee's gaze switches between me and her ex, before fixing on me as she reaches the entryway, all color drained from her face. "Okay. Flynn, this is Rhodes. Rhodes, this is Flynn."

My lips twitch. "We've met."

"Oh, yeah, right. Shit. Okay. Um . . . it's kind of a big deal to say 'by the way, I live with my ex-husband and we co-parent our son together.' It's not exactly pre-first-date conversation."

She's not wrong.

"True." I drag my eyes over her face then down her body and back up again, my lips curving into a hopefully reassuring smile, because right now Dee looks like she wants to run back into her room and lock the door. Reaching out, I lace my fingers with hers and give her a gentle squeeze. "It helps that Flynn doesn't think I'm a dick either."

Dee's narrowed gaze jerks Flynn's way. "What did you say? Flynn Michael Duncan, I swear——"

I chuckle and shake my head. "As far as meeting ex-husbands on a first date goes, this *is* a first for me, but he was gentle, I swear."

She scrunches her nose and meets my gaze. "You're . . . okay with this?"

"Well, he's not a dick either, so once I got past the shock, it was all good."

"Yeah."

"You look gorgeous, by the way."

Dee steps back, not letting go of my hand as she looks me up and down slowly in the same way I did to her. She shrugs. "You'll do." A smile tugging at her perfect, pink-painted lips. There's this pull to Dee that I didn't expect, and in person, it's so much more powerful than when I was mesmerized by her eyes and her infectious smile in her videos.

Flynn clears his throat, and as if in slow motion, both Dee and I slowly swing our heads his way as Harvey comes running down the hallway toward us. "Hey, Rhodes. Hey, Mom. Hey . . . Dad?" the boy says, his eyes switching between the three of us. "Is Jake here too?"

A snort escapes me, and I huff out a relieved breath. Never have I appreciated the cluelessness of a ten-year-old more than I do right now. "Hey, bud. Jake's at home. It's just your mom and me going out today with Marco and Renee."

"Damn."

"Harvey," Flynn and Dee warn in unison. The boy bites his lip and shrugs his shoulders in an 'I'm cute. Love me' kind of gesture, and I have to swallow down a laugh.

Then, as if this weird scenario rolls right off his back, Harvey looks to his father. "I'm ready to go, Dad."

"Right. Okay. Then grab your gear bag and let's hit the road."

Harvey tackles Dee's legs, hugging her goodbye then waves at me before disappearing down the hall.

Flynn pushes off the doorway and holds out his arm. "Nice to meet you, Rhodes." He shakes my hand again, his lips quirking. "And sorry for the awkward yet probably memorable introduction."

"Good to meet you too. Thanks for not being a dick," I reply. We both chuckle, looking to Dee, who is watching our exchange with wide eyes and a gaping mouth.

"See ya, Dee. Don't do anything I wouldn't do." Then Flynn gives us a chin lift and walks in the direction his son went.

Dee's cautious gaze locking with mine. "Um . . . wow. That was . . ."

I purse my lips to stop myself from laughing at her. Fuck I wanna kiss her. Before our date. Before we leave the house. It may be backward, but it's all I can think about now.

My attention goes to her mouth, her tongue darting out and tempting me more. When I look up, I'm met by her hooded emerald eyes, and I lock my knees to stop the urge to wrap my arms around her shoulders, pull her close, and kiss her till she's dazed and her mind is clear of anything else but me. It's a surge of possessiveness I wasn't expecting—one I haven't felt in a hell of a long time.

I dip my chin and watch the emotions flit across her face. It's like turning pages of a book to sneak a peek inside, and I love how she's not holding anything back. Her lashes flutter closed, and I fight against the almost overwhelming urge to brush my lips against hers. But I want to take my time, build it up until that moment comes when we're both consumed with the need to taste more than we need to breathe.

Poised with my mouth less than an inch away from hers, I wait as her eyes slowly open.

"Rhodes?" she whispers, making my lips curve up.

As I straighten, she scrunches her nose and frowns, looking adorably confused. I grab hold of her hand. "We'd better get going. We wouldn't wanna be late, would we?"

Her eyes widen before narrowing on mine. "You're a tease, Rhodes Anderson."

I can't help but laugh under my breath as I open the front door and usher her outside. "I promise I'll make it worth your while, Dee Duncan."

"You'd better."

Chapter 8

Dee

I'm still trying to recover from the events of the last ten minutes when Rhodes leads me to his SUV and closes the door behind me before rounding the hood and hopping into the driver's seat beside me.

I click my seat belt on in autopilot, my mind going a million miles a minute, trying to work out if there's a worse way this date of ours could've started.

"So . . ." Rhodes says, leaving my street and driving toward the freeway. "Flynn seems nice."

I do a double take to make sure I heard that right. "*That's* your reaction?" I spin in my seat and bug out at him.

His lips twitch. "Am I supposed to be mad? Maybe cancel the date and call it quits now when I've been looking forward to today all week and the highlight of my day was watching you walk down the stairs wearing a smile that could light up a room and knowing it was just for me?"

"Well, when you put it that way, I guess I—"

"Those jeans help though."

My mouth drops open, but it's half-assed indignation because he likes my butt, and I *like* that. A *lot.*

When I don't say anything, Rhodes frowns and reaches over the center console and rests his hand on mine. "Did you expect me to run for the hills? Was I surprised to meet Flynn? Yes and no. You said he was going out with Harvey today, I just figured they might've left already. Was it a little awkward at first? Sure. But we said we weren't going to censor ourselves, right?" He squeezes my hand before putting it back on the wheel and driving onto the freeway onramp heading downtown.

"We did."

"And we also agreed not to agonize over it. I meant what I said. Flynn isn't a dick, and I like that. It would make it a lot harder if he was. Let me tell you though, your son has impeccable timing."

I giggle at that. "He's adorably clueless, and I'll be a little sad when he realizes that how we live isn't the norm."

Rhodes shrugs. "So, tell me how you live then?"

Now this I can do. Leaning my arm against the door, I look over to the driver's seat. "Long story short, and probably not a fun first-date talking point, but I live my life with no regrets and I've already said I'm nothing but honest."

"And believe me, I appreciate that."

"Right. Okay. So, the *Cliff Notes* version is that Flynn and I had a come-to-Jesus moment when we were overseas and we decided that after being married for twelve years, having a mortgage and an amazing son together, we were better friends than lovers and better parents than husband and wife." I study Rhodes's expression, curious—but no longer worried—about how he'll react.

"Wow."

My head jerks back. "Really?" I ask, earning a quirked brow.

"Yeah. That's really responsible and self-aware." He glances my way. "If I wasn't already impressed with the two of you and how you interact, I am now."

"Who are you, Rhodes Anderson?" I ask, my voice filled with awe.

His brow furrows, his lips twisting into a cute half-smile. "What you see is what you get with me."

"Just when I think I've got a read on you, you go and blow me away. Are you the knight in shining armor who came to my rescue when I was mugged or the guy who chases a homeless kid down and lets him go with a bed and meal arranged at a local shelter. Or, the cool single dad who gets set up with the woman he's been watching online and barely blinks? And don't even get me started on the awesomeness that is your son."

"Honestly, what you see is what you get. I'm a firefighter, a dad, and I guess your everyday average Joe," he replies.

"There's nothing average about you. *Believe* me. Rhodes?"

"Yeah?"

"As long as you know that I'm looking forward to discovering everything else about you. I think I might make it my new mission."

"Have at it, baby. At least then we'd be even."

RHODES PULLS into the parking lot of the Showtime Entertainment Complex. I'd heard about this place when it first opened and always wanted to go.

Rhodes laces his fingers with mine as we walk inside the venue, spotting Marco and Renee standing to the side waiting for us.

Marco's eyes drop to our joined hands, a grin covering his face by the time we reach them. "Hey, you two."

"Hey," Rhodes replies, looking around. "This place is mind-blowing."

"Yeah. We came here a few months ago and had a blast." Renee looks between the two of us. "And what better place to come for a double date?"

Marco turns his warm gaze on his girlfriend. "Right. Let's go. Our booking starts in ten minutes, which is enough time to get drinks and find our table."

"We'll follow you guys." The other couple move ahead of us and I step forward, stopping when Rhodes turns my way. I meet his eyes with curiosity.

"You okay?" he asks.

"Yeah, of course. Why do you ask?"

"For a first date that hasn't even started yet, you've had a lot to think about."

I melt inside, and I let it all hang out, not hiding the fact I like his thoughtfulness, again asking myself how this man is single. "I'm good, honey."

He lifts his brow. "Would you tell me if you weren't?"

"Oh, yeah. Something to know about me—I'm a talker."

"Maybe Flynn can give me some pointers," he muses.

I struggle not to laugh as I roll my eyes. "And he's got ex-husband jokes."

"He's a bigger man than I would be."

"Oh really?

"Yep. If it was me meeting the guy wanting to date my wife—knowing what a catch she is—I'd totally be a jerk."

My lips twitch, trying to imagine a scenario in which Rhodes Anderson would ever be an asshole. "Is that so?"

"Hell, I want to be a possessive jerk now to the three guys I've already caught checking out your ass."

I lean in, tipping my face to his and smirking at him. "What I wanna know is why the guy I *want* to be ogling me isn't doing that instead of watching others do it?"

His brows lift, his eyes flashing with surprise. I like keeping him on his toes. Sometimes my frank honesty can be refreshing, sometimes not so much. I'm happy in this instance, Rhodes gets me.

Rhodes quickly recovers and closes the remaining distance between us until our chests are almost touching. His spare hand is now resting on my hip, the heat of his touch making a tremble course through my body.

"How about we make a deal, just for tonight?"

"Okay . . ." I murmur. I might get into trouble here, but I find myself willing to do anything he might ask of me.

"Let's live in the moment? No pressure. No expectations. Just you, me, Marco, and Renee, hanging out with friends and enjoying ourselves. Drinks, food, and good old-fashioned fun where I will— more than likely—beat the pants off you at whatever game we play."

"Is that so? You think you can beat me?"

His eyes turn molten. "Depends what we're playing . . ."

And damn if *that* doesn't warm me from the inside.

"C'mon, love birds. You coming or what?" Marco calls out.

Rhodes rubs his hands together. "Oh yeah, this is gonna be fun."

"Well, after you teased me back at my house, I say you might be right. It's only fair." I shoot him an amused glance and let him go before walking away with an extra spring in my step and swaying my hips knowing he's watching.

The rumbling growl coming from the man behind me makes me smile.

A chirpy, mid-twenties, hipster-looking dude approaches the four of us with a huge grin on his face. "Hey, ladies and gents. My name is Trent, and I'll be your trusty, talented, and sometimes funny ax coach for the next hour or so." Trent goes over the safety precautions before launching into an explanation of how the game works. "The goal is for an individual to beat their competing player or for a team to get to a certain number of points first. There are three rounds of five throws per person, but even if a winner is declared after the second round, we'll still go ahead with the third, because who doesn't wanna throw axes at a bullseye for fun, am I right? Although, you two boys look like you've chucked more than a few axes in your time."

We all laugh and nod our heads. Trent's upbeat attitude is infectious, and it has me itching to give it a go.

"Right, so I'll be off to the side observing and I won't intrude or step in unless someone asks or I have to. But first, let me demonstrate how to hold and throw this auspicious little wood chopper." He grabs an ax from the holder and twirls it in his hands before holding it up in front of him. "Dominant hand on top, the other one below, then all you gotta do is face the target . . ." He turns around and steps to the edge of the throwing lane, looking back over his shoulder at us. "Then you lift it over your head like this, and it's a case of rocking your hips forward and sticking your butt out, using your body to catapult the ax forward, and *hopefully* lodging the blade in the target."

God, he makes it sound and look easy. Lucky I've never been afraid to make a fool out of myself in the name of having fun.

Marco and Renee stand back and let us go before them.

The first ax I pitch down the lane spins end over end before hitting the target with the metal butt. It drops to the floor like a lead balloon and I huff out a frustrated breath. "This is a lot harder than it looks."

Rhodes appears beside me, shooting me a hot-as-hell smirk. "If it helps, I did the same thing my first time?"

I roll my eyes. "Of course, you did. And let me guess—you're about to tell me you are classed as an expert-level ax-thrower now?"

He chuckles behind me as I walk toward the target and bend over, taking my time to reach out and slowly pick up the ax. A quick check over my shoulder confirms what I'd expected to see—Rhodes's eyes pinned to my butt. *Maybe distracting him is the key to winning this damn game.* And if that doesn't work, at least we'll have fun flirting while he kicks my ass. With a little wiggle of said derriere, I straighten and make my way back to my date, dragging my gaze up his body without shame and flattening my hand on his shoulder when I reach his side. "You're up, honey. Maybe you can show me how *good* you are at this game."

His attention drops to my lips then up again and damn, just the heat in his eyes has my body sparking to life. *How does he manage to do that to me with just a look?* I keep wanting to grab his face and kiss the hell out of him.

"What game is this again?" he asks, his deep, hoarse tone making my knees weak.

"Why, ax-throwing, of course," I say innocently as I flex my fingers against his shirt. "It *is* our first date, after all. And unlike *some* people, I'd never *tease* anyone without knowing I was prepared to follow through. That would be kinda cruel, don't ya think?"

Rhodes shakes his head slowly, his eyes dancing with amusement. "Oh, we're playing now, sweet cheeks."

My brows jump up and I grin. "Sweet cheeks?" I lean in, bringing my face so close that his heavy breath washes over my skin. "But how will you ever find out how *sweet* my cheeks can be if you don't win . . .?" I blow him an air kiss and walk to the table where Marco and Renee are standing.

Renee is beaming, and Marco's head is dropped, but there's no missing his smirk. "You right there, brother?" he calls out to my date, grabbing an ax from the rack outside the throwing area.

"Yeah . . ." Rhodes answers rough and low before clearing his throat and looking over his shoulder at us girls, his eyes locking on mine. "If we didn't need to win before, we need to now. I'm finding myself somewhat . . . *motivated*."

I can't help but snicker.

"Now I need to know," Renee says, leaning onto the table and turning her body toward me. "Because I was already thinking of making this interesting. I mean, girls versus boys seems fair. Unless you want to pair up with Rhodes. it *is* a date, after all."

"Oh no. It definitely needs to be a battle of the sexes."

"Awesome. At least then I can have a little fun with Marco. They may be the boss men at work but believe me. You've gotta make sure things are equal at home." Renee waggles her eyebrows.

"I *can* hear you, princess," Marco says, not looking back.

She winks at me. "I know, Lieutenant. Why do you think I said it?"

Rhodes grips the handle, one hand slightly higher than the other, planting his left foot in front of his right in the 'expert' stance our games ax coach showed us. Then he lifts the ax and throws it at the target, a sigh escaping my lips as I admire his flexing arm muscles

"Girl . . ." Renee says, holding her fist out in front of me and bumping her knuckles with mine. "You get your eye candy, and I get mine. This double date thing is the best. Idea. Ever."

Between rounds two and three—with the score being one win apiece, girls vs boys—Marco and Renee head over to 'Food Truck Alley' on the far side of the warehouse to get us some snacks, leaving Rhodes and I alone with newly fetched drinks in hand.

"Having fun?" he asks.

My mind is a little distracted by his leg brushing against mine. So far, this game of ours has morphed into a challenge to see who can drive their date crazier. Accidental touches, soft hands resting on arms, shoulders, hips, the small of my back—anything and everything *decently* possible to distract one another.

And by god is Rhodes good at the art of distraction.

"Yeah, I am. It helps that Renee's damn good at this ax-throwing thing. Otherwise, it would've been a thrashing by now."

"Oh, I don't know. You seem to be getting better."

I snort at his massive overstatement. "If by getting better you mean hitting the target once in that last round."

"Definitely better," he says, his lips curving up into a wicked grin.

"At least I don't mind being beaten when I like the view of my opponent."

Rhodes chuckles. "I'll make sure to tell Marco you think so."

Rolling my eyes, I giggle and nudge him with my elbow. "Take a compliment, Rhodes."

"I'll take anything from you, sweet cheeks."

"How about dinner this week then? I still owe you that thank-you meal, and I'd love to cook for you."

His gaze goes soft. "And a restaurant full of other diners?"

I lean in and drop my voice to a whisper. "You see, the perks of being the boss is that I can delegate and use the kitchen I have for filming in for private guests."

Rhodes's brow arches. "You entertain a lot of private guests?"

"Not so far. Only Harvey and my parents, and now, hopefully, you . . ."

"I'd be honored then," he replies, reaching over and placing his hand in mine. "My shifts probably don't fit in well with you this week though. I'm working tomorrow, then Tuesday and Wednesday I'm off. Thursday—work, and Friday and Saturday I'm free."

I purse my lips. "Why wouldn't they work for me? I have staff. My kitchen runs like a well-oiled machine. I'll let my restaurant manager, Suzy, know that I'll be there but not *be* there. I've been looking forward to feeding you since we first met."

His brows jump up. "You have?"

"Oh yeah. I use my food to express myself."

Rhodes leans in, his leg pressing firmly against the length of mine now. "I think you're expressing yourself just fine so far. It helps that you uploaded a new video today with 'How to Win Your Date Over One Meal at a Time.'"

I wink at him, my smile widening. "Glad you liked it. Let's say dinner next Monday, that would be your day off, right?"

The smile he gifts me is so big it's blinding. "I'd love to."

"Now. . ." My lips twitch. "We haven't discussed what the prize is when I beat you at this game."

Rhodes's eyes roam my face, pausing on my lips before lifting to mine. He shoots me a slow-growing smirk. "Winner's choice," he murmurs, and the rough rasp of his tone has my thighs clenching together out of instinct alone.

"You've got yourself a deal."

"I've got my eyes on the prize, sweet cheeks," he says, not looking away from me—even when Marco and Renee slide a couple's platter of bar snacks on the table in front of us.

Rhodes proves his point by stepping up for his final throw, and with his eyes locked on mine, he heaves the ax over his shoulder, scoring a bullseye and making my heart race and soar simulta-neously.

After a great evening, we bid farewell to Marco and Renee. And with Rhodes's hand in mine—something I find he likes to do a lot—we make our way into the parking lot.

When we reach his car, he unlocks the doors and lets me go. Then without a word, he's facing me and slowly pressing my back against the car.

I slide my arms around his waist and rest my palms on his

shoulder blades. "You finally going to claim your prize?" I whisper, sounding like a wanton woman ready to mount her man. It's not like I'd say no, but nothing between us feels the slightest bit casual. And at this stage in both of our lives, I'd hazard a guess that after waiting this long, Rhodes isn't about to screw around just to get laid. Lord knows it's not worth adding sex onto my already full plate unless it comes with all the benefits of a committed relationship as well.

He braces his forearm on the door above my head, bringing every inch of his hard body flush against mine. He's toned, but he's also got shape. Fit, but without angles that'll poke an eye out.

"If I had my way, I would've been kissing you all night. Every time you licked your lips or smirked at me, I wanted to sink my teeth in and steal a taste."

As if punctuating his point—or simply taking his time to play with his winnings—he runs his palm up my side, grazing the side of my bust, leaving goosebumps in his wake. His hand slides to my neck before cradling my jaw, the pad of his thumb tracing the edge of my mouth.

A whimper escapes my lips, and his eyes flash molten and hot, ready to burn me alive.

Holy God. Bucket needed in the parking lot. A woman is about to spontaneously combust here.

We stay there staring, our breaths shallow and fast, our hearts racing in sync with the other, our bodies touching chest to thigh and every delicious inch throbbing incessantly between us. It's like time stands still. The world is revolving around us, yet we're still here stuck in an augmented reality, waiting for that final push to take what we want.

"Please," I whisper, and his resistance snaps. He gives me his weight, his hands clutching my head, holding me in place, tilt my chin up. Locking our eyes together, he ever so slowly lowers his mouth toward mine—the wait to feel his lips on mine so exquisitely painful. I can't take it anymore, and I grip the back of his head at the same time I surge forward, and we crash together in a tangle of mouths and lips and tongues and teeth.

It's not soft and slow. It's hard and fast, desperate, and completely honest. I want to dance in the rain and offer thanks to the universe above. There's no pretense, no pretending. This isn't a precursor to get me into bed. This is the pent-up passion that has been building all night—if not all week.

My nails bite into his scalp as he rolls his hips against mine and groans as he plunges deeper, his tongue exploring my mouth, tasting me and making me moan. It's seven at night, and we're making out against his car—in a parking lot, no less—and it's still as hot as it was when I used to do it as a teenager.

As far as memorable first kisses go, this has jumped straight to the top of the list. Bar none.

Desperately needing air, I suck in a breath when Rhodes tears his lips from mine. "Damn, sweet cheeks. You can kiss."

"Believe me, you're the master of anticipation. You made *me* nearly jump *you*."

"I like to delay gratification. What can I say?"

"Well, I'll tell you one thing. I may like to win, but if that's my reward for losing, I'm winning regardless."

His eyes sparkle with amusement as he grins down at me. "I've been wanting to kiss you for a fuck of a long time."

"And now that you have?" I ask, resting my hands right over his racing heart and looking up at him.

He runs a finger down my cheek, his big hand cupping my jaw. "Now, I'm gonna be doing it a hell of a lot more often."

"Promise?"

He laughs as he brushes his lips against mine once more. "It's a god damn guarantee."

Chapter 9

Rhodes

After a crazy, busy week, Jake and I meet up with Marco, Gio, and Luca—the other Rossi brother—for a run around the Busse Woods Trails. It's all for a good cause though, because in five months, we're all running in the annual Ovarian Cancer Charity Run—something we've done for the past four years. At first, Jake and I did it to honor Lily's memory and help others battle the horrible disease that took her from us. Now it's a way to memorialize her and help raise money that can go toward one day finding a cure, so that no one else has to be lost.

The plan today is to do an easy five miles, but Gio and Luca have been known to do crazy distances whenever the mood hits them. As we stretch against the car in the parking lot, I'm mentally preparing myself to be guilted into running the full course today, which would mean a whole world of pain tomorrow.

At least if I can't walk after this, I'll have two days to recover before my dinner date with Dee on Monday.

We've been like ships in the night this week, but we've stayed in touch. That's not to say I didn't send a bunch of flowers to the restaurant on Monday morning after our date.

I'd been ready to take her and claim her as mine right then and there. I've never felt that before. Not with anyone, but everything feels so natural with Dee that I'm making a point *not* to question it. I'm going to enjoy it.

This is not a quick slam and scram scenario for me. I like Dee. She's funny and smart, ambitious, and caring. Her sexy body, stunning smile, and husky moan have a lot to do with it as well.

I swear she almost had me embarrassing myself when we were making out against my car. So fucking hot, and responsive, and greedy—I loved it.

"Earth to Dad?" Jake says, snapping me out of my daze.

"Yeah, kid?"

"Stop mooning over your *girlfriend*," he says with a shit-eating grin. The problem with raising a kid who's the perfect mix of me and his mother is that he's quick off the mark and doesn't miss a thing.

"She's not my girlfriend yet. We're still getting to know each other."

"Look, Dad. I know it's been a while for you, but when a guy likes a girl and a girl likes a guy, you lock that girl down before someone else snaps her up. When it's someone as cool as Dee Duncan, you do that quickly. You get me?" he says, his expression serious.

"Relationships don't work that way. You can't just 'lock someone down,' Jake."

The teenage love guru rolls his eyes. "Yes. You do. You said her ex was cool with you. Her *kid* likes you. *I* like *her*, and whenever you two message each other, you get this weird smile on your face I haven't seen since Mom. Admit it, Dad. You're *really* into her."

Gio wraps an arm around Jake's shoulder. "Yeah, *Dad*. Tell us you really, *really* like her."

"God. Here we go." I roll my eyes and search the sky for some divine intervention.

"Who do we like?" Luca says, walking into the conversation without a care in the world, Marco following him and standing beside me.

"Oooh, are we talking about girls? Can we do it while running? Or do you guys wanna sit around with your fingers up your asses while we discuss Rhodes's love life?"

I jerk my head Marco's way. "Yeah. What he said. Let's go." Leading by example, I jog away from them toward the start of the official trail.

"Dad, no pressure, but you know the third date is important, right?" Jake says, moving beside me.

I give him the side-eye. "You been watching those YouTube dating videos again?"

"Look, he's got some good advice," Marco says.

I snort. "It's not my first rodeo, kid."

"Well, in fairness to Jake, it's not like you've had to date for a while," Gio says from where he's running behind me.

Luca bursts ahead and turns to face us, running backward as he does. "I'm an expert at modern dating. Ask me anything—I'll help you out, brother."

"When did you last have a girlfriend?" I ask, earning a middle finger from him.

"Not all of us are as lucky as Marco, who goes to a damn house showing and ends up meeting the love of his life. Sheesh. That shit only happens in books, I swear."

"Or movies," Jake adds.

Luca nods. "Exactly."

"And you would know this how?" Gio asks, not even breaking a sweat as we hit the one-mile marker.

"Reading romance novels. They're surprisingly enlightening." Luca says this like it's completely normal. For others it is. For Luca Rossi—fuck no.

"Is that right?" Marco muses. "Let me guess. You've been stealing Mama's bodice rippers? The ones with that long-haired, shirtless guy on the front?"

I turn my head. "Wait, are you talking about Fabio? My mom used to have those too."

"Are we *seriously* running five miles talking about fucking romance books? Or are we gonna find out the goods from Rhodes about his love life?" Gio says, sounding far too interested in whether I'm getting laid or not.

Thank heavens for Jake tagging along. "Hello? Son here. Don't wanna know deets about what Dad is or is not getting up to. As long as he's happy—that's all I need to know."

Marco snorts. "Dude, you *wanted* your dad to meet someone."

"Yeah. Doesn't mean I need to hear the locker-room talk. Jeez," he says, running ahead and leaving us in his dust.

"What's that about?" Gio asks.

"He's all good."

Gio looks from Jake to me, arching a brow. "You sure it's not all becoming too real for him?"

"What do you mean?" It hits me. *Lily.*

I shake my head. "He's good. He's even told me what to wear for my dinner with Dee on Monday. Right down to booking me in for a damn haircut in the afternoon."

That makes my friends chuckle.

Marco smirks at me. "Then he really doesn't wanna hear how you made out with Dee against your car."

I narrow my eyes at him.

Gio spits out his mouthful of water. "Damn, Rhodes. Keep the goods from Jake, but don't hold out on me."

"Yeah. It's not like G has anything going on in *his* love life. He has to live vicariously through yours," Marco teases as we pick up the pace to catch Jake and Luca. My muscles are starting to burn in a good way.

"Better than listening to Luca's exploits. That guy needs to look for quality over quantity."

I snort. "Maybe not hitting the clubs with Scotty would be a good start."

"He'll figure it out," Marco says, sounding all sage-like. For a man who waited years to find his showstopper, he's a relationship man now through and through, and I couldn't be happier for him.

Seeing him fall in love gave me hope, and the more time I spend with Dee, the more hope I have that we do get a second chance to find happiness.

It doesn't take away from what Lily and I had. It's just a different path with another fantastic woman, who could potentially change my life for the better. Only time will tell.

I'm looking forward to finding out.

By the time we do six miles then walk a couple more back to the parking lot, we are all dead on our feet.

Then it's home to chill out with Jake and do chores as per our usual weekend routine when I'm not working or sleeping.

It's when we take a break from working in the backyard that I tackle Gio's point about Jake and Lily and how he feels about Dee and I dating.

I sit down on the porch steps and nudge him with my shoulder. "You all good, kid?"

He screws his lips up, looking at me strangely. "Well, yard work sucks and my muscles are a bit tight, but other than that, I'm good. Why?"

"G seems to think you might be feeling a bit weird about me dating Dee."

He jerks back, his brows lifting so high they almost touch his hairline. "God no," he says, and I let out the breath I was holding. "I *wanted* you to start dating. In a million years, I didn't expect Uncle Marco to set you up with Dee Duncan, but she seems nice, and I hope I'll get a chance to know her better. She obviously makes you happy, so how *can* I be weird about that?"

"Because of your mom . . ."

He shakes his head. "Look, Mom is a hard act to follow, but I *want* you to meet someone and be happy. In a few years, I might go away to college, and I don't like the idea of you being in this big empty house without me. You're not *that* old, you've still got a lot of life to live. And I appreciate you working hard and focusing on me, but you're a good-looking dude. You deserve a good woman who'll be there for you, just like you're here for me and like you were for Mom."

"Damn, kid. Hit me right in the feels," I mutter, lifting my beer to my mouth and taking a long sip to swallow the growing lump in my throat.

"Besides, she's a good cook. What else could a growing kid ask for?" He pats his flat stomach. "I *am* jealous that you get to go to Delish before me though."

"You wanna tag along? I'm sure Dee won't mind."

He snorts. "And be the proverbial third wheel? Thanks, but no thanks. Seriously, Dad, I want to see you happy again. If that's with Dee, all the better. If it doesn't work out and you meet someone else, so be it. The main thing is that *you* start living again, because you've put in the hard yards with me, and Mom wouldn't want you to be alone. She said that."

My head spins around so fast I almost keel over. "You remember that?"

"Of course, I do. She also made me promise that we'd look after each other, and this is me doing that. Mom was a rock star. What's to say Dee won't be the next headline act in the concert that is your life?"

What on earth did I do in a past life to deserve him. "Love ya, Kid."

Jake's lips quirk up on the side. "Yeah, Dad. Love you too. But are we done with the *D* and *M* now, 'cause I'll never get a chance to practice my driving with you today if we sit out here gabbing all day."

I roll my eyes. "Okay, okay. As long as you know you can talk to me anytime, yeah?"

Jake places his hand on my arm. "Dude, relax. I'm cool, you're cool, Dee's cool. Don't screw it up, and I'll be happy."

"Why do you think I'll be the one to screw it up?"

"'Cause times change, old man. My job is to help you get up with the times."

I laugh at that. "Right. Good to know you've got my back, kid."

"Always." He smirks before putting his bottle of water down and moving to his feet. "But I won't complain if you bring me home some of Dee's cooking after your date. Just saying."

I snicker. "Duly noted."

"I mean . . . it's only fair, right? Call it payment for services rendered."

My lips twitch and I lift my brow. "Right. So, it's gonna cost me to get your sage dating advice?"

He shrugs. "Hey, it's cheaper than a hooker, Dad."

Then he's walking away, leaving me speechless.

RHODES: Hey, sweet cheeks. How's your night going?

Dee: Hey. It's good. Chilling with Harvs at home after teaching him how to make potato gnocchi with a pesto cream sauce.

Rhodes: Damn. Do you offer lessons? 'Cause I know a sixteen-year-old who loves to eat. Would be great if he could cook as well. Haha.

Dee: I would for Jake. He already asked me at the BBQ.

Rhodes: Shit. He doesn't waste time, does he?

Dee: It was after he told me to go easy on you.

Rhodes: And how's that going for you?

Dee: After the way you kissed me last Sunday, I'm starting to think there's nothing rusty about you at all.

Rhodes: You're not too bad yourself.

Dee: Good to know. Feel free to leave a Yelp review online for future kissing recipients.

Rhodes: Grr.

Dee: I knew I'd get the caveman to make an appearance.

Rhodes: If you're not careful, he'll come out next time I see you.

Dee: I'll look forward to it. I've designed a special menu for our date on Monday.

Rhodes: Care to share?

Dee: Oh no. That would ruin the surprise.

Rhodes: You could serve me boxed mac and cheese, and I'd still enjoy it

Dee: I'm screwing my nose up right now. You do know you're dating a chef, right?

Rhodes: Haha. I was trying to be charming.

Dee: You don't have to try, honey. You probably charm the pants off women without breaking a sweat.

Rhodes: I wouldn't know. Might be interested in testing that theory with you though.

Dee: Damn. Is it Monday yet?

Rhodes: Sweet dreams, sweet cheeks.

Dee: And there you go again. Good night. Stay safe at work tomorrow. I have plans for you, Rhodes Anderson.

Rhodes: I have plans for you too, Dee Duncan.

Dee: Can't wait. And, Rhodes . . .

Rhodes: Yeah?

Dee: Can't wait to taste my cooking on your lips either.

Yep. Dee Duncan has me hook, line, and sinker. And I, for one, am *not* complaining.

Lils, I've got a live wire on my hands. Lucky for me, you got me used to it. Lucky for me, I have a chance of getting used to it again.

Chapter 10

Dee

Rhodes: This is Jake. I know Dad won't ask, but I have no shame. If you make anything good, PLEASE take pity on me and send a doggy bag home. I promise I'll love it. Especially if it's that risotto and your chocolate lava cake you demonstrated online today. That looked AMAZING.

Rhodes: Although, kinda weird when I know the title 'From First Date to First Mate: How to Turn Him on With Food' is about my dad.

Rhodes: Also, this message will self-destruct, because I cannot have Dad knowing I hacked his phone again. He's running out of pin combinations that he'll still remember. Take pity on him. He's old.

Rhodes: Wait . . . not THAT old. I mean . . . he's hot for a thirty-nine-year-old, right? Okay, I'm going now, 'cause he's just getting out of the shower, which means phone fun time gone. BYE.

The first text stops me in my tracks. The second and third throw me over the edge and have me laughing my butt off as I walk out of my office and toward the front of house to check-in. I managed to squeeze in a quick shower and outfit change too, because there's a difference between serving guests in chef whites and trying to impress the man you want to kiss again—maybe *more* than kiss again —on a date where you're cooking for him.

And why the hell am I nervous about making Rhodes a meal tonight? I've cooked for politicians and royalty—well, it was some third cousin twice removed—and even celebrities. I've made dishes for other chefs I've admired and looked up to for years. Yet cooking for Rhodes for the first time has me on edge?

Knowing I need to calm down, and with thirty minutes to go before he's due to arrive, that leaves me with two options: drink or call someone to give me an ego boost.

I save the former as a last resort and opt for door number two in the form of a group text recently formed between Renee, Skye, Gilly, and Faith.

Dee: Quick. Someone tell me I'm the best chef you've ever met.

Faith: What do I get out of this text-a-compliment service?

Skye: Your buffalo wings were pretty damn good.

Faith: Skye, you're pregnant. You're at the 'eat anything' stage.

Skye: Amen to that.

Renee: Dee, that man would eat anything and everything you offer up to him on a plate.

Skye: That's what she said!

Renee: Oh my god, I didn't mean THAT.

Skye: Why not? I would mean that. Tonight's the third date, isn't it?

Faith: Technically the second. BBQ with firehouse and family doesn't count.

Skye: True. No chance for anything sexy to go down at my place. So, second date rules apply then. Easy peasy.

Dee: Wait, there are rules for different dates? When did that become a thing?

Faith: Probably around the time you were graduating high school and shacked up with your husband.

Skye: BOOM. She kinda has a point there.

Dee: Says Faith who MARRIED her childhood sweetheart!

Faith: And thank god I did! He doesn't care about first, second, or third date rules. He's a take what he wants kind of guy.

Gilly: Ezra is an any way he can get it guy.

Dee: Eww.

Faith: Double eww. That's our brother.

Gilly: Yep. And thank god for him.

Dee: Have any of you got some actual advice? I'm on the verge of freaking out. What if I screw up the risotto and he thinks I'm all show and no substance?

Renee: Babe, he calls you sweet cheeks. According to Marco, that's not a Rhodes thing to do. He's also whistling at work.

Skye: It's true. Rhodes isn't a whistler. He might hum along to some song on the radio or something, but he doesn't whistle like he's a man who's got the girl.

Dee: He hasn't got me yet.

Gilly: Not what I heard.

Renee: Not what I SAW.

Dee: Damn.

Faith: Busted.

Skye: Haha, this is gold. Delilah Baker, one word: RELAX. And another word: ENJOY. Rhodes wants you, not your damn risotto.

Faith: In all fairness, Skye. It is a damn good risotto.

Skye: Damn. See, if I send Cohen to the restaurant, can we buy your best offering?

Dee: Sure.

Faith: Skye, can you still see your toes? 'Cause after Dee's risotto, you won't be able to.

Surprisingly, I'm a lot less tense after that little five-minute pep talk. And Skye is right. Rhodes is not with me because of the videos or the profile or the rave reviews about the most popular rice dish on my menu. I know that. It was a momentary speed wobble. A little self-esteem reality check. Maybe it's because I really like Rhodes. It's been a long time since I've doubted my ability to deliver a mouthwatering, rave-about-it-for-days meal for anyone I've cooked for.

I may not have seen Rhodes coming into my life the way he did, and I certainly didn't expect my brother to set us up together, but I have absolutely zero regrets about it now. He makes me smile, he makes me laugh, he turned me on with an almost kiss, and then *definitely* delivered on everything he promised at the end of the night.

He's smart, he's honest, and he's a good dad. Oh, and he wasn't a dick to Flynn, which means he got my ex-husband's tick of approval. *Apparently that's a thing.*

Which makes me wonder if I'd have gotten Rhodes's wife's acceptance too? I don't let myself go too far down that path, because I haven't asked about her yet. And Rhodes hasn't said much about her either. I'm hoping tonight could allow us to broach the subject. I think it's important, for him and for me. Maybe I'll bribe him with Jake's doggy bag.

With a quick time check, I quickly make the rounds and touch base with Suzy, then move toward my filming kitchen and get the risotto started. I leave it to cook before waiting for Rhodes to arrive at the back door, which he does, not even a minute late.

When I lay eyes on him, I instantly feel a whole lot better for seeing him. "Hey."

He smiles and steps in, looking over my shoulder before wrapping an arm around my waist, holding his hand against my hair, and lowering his head. Then he's kissing me surely, thoroughly, and only pulling away when I sag against him. "Hey. How are you?"

"A hell of a lot better now." I run my hand down his chest and lace my fingers with his, feeling lighter than I have all week. It's funny how being around someone can lift your mood. Although in Rhodes's case, it's just the thought of him lately. I'm like a giddy teenager. It would almost be embarrassing if I wasn't enjoying it so much.

He laughs, his eyes crinkling at the sides. "Funny that. I am too."

"Let's see if I can make you feel even better," I say before leading him along the hallway and through the open door to my filming kitchen. "Welcome to the chef's private dining room." I stop to close the door behind us, letting him walk inside and look around as I engage the lock. I follow him over to the big stone-covered center island that doubles as a workstation, and watch him run his palm over the countertop.

"You film in here, don't you? I recognize it."

"Oh yeah, I forgot you're a fan," I tease.

He glances over at me with a wry smile as I move to the other side of the bench.

"You might say that. Is that a bit weird for you?"

"If you'd stalked me, I'd make you wait for my cooking."

His eyes widen. "I didn't—"

I wink at him and giggle. "I'm joking. Besides, you're far too cute to let a little fan-boying hold me back."

"I'm going to have to watch myself around you," he replies with a shake of his head. "Something tells me you're gonna keep me on my toes for a while."

I beam at his intimation that he plans on whatever this is between us going on for 'a while.' "Mayyybe . . ."

"Right, now tell me what I can do to help." He starts rolling his shirt sleeves up and moving around to join me.

It shocks me—but given it's Rhodes, I don't know why I'm surprised. "No, no. This is supposed to be *me* cooking for *you.*"

He rests his hands on my hips and turns me toward him. "Would you deny me the chance to assist *the* Dee Duncan in her kitchen?"

"Well, when you put it like *that* . . ."

After bringing his face closer, he brushes his lips against mine. "Let me help you, sweet cheeks. I've been looking forward to it all day."

Rhodes might've been a fan of mine, but I'm fast becoming an *equally* big fan of his, *especially* if he keeps touching me every chance he gets. Cupping his face in my hands, I flex my fingers against his stubbled cheeks and smile. "Will you help me cook us dinner, honey?" I ask, loving the gentle look he's giving me.

"It'd be my honor, chef."

Wanting to kiss him again, I lift on my toes and press my mouth to his, moaning when he wraps me in his arms and takes over the kiss. When we pull apart again, he rests his forehead on mine, our eyes locked. "Lucky I locked the door. At this rate, we'll *never* get fed."

"Not complaining, sweet cheeks."

"Okay, then. Let's get started."

"Yes, chef," he says, shooting me a cheeky smirk before looking around at the numerous bowls of pre-prepped ingredients.

I move to the big industrial refrigerator and start pulling out what we're going to need. "Because I'm an overachiever, who wanted to impress my date, I may have gone a little overboard with the menu," I explain, handing things off to Rhodes when he holds out his hands to help.

"This date of yours must be one hell of a guy," he muses.

I laugh. "Yep. He's a firefighter, like you. Rather handsome and claims to be rusty at dating, but so far he's proving that to be a lie."

"Is that so?"

"Yep. At least he's a great kisser though. *Really* good. I'm hoping he plans to kiss me *a lot*. His nice butt doesn't hurt his case either," I continue, earning a deep chuckle that I feel everywhere.

"He sounds like a catch."

"It seems that way, yes." My face starts to ache from grinning too much.

When I return to his side, he bumps my hip with his. "I'll stop seeking compliments if you tell me what culinary delights you have in store for us tonight."

I roll my eyes and sigh melodramatically. "Needy men, I dunno. Lucky I really like you, Rhodes Anderson." I turn around and hold up my handwritten list of dishes for him, putting on my best presenting voice. "So, tonight, we're starting with a little snack of grissini with goat cheese and black-truffle dip. For the appetizer, there's oysters three ways—mignonette sauce, a Vietnamese chili dressing, and Oysters Kilpatrick."

"Wow," he says, sounding genuinely impressed.

Happy that he is—*and* that he's not averse to seafood, which was a big risk—I continue. "And over there in the pot I should be stirring, is our main of sweet corn and crab risotto."

"Damn."

My lips twitch as I glance over at him. "Either I've reduced you to single-word answers or I haven't done my job right."

He lifts his brow and smirks. "Or maybe I'm wondering if I have a shit-show in hell of keeping up with you to help cook this delicious meal."

"Don't worry, honey. I promise I'll go easy on you . . . with the cooking anyway."

"Honestly, I've watched you cook online, and I was mesmerized. Seeing you do it in front of me might be a dream come true."

"Oh, you wait. If you're impressed with all of that, then dessert is gonna knock your socks off."

"Just my socks?" he says with a sexy smirk so hot I momentarily consider delaying our meal.

"Behave. I can't cook and be thinking about everything I wanna do to you."

"Now *this* I want to hear. How about you keep going, and I'll sit over here far away from you while you tell me all these things you've been thinking about doing to me."

"Maybe I wasn't always the one *doing*."

"Even better. Because I've got my own little mental wish list going too."

"Do tell me about these plans you said you had for me . . ."

He chuckles, his eyes alight with an equal measure of humor and heat. "Where's the fun in that? I've been looking forward to seeing the master at work in her element."

"Flattery will get you everywhere."

Then he languidly runs his eyes down my body and back up, sending a wave of heat in its wake that makes me lock my knees to stay upright. When his hooded gaze meets mine again, there's no mistaking the direction his mind has gone. *By god, I like where it's going, too.* Although, if this keeps up, dinner will be out the window and we'll be dining down on each other.

"How about we keep adding to our wish lists while we cook, because that risotto smells amazing and everything else you've described sounds just as good. And *maybe* . . ." he says, leaning in close. "Maybe one of my fantasies has been to cook with you, too."

That makes my chest warm and my lips curl up. "Okay then.

You can grab those two ears of corn and strip off the kernels for me while I stir the rice, make the dressings for the oysters, and pour us a glass of wine."

"How about *I* get us the wine, and then I'll strip the corn. But first, I have to do this." Then his hand is wrapped around the back of my neck and he's closing the distance between us for a long, wet, thorough kiss—something I'm learning Rhodes does *very* well.

He grins at me when I moan at the loss of his mouth. "Like that," he rumbles.

"Not as much as I do, honey."

"Debatable," he murmurs, his eyes drifting to my mouth again.

I flatten my hand on his chest. "You're gonna have to stop looking at me that way if you ever wanna eat."

"Yeah . . ." he says, *not* changing the way his eyes are eating me up. He shakes his head as if trying to snap out of a daze. "Right. Wine then corn."

"Sounds good." I smile before flexing my fingers against his heart and moving away to finish the main course.

"DAMN, DEE. THAT WAS FUCKING AMAZING," he says, placing the cutlery on his empty plate and leans back in his chair.

Having gorged ourselves on all three courses so far. It's fair to say we're well-fed and happy, especially if the satisfied grin on Rhodes's face is anything to go by.

I lift my glass to my lips and take a sip of the 2018 Far Niente Chardonnay I paired with the risotto. "Glad you enjoyed it."

"I knew it would be good, but I don't think I've eaten that well in years, probably since before Lils got sick." He wraps his fingers around his glass before freezing, his gaze jumping to mine. "Shit. Sorry."

Tilting my head, I see his bunched brows. "For what? You had a wife, Rhodes. You have a son. I have a son and had a husband. The difference is that mine is still in my life on a daily basis, and you lost yours far too early."

His eyes soften. "Yeah. But it's not good form to bring her up during a fantastic date with a woman I hope to see again."

"You wanna see me again?" I ask, my lips quirking into a small smirk.

"Well, you're cooking doesn't suck."

"Nice to know."

"And you make the art of cooking a hell of a lot more interesting."

I shift forward in my seat, leaning into an elbow on the table. "That was because I had a sexy man in my kitchen cooking with me."

His eyes flash again. *Fuck I like that look on him.* Then his expression turns serious again. "But I am sorry. Jake and I talked about it after Lily passed away, and we agreed we would never forget her, and part of that is by talking about her."

I reach over and hold my hand out, the weird tightness in my chest easing when he laces his fingers with mine. "I love that though. I can't imagine what it must've been like to live through losing the love of your life, and to have Jake to think about while all of that was going on. But I also can't imagine you'd ever forget her, Rhodes. I'd want to hear about her."

His body jolts. "You do?"

"She's as much a part of you as Jake is. And to state it plainly, so there's absolutely no doubt in your mind, I like you, Rhodes. A lot. And I want to spend time with you—and Jake—and want you to meet Harvey again too."

"I want that," he says with no hesitation, no uncertainty.

This man, god, he kills me with his honesty. It's so fucking good.

Flynn and I lived in denial for such a long time, trying to keep a steady ship and not rock the boat by admitting what we both knew to be true. Since then, I made myself a promise to always be honest and put my needs way up the list.

Rhodes isn't finished. "I also want it known that I don't date—not until you—and I know it hasn't been long, but this feels right between us and I'm not a fan of sharing, so—"

"You asking me to go steady, honey?"

He chuckles and shakes his head at me. "Yeah, I guess I am."

"Then do I get your class ring or letterman jacket?" I tease.

"Haven't had those for a long time. I could probably give you one of my CFD tees."

I giggle and sigh dramatically. "Oh, I guess that'll have to do."

He rubs his thumb over my knuckles. "I'll try to limit bringing Lily up."

"Don't you dare."

His eyes widen and his glass stills.

"I'm serious, Rhodes. We said we wouldn't censor, and with all indications being that I'm going to want to see you for a while, you'll have to interact with Flynn, because he's still a big part of my life too." I squeeze his hand to make sure I have his attention. "You accepted meeting my ex-husband and barely skipped a beat. You've gotta trust that I can do the same. Lily was your wife and Jake's mom. She's important, and I wouldn't be the woman you deserve if I can't accept that."

"Fuck I wanna kiss you right now."

I arch a brow. "What's stopping you?"

"Absolutely fucking nothing," he spits out as he surges up and rounds the table before pulling me to my feet, wrapping me in his arms and slamming his mouth onto mine. My lips part and my tongue seeks his. My hands glide through his hair and hold him in place, my body threatening to overheat as we make out like teenagers, the world around us fading away. It's sublime.

A little while later—after feeding each other my famous chocolate lava cake and tasting it on each other's lips, which might be my new favorite way to eat *anything*—Rhodes regrettably says he should head home.

"Before you go," I say, releasing his hand and walking over to the fridge. I pull out a paper bag with the Delish logo on it and move back to him where he stands watching me with a confused expression. "This is for Jake."

"You made my kid a doggy bag?"

I shrug. "It's nothing. We had leftovers, and it's better than letting it all go to waste."

"You know you're gonna be his favorite now, right? Probably more than me."

"You'll be the one delivering it so we might share that top spot. Not a bad place to be." I grin up at him. "Especially if it scores me brownie points with his dad."

"All you have to do is breathe to do that, sweet cheeks."

I huff out a breath, making him growl.

Hand in hand, we walk out to his car before making out against the wall. It leaves me pent up, and for a brief moment, I wish I could drag him back to the kitchen and say goodbye with other parts of my body.

"Thanks for dinner, Dee," he rasps against my lips, his body still pressed against me.

"You're welcome. Thanks for helping me cook it." I roll my hips, earning a deep groan that courses through me.

"Don't tease me when I'm on a knife's edge here."

"Oh, really?"

He turns to where we just came from, down the hall. "Any other time, any other place, I'd be showing my appreciation in more *creative* ways."

Absolutely nothing could wipe my grin off my face in this moment. I slide one of my hands down over his butt and push him against me. "I'll hold you to that."

"That's a promise, sweet cheeks."

My lips quirk up. "Feels to me like it's *you* with sweet cheeks right now."

Rhodes chuckles and kisses me while doing it. "Check with Harvs about mini-golf this coming weekend. And since Jake's license test isn't for two more weeks, he'll be up for an outing too."

"Big step," I murmur, looking deep into his soft blue eyes. "Going out with our kids."

"I think we're old enough and wise enough to know not to waste time when it comes to something that feels this good and this right. We'll go at whatever pace feels right between the two of us, but nice and slow with the kids."

My heart stutters before it melts into a puddle at my feet—pretty much the same thing my entire body is threatening to do. "Rusty my ass," I murmur, earning a panty-dropping grin from the man.

He leans in so our lips are barely touching, his warm breath fanning over my skin and making me tremble. "Seems I'm finding my groove when it comes to you." Then he kisses me once more—this time soft and slow and gentle. He pulls away and gifts me a smile that makes me feel like the luckiest woman in Chicago.

Thank heavens for knights in shining armor and matchmaking brothers, because holding Rhodes in my arms, I never wanna let him go. And though that should scare me, it absolutely does not.

Chapter 11

Rhodes

As much as all the guys at work have given me 'advice' about what to do, when to do it, and Scotty's constant questions about whether I *have* done it, I'm not going to wait X amount of days to call her. I'm not gonna play games, because I'd hate for her to do that to me, and in the three weeks since the setup, there's been absolutely nothing but straight-up honesty. This thing that's building between us is as easy as breathing. Even accidentally mentioning Lily didn't annoy Dee. In fact, she was fucking perfect in her response to it.

It's a hard thing to discuss, and not because I've been holding myself back for six years or grieving my wife. Jake and I gave ourselves to the end of the year that she died to simply grieve, processing everything as it came flying at us; the missed milestones, birthdays, family traditions, and the little things. Like no longer coming home to a house filled with delicious baking smells or crawling into bed after a twenty-four and just holding her in my arms for the peaceful ten minutes we'd get before Jake would wake up or Lils would have to get ready for work.

After that year, we shifted to celebrating her life and remembering all the good things. Now in almost everything we do, we carry her with us.

Then there's Dee, and I don't know what it was that first drew Jake to her videos, but when he showed me that first one where she was talking about box food being sustenance for aliens, it was like I had been lost and suddenly found again. It's the only way I can describe it. It wasn't love at first sight, but it was definitely a case of interest, intrigue, and many hours spent watching her old videos.

After meeting her, kissing her, and dreaming of all the things I wanna do to and with her, that feeling has only intensified.

Checking the time and noting I've still got a good three hours until Jake gets home, I consider asking her for an impromptu lunch date. Maybe a burrito or hot dog and quick walk around Grant Park. Picking up my phone I dial her number.

"Hey, handsome. I was just thinking about you."

My brows go up. "Is that right? Funny that. I was thinking about you too."

She laughs. "Hence the call."

"Uh huh. How are you?"

"I'm good. Been hanging at home this morning. I had a late night in the kitchen since my manager called in sick, so the struggle to get out of bed this morning was very real." She sighs. "Thankfully, Flynn has consultations all day, which means he was able to see Harvs off to school and let me sleep."

"You work long hours. It's good he's there to help." And the only jealousy I have is that fact that it wasn't me there for her.

"And now you see the beauty of my ex and I getting along and co-parenting in harmony.""

I chuckle. "Maybe I should entice you to come over with the offer of a massage."

"God," she moans, and I feel that sound right in my dick. "That would be amazing."

"My hands are always willing and able, sweet cheeks. They're yours if you want them.

She falls silent. "You shouldn't tease me, honey." Her voice is warm and low and reaching me in all the right places. *Damn, she's good.* "I know how you make me feel when you're hands are on me, so I can imagine how they'd be *all* over me . . ."

Yep. My dick is definitely wide awake and eager to please now.

"Are you home alone?" she asks curiously.

"Sure am. Why?" I smile. "You wanna come keep me company?"

"I'd love to."

I wait for a but that doesn't come.

"On one condition . . ."

"Name it. I'll do it," I say.

If it was any other guy at work saying this stuff, I'd be ribbing the crap out of them. But instead of Dee and I being at the three-week stage, it honestly feels like we're at the two-three month one already. Maybe it's the fact we're older and wiser and over the whole dating bullshit that goes along with new relationships. *Or maybe it's 'cause she's Dee, and she makes everything easy.*

"I've arranged cover for the restaurant tonight, thank god, but I've gotta go drop some keys off, so my condition is that you let me bring you lunch."

"You're honestly asking if you can feed me? Dee, you can do that anytime."

"Good. 'Cause that means it's up to you to provide the enter-tainment . . ." She lets her statement hang between us and my brain and dick yell 'hell yeah' while my heart is lying back in its deck chair sipping a piña colada.

I go for subtlety. "It's past noon . . ."

"Oh, Rhodes, don't you know it's called an afternoon delight for a reason?"

"Sweet cheeks, I said I didn't date. Didn't say I've lived the life of a monk . . ."

"Oh, thank god for that," she says.

And for a moment, I think she's joking. She's not.

"At least one of us has recent practice with anything, 'cause I'm at twenty-five months and counting." She laughs but my brain is stuck on her confession. "And now he goes quiet . . ."

Ever since I left her in the doorway to the restaurant, I've been consumed with finding a way to continue our hot make-out session in private. It's not like sleepovers are an option—not an easy one anyway—she has Harvs to worry about and a restaurant to run, and I have my own list of obstacles. I'm not against her staying overnight, but I'd want to prepare Jake for that since it's never happened before. I'm willing my heart to slow down and my balls to loosen up a bit when she speaks again.

"Rhodes, I wasn't meaning I was gonna come over and jump you. I'm in no rush or anything. It's just—"

"You'd better hurry, baby. I'm in a giving mood, and you've opened the floodgates."

"Well, I *hope* it'll be *you* opening those, but I'm not adverse to lending a hand to get to that goal."

I growl earning a cheeky laugh from my girl.

"Down, boy . . . at least for thirty minutes, then you can be whatever you want.

"Dee, why aren't you in your car already?"

As soon as we end the call, I'm up out of my seat and stripping my clothes off as I walk through the house, across my room, and into my ensuite to clean up.

True to her word, thirty-five minutes later, I'm opening my door to a grinning Dee with a black Delish bag hanging from her fingers.

"Dee Duncan delivers Delish," she says with a sly grin.

"Damn, I should get delivery more often if it comes in a package like that."

She bats her lashes dramatically and clutches her chest. "Flattery will get you *everywhere*, Mr. Anderson."

"In that case, get your butt inside so I can eat that amazing smelling food with you."

"You definitely know how to sweet-talk a girl."

"Only the ones I like," I whisper as she walks through the door. I sweep her into my arms, earning a squeak before I steal a kiss from her and groan at the contact. It may have only been three days, but by my count, that's three days too damn long.

She laughs against my lips as she presses lightly on my chest. "Hey. I said I *brought* you lunch, not that I *was* the lunch."

"Well, that's disappointing." I hold out my arm to usher her into the living and dining area, chuckling to myself as she swings her hips in time with the bag hanging from her fingers.

"I didn't say I wasn't planning on being a sweet after-lunch-*snack* though."

Fuck. I follow her like a drooling puppy dog, not embarrassed by it at all. It's then that I get it—what first drew me to Dee—it's her sparkle. That's corny as hell, but it's the pizazz she has, her laugh, her effervescent love of life that she shines far and wide. In person, it's with her smart mouth and wicked sense of humor. At the restaurant, it's her personality and passion for good food that you can sense in the air and taste with every bite. In her video blogs, it's her determination to teach the world how to make quick, easy food instead of ready-made alternatives. All of this runs through my head while Dee moves into the living room.

God, I thought I was a little obsessed over her before we met. Now I might be a lost cause.

Being with Dee makes me feel on top of the world, and I'm determined to stay here and work hard to keep her by my side.

But before that, I need to eat.

Walking through to the dining room, she stops and looks at the bookshelf where there are photos of Jake and I, family, friends, and finally, Lily.

She glances over her shoulder at me. "I thought Jake was you through and through, but he has her eyes."

"Yeah. They changed. Sometimes they'd be blue. When I'd pissed her off, they'd be electric green—something Jake also inherited. It was hard to stand my ground when she'd point those my way, and I find Jake has that trick up his sleeve too."

Her lips curve in a knowing smile. "I bet you give in every time."

I chuckle, looking at the ground and shaking my head. "Pretty much."

"Wish I could've gotten some tips. Might come in handy one day." She shoots me a wink before continuing to the kitchen.

I stay there, dumbfounded and amazed, staring at Lily's photo, partly kicking myself for not thinking about the fact that my new girlfriend kinda got slapped in the face with my past. She just took it in stride and didn't even miss a beat.

"C'mon, honey. This food may travel well, but I promise you won't wanna wait," she calls out from the kitchen, snapping me from my thoughts.

As if she has a sixth sense, by the time I reach her side, she's already found the plates and cutlery.

I move behind her and brush my lips against her neck, pressing my front to her back, nuzzling against her skin and breathing in the sweet scent of her jasmine perfume. "Sorry, I didn't think."

"About what?" she says quietly.

"The photos."

She stops what she's doing and covers my hands wrapped around her waist with her own, leaning her weight into me. "Honey, I'd be disappointed if you *didn't* have photos. You said you live your lives now memorializing her. You wouldn't be the man I'm coming to know you are if you hid her away."

"Fuck, Dee. Are you real?"

She releases a contented sigh. "As real as it gets, honey."

"That's good. Because I think I'm fast becoming addicted to you."

She tilts her head, giving me better access. "You sure you're not just horngry?"

I chuckle below her ear, sucking gently. "I'm definitely that. But it's not food making me feel that way."

"There are worse things to be addicted too," she rasps, a soft moan vibrating in her throat.

I nip her collarbone before soothing the sting with my tongue. "Like?"

"Anything and anyone that's not me."

I drop my forehead to her shoulder and laugh. "Yeah, I think you're right about that."

She snickers and steps away from me, leaving me in a rather uncomfortable predicament. She looks down, her gaze flashing with heat, definitely looking pleased with herself before she narrows her eyes. "Now stop trying to nail me in your kitchen before I can feed you."

My brows lift up. "You saying I can nail you in my kitchen *after* you feed me?"

"Well, shit, I walked right into that one, didn't I?" She giggles.

"Let's save that until we have a lot of guaranteed uninterrupted time, yeah?"

"Isn't this only our third date?"

"Didn't know you were counting," she says with a smirk. "Isn't that usually the girl's job?"

"You calling me a girl?"

"Noo . . ." Her smirk widens before her eyes soften. "It's nice. But also, I don't think the 'third date rule' applies to us."

I frown. "It doesn't?"

"Nah. 'Cause it's starting to feel like I've known you forever."

"I agree."

"See, it must be right. Look at us—we're already thinking the same."

I almost drool as she spoons out a roast pumpkin, prosciutto, and pearl couscous salad she made on a video last month.

She glances sideways at me and her lips twitch. "I'm guessing you saw my video where I made this?"

"Yeah, and then Jake and I tried to make it and I still managed to fuck it up."

"Then I made a good choice. It was between this or a moussaka my sous-chef, George, had just pulled out of the oven."

"Damn," I frown, peering into the unfortunately empty Delish bag. "That didn't fall into your hands as you were leaving?"

"Next time, I promise."

"*I* might hold *you* to that before we even get a chance to have sex in my kitchen."

She hands the plate over to me. "Get away, you horngry animal."

"Grr."

"GOD THAT WAS AMAZING."

Dee shrugs, putting her empty plate on the coffee table in front of us. "It's pretty simple to make. I could show you some time."

"I'd like that. You know what I want more though?"

She looks over and arches a brow.

"A taste of that sweet after-lunch-snack you promised."

Her lips curve up on one side, her green eyes sparking with heat.

She turns in her seat on the couch to face me. "Well, what are you waiting for?"

I crawl over her and brace my hands beside her head before slowly lowering my body onto hers as she stretches out beneath me. "Hi," I murmur, placing a kiss on the corner of her mouth.

Her hands glide around my shoulders and flatten on my back, pressing me against her. "Hey there."

"Thanks for lunch."

"It's what I do."

"And what else do you do?" I trace her smile with the tip of my tongue.

"Kiss me and find out."

Don't have to tell me twice.

I groan against her lips, kissing her soft and slow before deepening the kiss when her fingers run into my hair and her nails scrape gently against my scalp.

She whimpers into my mouth, giving me as good as she gets as she spreads her legs wider and hooks her calves behind my thighs, allowing my hips to fall in between. My hard cock presses against her core, my pelvis rocking into hers. She thrusts on an upward glide, increasing the pressure. Her body trembling, her grip in my hair tightens.

I tear my mouth from hers and kneel between her legs, dragging my fingers to the hem of her top and jerking it over her body before throwing it onto the floor. I do the same with mine, loving the way her eyes rake over my chest, her gaze falling with need and heat.

When she pulls me back to her, our skin on skin for the first time, it turns wild like a spark has been lit, the fire between us roaring to life.

As our mouths fuse together again, her hands are everywhere, running up and down my back, gripping my ass and rocking my hips harder and faster. Her whimpers turn into moans, and I'm desperate for more. I bury my face in her neck, nipping and sucking the soft, silky skin there, loving the way she's going wild and fucking thrilled I'm the one doing it to her too.

I shift my body lower, reaching between us to pull down her black satin bra. Cupping her breast in my hand and wrapping my lips around her nipple, I draw deeply, making her arch into me.

"Honey . . ." she rasps, the sound shooting straight through me to settle in my balls as they draw up, my cock throbbing, begging for release.

"Baby, you're fucking fantastic," I groan, needing to taste her mouth again.

"Rhodes . . . I'm close."

Even fucking better. "So fucking sweet," I murmur, raking my teeth against her lip before delving deep. My tongue rolls around hers, our hips thrusting harder and faster now. It's exquisite torture.

I reach between us again, but this time I lift up and lock eyes with hers. Her blown pupils show me how far gone she is and drives me to see just how much more it'll take for her catch fire for me.

I make quick work of the button at her waist before tugging the zipper down and diving my hand inside her underwear, closing my eyes and releasing a loud guttural groan when I find her swollen and wet for me. "Fuck baby."

"*Yes* . . ." she moans as I stroke her core, my thumb swirling over her clit. Her movements turn erratic, her eyes hooded. She hooks her hand around the back of my neck, crushing her lips to mine, and this kiss turns feral. It's all teeth and tongue, groans and moans, whimpers and growls. "I'm gonna come. Fuck."

"Yeah, Dee. I wanna hear you. I want to hear you scream my name down my throat as I make you come all over my hand."

"Yes. Jesus. God. So good."

"Not god. Just a man who loves the feel of you and wants to feel more. Give it to me, Dee. Take yourself there." I push two fingers inside her and flick her clit with the tip of my thumbnail, and she's crying out, her body convulsing with wave after wave of her climax.

"Rhodes. Honey. Yes!"

And my chest swells, my heart racing as she comes apart at the seams under my hands.

I slowly ease her back down, gliding my hand out of her pants and locking eyes with her as I bring my fingers to my mouth and groan deeply as her taste overwhelms my senses. "Best fucking after-lunch-snack I've ever had," I murmur before I lose myself against her and kiss her soft and slow and sweet, her hands lazily rubbing over my shoulders and back.

"Now *that* is an afternoon delight," she says when we pull apart, both trying to catch our breath.

"Sign me the fuck up," I mutter, touching my lips to her neck.

There's a noise at the front door, and we both go completely still. At the sound of a key sliding into the lock. My eyes nearly pop out of my head as I realize we're about to be sprung and Dee's half-naked body is still pressed to mine.

"Fuck." I scramble off the couch as Dee does the same. I quickly snatch her T-shirt from the floor as she rights her jeans and bra, and together we manage to get her tee over her head. We both quickly sit and try to act casual while I think about anything and everything completely unsexy to get my angry hard-on to calm the fuck down.

Jake walks into the living room and stops in his tracks when he sees us sitting on opposite ends of the couch, looking as guilty as hell.

"Well, well, well. What do we have here, kids?"

I narrow my gaze, staring daggers at the shit-eating grin he shoots me before he laughs under his breath and shakes his head. "What have I told you about having girls over, Dad?" he says, enjoying this far too fucking much.

I roll my eyes. "Yeah. What *have* you said, Jake?"

He points to us. "Ah ha! Sprung. Kids these days. And what about you, young lady? Do your parents know where you are?"

"Jake . . ." I warn half-heartedly, struggling not to burst out laughing with the taste of her still lingering on my tongue. Just my luck Dee and I get interrupted the first time we get it on. I was enjoying the hell out of her too.

"Hi, Jake. It's nice to see you again," Dee doesn't even try to hide the humor in her voice.

"You too, Dee. Probably didn't expect it to be like *this* though. But what's a guy to do, right? I come home early from school, looking to take a load off and relax, and I walk into *this*," he says with an over-dramatic sigh.

I raise a brow. "What *are* you doing home so soon?"

"No driver's ed training today, remember, Dad? Maybe you had *other* things on your mind?" he says, waggling his brows.

"Yeah, yeah." I rub the back of my neck. *Have kids they said. It'll be fun they said.*

"Right. Well, I'll leave you two *lovebirds* alone. But see you Saturday, Dee. I've decided Harvey and I are gonna team up and kick your asses at mini golf."

Dee's eyes soften. "Looking forward to it."

"And thanks for the doggy bag. That risotto was the shit." And with that poetic compliment, he's walking out of the room, waving his hand over his head.

I shoot a cautious look Dee's way, only to find her grinning from ear to ear, her lips twitching. I lift my arm as she struggles and fails to hold in her laughter. It's when she snuggles into my side and dissolves into a fit of giggles that I press my lips to her hair and chuckle against her temple. "Told you we need guaranteed uninterrupted time."

She lifts her head and tilts her face toward mine. "Let's organize that as soon as we can. Although . . . sneaking around like teenagers could also be fun."

"Jesus. You might just be the death of me," I mutter, touching my lips to hers. She smiles and kisses me softly. "But what a way to go."

Chapter 12

Dee

Rhodes and I had agreed that the best course of action would be to play Saturday really low key. It's a chance for Harvey to see Jake again—something he'd been asking me about a lot—and also a casual introduction to the whole 'Mommy has a boyfriend' concept.

I may be taking this really slowly with my son, but I really like where things with Rhodes and I are going in a way that I don't see it being a short-term thing, which means Rhodes and Jake could become regular features in our lives. I wanted to make sure Harvey had absolutely no reservations.

So, when Flynn and I sat down with him to discuss the 'day date with the kids' idea, Harvey's reaction made my eyes sting. "I always wanted a big brother. Billy Nelson doesn't have a big brother. He's only got a sister, and she never lets him do anything with her. I bet Jake would let me do stuff with him."

I ruffled his hair while Flynn just grinned at him then looked over at me and winked.

"Is it time to go yet?" Harvey asks me for what seems like the tenth time this morning.

I make a point of slowly looking at my watch and humming and hawing while he bounces excitedly in front of me. "Moooom . . ." he groans.

Laughing, looking him up and down, taking in his black shorts and bright red T-shirt. "Well, I think since you look so handsome, and you even have your shoes on. We are ready to hit the road."

"Yes!!" he says with a fist pump before tackling me with a hug and running back out of the room. "Dad! We're going now."

"Have you got your shoes on?" Flynn calls out, making me giggle. If Harvey doesn't have to wear footwear, he won't. He's been that way since he was a toddler.

"Yeah, Dad," He sighs, giving me a glimpse of what a future will be like with a tween and then teenager. At least if things go the distance with Rhodes and I, he'll have already survived the teenage years with Jake and will have hopefully learned a few tricks and tips to pass on to me.

With a last look in the mirror, I move downstairs to find Harvey waiting impatiently by the front door and Flynn leaning against the door shooting me an amused smirk.

"Ah, and she goes with *those* jeans. There's no way you're gonna win now," he teases.

"They're my Lucky jeans." Casual date means comfy yet still sexy enough to distract Rhodes from kicking my ass, so I paired a loose-fitting Delish V-neck tee with my favorite butt-lifting jeans— because I'm almost thirty-seven, and gravity doesn't care how much you lunge or squat or Zumba.

Flynn's grin widens. "Lucky by brand, not by nature. At least Rhodes will learn about your never-give-up attitude.

"Thanks for the encouragement," I mutter.

Harvey steps forward and grabs my hand, giving me a squeeze

and looking up at me. "It's okay, Mom. I can be your partner if you want? The Duncans vs the . . . What's his last name again?"

"Anderson, baby."

"Right. The Duncans vs the Andersons. We can make it a competition, and then I can win for you."

"Damn, kid. Maybe we should do that."

"Then again, Jake might want *me* to be his partner, and then I'd have to decide if it's kids vs parents."

Flynn chuckles and I join him. "Let's hit the road, and we can decide who partners with who when we get there. How does that sound?

"Yeah! Let's go then." Harvey turns and gives Flynn the same tackle-hug he gave me earlier before grabbing my hand again. And with a goodbye wave and a mouthed "just relax" from my ex-husband, Harvey and I walk out the door—destination City Mini Golf.

Forty minutes later, we've parked and fed the meter on the east-side of Columbus Avenue and are walking hand in hand toward Millennium Park before spotting Rhodes and a glued-to-his-phone Jake waiting for us.

"Hey." I step forward to give Rhodes a hug.

"Hey, sweet—Dee." He catches himself, and I snort, earning myself narrowed albeit amused eyes before he turns to Harvey. "Hey, Harvey. Good to see you again."

"Hello, Mr. Rhodes. Hey, Jake," my son says, almost vibrating with excitement and anticipation. When I say he was so looking forward to seeing Jake again, I caught him practicing conversations in the bathroom mirror last night. It was equally adorable and heartwarming.

Jake slides his phone into his back pocket and grins. "Hey, bud. I hear you and I are gonna kick some serious parent-butt today."

Harvey's chest swells. "Yeah. My dad and I play all the time, and sometimes he lets me win. I don't tell him I know that. I pretend I'm super good and he must be bad for losing to a kid."

"Oh yeah, Harvs. You and I are going to get on so well." Jake jerks his head to the side. "Wanna come in and we'll make sure we get the good putters. Winners need the *best* equipment. Right?"

Harvey nods excessively before the two of them walk away.

"Now"—Rhodes closes the distance between us—"I can give you a proper hello."

I open my mouth to say something, but he uses the opportunity to wrap an arm around my waist before gently gripping my chin and kissing me like it's leading to the bedroom, not that we're standing in a central city park outside a mini-golf course. I have to grab his biceps and hold on as he kisses and nips and explores every inch of my mouth with his tongue. I fight to keep up and give as good as I'm getting back from him. "Damn, honey. *That* is a welcome."

He grins, his eyes crinkling at the sides as we stand close in each other's arms. "We didn't talk about PDA and Harvey, so I decided to go for friendly not intimate."

My stomach flips, and warmth fills my chest. "Thank you. I guess tepid warmth would be a good approach. Slowly but surely."

"Sounds like a plan. I'm onboard for however you want this to go today. Harvey knows we're dating, right?"

I nod, and he continues.

"And Jake is old enough to get what's what. So, I'll follow your lead on all of this. Making sure you're comfortable and Harvey is okay with everything is a priority, yeah?"

"Stop making me want to kiss you again," I murmur, melting against him. He chuckles and brushes his lips gently against mine.

"Not going to happen, sweet cheeks. I'm going to get you addicted to me as much as I am to you," he says quietly, moving to press a kiss on my jaw. "But until I can do *more* than this . . ."

His voice is soft and low and my body is demanding everything and now.

Giving my libido whiplash, he straightens and tangles his fingers with mine. "We should really get inside, because Jake is a good kid, but there's no telling what tricks of the trade he's passing on to your son."

I giggle and shake my head. "Right. Let's go stop the teen from corrupting the tween, shall we?" Rhodes leads me inside the gates and toward the concession booth where we find the kids waiting for us.

"Jeez. Take your time, slow pokes," Harvey says with a laugh. "Right Jake?"

"Maybe they're scared that they're going to get beaten by a couple of kids."

Harvey looks up to Jake, and I'm already seeing hero worship at play. "Yeah."

"You paid?" Rhodes asks Jake, who scoffs and shakes his head.

"You think I'm going to pay when I know you will anyway. You always said, you date, you pay. So, Daddio . . ."

"Yeah, yeah," Rhodes muses, laughing under his breath as he steps up to the window. "Two adults, a student, and a child."

"You want a family pass? It's cheaper," the booth attendant asks.

"Sounds good," Rhodes pays for all of us, and we're directed to the next window over where the young guy behind the counter goes to Harvey first.

"Hey, dude. I can tell by looking at you that you're a bit of a putting shark. Am I right?"

Harvey blushes a little and bumps one shoulder. "Yeah. I'm not bad."

"Oh, you're one of *those* guys. The ones who make you *think* you've got a chance when really they're going to whip your butt."

"That's me." He stands a little bit taller under the attention.

"Better get the best putter for the best player," the attendant winks at Harvey before looking the rest of us up and down then turning away. He returns with four putters and four different-colored golf balls a minute later.

He hands me the scorecard and pencil. "And for the lady, 'cause we all know these guys will try and cheat to impress you."

"You're not wrong there." I laugh when my three playing partners big and small scoff in defense.

The attendant holds his fist out to Harvs. "Good luck, putting shark. Make sure you do a victory dance at the end when you win, okay?"

And after an exploding fist bump—from both of them—Rhodes runs his arm around my waist and the four of us follow the signs toward the first hole of eighteen.

Halfway through our game, I'm starting to think Brad was right about Harvey. Or else Rhodes and Jake are playing bad for his benefit. Whatever the case, I don't think I've laughed more on a family outing in years. Jake is a born entertainer, and you can tell the relationship he has with Rhodes is rock solid. They look out for each other. They're always joking, teasing, or cheering each other on.

Whereas Harvey has been focused on two things: impressing Jake and winning.

But I'm relaxed, I'm happy, and I'm definitely enjoying the subtle and sometimes discreet ways Rhodes has been flirting and touching me. The current hole we're on has a windmill that rotates to block a ball-sized tunnel through to the other side, and so far I've missed it three times, much to Jake and Harvey's glee.

Rhodes comes up behind me, cloaking my back with his and holding me close as he mimics my stance and reaches around to cover my hands over the grip. "Now *this* is how we *should* be playing mini golf. Definitely much better," he croons in my ear, sending a shiver through me. I discreetly push my ass into his pelvis, my lips curving into a smirk at his barely audible groan and the growing hardness I find.

"Behave, sweet cheeks."

I turn and meet his eyes over my shoulder. "And where's the fun in *that*?"

"Oh, we'll have fun in this position, just not when our kids are right there." Rhodes's voice is laced with humor and heat, which makes me laugh and clench my thighs together in the same breath.

"Step away from your teammate, Dad. No cavorting allowed," Jake announces rather loudly.

Rhodes groans and shifts back, taking a deep breath as he does. "Damn smartass."

"Pleased to be of service, Dad," he says with a smirk before turning back to me. "C'mon, Dee, chant the rotations in your head and hit the ball on the count of three so that you're through the gap before you hit four. Get it?"

"Yeah. Let's give it a shot, right?"

"Ha, get it, Mom? Give it a *shot*," Harvs says, hilariously stating the obvious and making us laugh.

"See, I'm not just a pretty face."

"No, you're a damn sexy one too," Rhodes murmurs behind me.

I whirl around and point a finger at him, narrowing my eyes. "Behave, Mr. Anderson. You're not supposed to distract your own teammate. Besides," I say, lowering my voice, "if I don't get the ball in the hole, you won't get the pleasure of watching my ass when I bend over to collect it."

"My eyes have been glued to your ass since the minute you first arrived, *Ms.* Duncan. So don't worry about me."

"Good to know these jeans are appreciated," I say with a wink.

"Everything about you is."

My breath hitches, but I quickly cover up my reaction. There will be time for that later, whenever Rhodes and I can arrange our adult alone time. Something that is *definitely* overdue.

"C'mon, Mom. Hit the ball already," Harvey calls out, making me roll my eyes.

"Kids these days, I dunno . . ." Then I bob my head in time with the rotations, taking Jake's advice and counting. When I hit three, I tap the ball hard with the head of the putter, and thankfully it slides past the blade of the windmill in time to a chorus of applause from my three male cheerleaders.

Harvey runs and hugs me tight before straightening and trying to look cool again. Jake offers me a high five, and Rhodes wraps his arm around my shoulders and pulls me into him, touching his lips to my temple.

God, I could get used to this.

We've just finished the horrible windmill hole when a familiar voice calls my name. Turning around I spot Faith and Bryant walking toward us, golf clubs in hand.

"Hey, sis," I say as we hug each other. "What are you guys doing here?"

"Curing world hunger." Bry embraces me after his wife. He shakes hands with Rhodes and Jake before ruffling Harvey's hair.

"They're playing mini golf too, Mom. Jeez." Harvs states the obvious, yet again.

I roll my eyes at him and return to my sister. "I mean, where are the kids?"

"We left them at home. I mean, they're old enough to watch each other now, right? Toddlers are so mature these days," Faith teases. "They're with Bry's parents. They offered to give us a break for a day date. It was either this or day *drink*, and we opted for the more responsible adult option." Her eyes dance with amusement as she looks between the four of us. "And how about all of you? Who's winning, Harvs?"

"Me! But Jake's helping. Mom and Rhodes aren't playing very well."

"Is that so?" my sister replies with a laugh. "Let me tell you, I kicked Uncle Bryant's butt." She holds up her hand, and Harvey doesn't leave her hanging, smacking his palm against hers triumphantly.

"You rock, Aunty Faith."

"I know, but not as much as you, Harvey Duncan. You're a rock star." She smiles warmly at my son. "You'll have to come out with us to the driving range one day. We can see how far and how hard you can really hit a golf ball."

Harvey turns to me, his eyes pleading. "Please, Mom. That would be *so* cool."

"Of course, bud. Anytime you want."

"Right." Faith looks at me. "We won't hold you up any longer." I can see the questions in her gaze, all of which I cannot answer.

Rhodes's gentle laughter from beside me grabs my attention.

"Yeah. Prepare yourself for a big phone call later, Bry. I think your wife is expecting a date debrief tonight."

My brother-in-law pulls my sister into his arms and chuckles. "I'm used to it with these two. Even as kids they'd sneak into each other's rooms and whisper all night until Patricia would catch them out and send them to bed."

"Hey. It's not our fault they separated our bunk beds and made us get our own rooms."

"Faith," he says, trying to hold back a laugh. "You almost made her pass out when you were trying to test a hypothesis about hanging upside down for too long."

Faith's eyes meet mine, and we both dissolve into giggles.

"Oh no. Now we'll never finish the game," Harvey says.

"Why's that?" Jake asks.

"Once Mom and Aunty Faith start giggling, they're lost forever," he replies dryly.

I simmer down and quirk a brow at my son. "Hey, mister. You do know I can hear you, right?"

His lips curve up, and suddenly I have images of a teenage Harvey doing the same thing to me. Dammit. Why do kids have to grow up?

"Well, we'll leave you all to it. Have fun. And, Rhodes, you should come over and see the renovations we've done," Bryant says, shaking Rhodes hand again.

Rhodes's head jerks back. "You're renovating *again*? Jeez. I haven't even completed renovation round one on my place"

Bry shrugs. "Whatever the wife wants, the wife gets."

"And this wife wanted to change my theme to mid-century modern, starting with tiles." Faith flashes us a beaming smile.

"Cool. I'll definitely call around for a beer on one of my days off then. Maybe I'll bring Dee and some of Faith's design ideas can rub off on her too. Lord knows I need all help I can get with colors and fabrics. That was always Lily's domain. Jake and I make do, but there's something to be said about a woman's touch, right?" He pulls me into his side again and, as if it's the most natural thing in the world, I wrap my arms around his waist, anchoring myself to him like he's doing to me.

I crane my neck to meet his gaze. "Oh, *maybe* you'll bring me along, huh? To my own sister's house. Jeez. Get set up, they said. He's a good guy, they said." I'm trying to hide my surprise at the ease in which he talked about me helping renovate while seamlessly mentioning his wife's name in the same breath. It's definitely an adjustment for me, but I'm slowly getting used to the fact that Lily is still a big force to be reckoned with in the lives of the Anderson men.

"Damn, I think I like it when you're a little feisty," he murmurs, snapping me from my thoughts.

"See you," Faith and Bry say, seemingly enjoying this show far too much.

I wave goodbye but don't look away from Rhodes's beautiful blue eyes, totally ensnared in his charming web. "You *want* me feisty? Oh, honey, you ain't seen nothing yet."

"Is that so," he murmurs, his gaze dropping to my mouth, my tongue instinctively darting out to wet my dry lips. The rumbling growl deep in his chest has me pressing myself closer to him.

"Um . . . guys?" Jake says.

We both turn our heads at the same time to meet the amused grins of both Jake and Harvey.

Jake winks at us. "We're just going to go get some snacks."

"You want my wallet?" Rhodes asks.

"Nope," he replies, jerking his head in the direction of the food carts we saw when we first arrived. "C'mon, Harvs. Let's go refuel for the rest of our butt-kicking mini-golf mission."

"Oh, man. I could kill a hot dog right now."

"Me too. And fries."

"And donuts."

"A mini-man after my own heart."

"Don't you mean stomach?" my son asks, and I bury my face in Rhodes's chest to stifle my giggle.

"That too, bud. Let's go," Jake replies as they walk away, leaving us alone, Jake looks back over his shoulder and shoots us a devilish, knowing grin. "Don't worry, parentals. We'll take our time." And then to Harvey, he says, "Had to get you away from the adults, bud. They're gonna kiss, and we don't need to see that, right?"

"Yeah. Eww. Girls are gross."

Rhodes is still chuckling when he cups my face and gently tilts it to meet his. "Lucky for me, I don't think girls are gross . . ." he murmurs against my lips. "In fact, I think *this* girl is a tease and a flirt, and I'm the one who's going to get lucky when I peel her out of these jeans later."

I arch a brow, my lips twitching. "Is that so? And when, pray tell, did you plan on telling *me* that you were gonna be peeling me out of *anything* later?

He presses his forehead to mine. "Adult alone time, sweet cheeks. Jake is going to a movie with friends tonight. That means—"

"That means adult alone time," I breathe, when inside I'm melting and swooning and doing high fives all around the joint.

"Fuck yeah." His eyes flash with heat before his hand is tangled in my hair and his tongue is in my mouth. It's definitely not the most *appropriate* kiss for the ninth hole of a mini-golf course, but then again, with Rhodes kissing me like an unspoken promise of all the fun we'll have later, I don't mind one single bit.

After downing hot dogs and fries and pop, Jake and Harvey *did* end up kicking our butts, winning by a clear five shots.

But with Rhodes by my side, it's safe to say that my mind was *not* on mini golf.

Chapter 13

Rhodes

Dee: So . . . still want me to come over tonight?

Rhodes: You think for one second I'm going to say no to adult alone time with you after teasing me all day in those jeans?

Dee: It was a few hours. Surely it wasn't THAT torturous.

Rhodes: Anytime I'm around you and can't touch you is torturous.

Dee: That's a yes to coming over then?

Rhodes: Why aren't you here already?

Dee: See you in twenty then.

"This is like living with a mooning teenager, I swear," Jake says sarcastically.

Looking up, I find him leaning against the doorway to the living room grinning at me.

Raising a brow, I drop my phone in my lap. "I think you're confused. I'm the dad, and *you* are the teen."

"Yeah. Yet you're the one grinning at your phone while texting, whereas my phone's on vibrate and I'm playing it cool by not responding straight away."

I chuckle. "Or maybe your phone's on silent so I don't know you're not getting any texts at all."

Jake clutches his chest in mock pain. "Ouch. That one hurt, Dad." His wide smirk makes me shake my head.

"You still heading out?" I ask.

He narrows his eyes. "Uh huh. Although *maybe* I should stay home and *supervise* . . ."

"Don't you da—"

He throws his head back and laughs. "Gotcha!"

"Why did *I* have to raise a smartass," I mutter, rolling my eyes.

"But to answer your question, yeah, Dad. I'm going out. Kyle's dad is picking me up and playing security guard for the night." I arch a brow and shoot him 'the look,' and he soon holds his hands up in surrender. "Yeah, I know. It's no skin off my nose. Saves wasting money on an Uber, and he's a bit like you anyway."

"How?"

"He's cool."

"Thank god. I can go to my grave having succeeded in being a cool dad."

"It's true. All my friends say so. Obviously being a badass fire-fighter doesn't ruin your cred either."

"Good to know. You need some money?"

"Nah. I'm good. So, Dee is coming over?"

"Yeah. You okay with that?" I ask, my tone turning serious.

Jake's head jerks back, his eyes flashing wide. "Dad, this is *your* house. *You're* the adult in this relationship." He waves his hand between us. "It's not up to me to say anything. But if it makes you relax, I'm fine with Dee staying the night. It's not like I'm a light sleeper, and I'm not naive enough to think you've been celibate for the past six years."

My mouth drops open, earning an amused gaze from my son.

"You're a grown man, you're not a virgin, and if anyone is gonna practice safe sex after all the lectures you've given me, it's you. So have fun. I'll text you before I come home to give you the head's up, and I won't be a smartass and embarrass you around your girlfriend. Deal?"

I look at him in wonder, again thinking that when god was handing out sons, I lucked out with mine. "You're a pretty good kid, you know?"

Jake's mouth quirks up. "You mean wise? Handsome? Pretty damn cool?"

"Humble too," I say with a laugh.

"Yeah that."

"Okay. So, you sure you're okay with it?"

He rolls his eyes. "Dad. Relax. Have your girl over. Don't act like I'm a ball and chain holding you back. I *want* you happy, and Dee makes you happy. It's as simple as that."

"You make me happy too, kid. And proud."

His chest puffs out a little. "Well, of course. I'm awesome." He looks me up and down. "Go have a shower and clean yourself up. You wanna make a good impression, don't you?"

I push myself to my feet and walk past him, bumping his shoulder as I go. "You're lucky I love you. Otherwise, I'd start to get a complex that my kid thinks I'm a lost cause."

"Nah. You're not *that* bad. A little direction is all you need."

"Gee, thanks," I scoff. "Let me know if Jeff arrives before I'm out. Okay?"

"Sure thing. Don't forget the aftershave. Chicks love that shit."

"Chicks probably don't like being called chicks either," I call back.

"Whatever. *Women*, then. Happy now? And I'll tidy up in here too. Can't have Dee thinking we live in a bachelor pad or anything."

. "Thanks, kid." I reach out and ruffle his already styled hair, earning a groan of protest. And as I walk down the hall to the shower, I'm smiling.

We did good with him, Lils. I hope I'm making you proud, baby.

And even not getting an answer to that, I know in my heart that she'd be smiling at me with her cute lopsided grin.

Fifteen minutes later, I see Jake off at the door, waving to Jeff. Us parents have a group chat where we fact-check and keep our fingers on the pulse of everything going on in our children's lives, and we all take turns at playing the cab of mom and dad. It's great for me given my work schedule and the amount of time Jake has with an empty house. Sometimes he stays with my parents or Lily's, but generally, he's home. I definitely hit the jackpot in the kid lottery with that one, because—touch wood—so far, apart from the need for a few minor attitude adjustments, Jake's never done anything to break my trust.

It's why his grandparents and I have all put in to buy him a Ford truck to give him when he passes his driver's test next week. He's been saving his allowance for it, but we all felt he deserved it, and we know he'll be responsible with it.

Just after Jeff pulls away, Dee turns into my driveway, grinning at me through the windshield.

When she gets out and walks along the front path and up the stairs toward me, her smile has me mesmerized. The pull between us is not only physical—it's more than that—a feeling that just continues to grow stronger the more time we spend together. And after today's seemingly successful outing with the kids, it's another tick joining the many others already marked off that have me thinking Dee was *meant* to come into my life. "Hey, sweet cheeks."

"Before I come inside, I have a question to ask . . ." she says, somewhat confusingly. "And I'll preface this by telling you that whatever your answer, it's totally okay and I'll still stay. Alright?"

My brows bunch together as I read her nervousness, something I haven't seen from Dee before.

"What's wrong?"

"Oh, absolutely nothing. It's just, well, your answer will determine whether I have to go back to my car or not."

"Okay, now you're confusing me."

"Sorry. Sorry," she babbles, scrunching her nose up. "Right. So, I talked with Harvey, and Sundays are Flynn's day with him anyway. So, I was wondering if I'll need the overnight bag I have in my car?"

I step forward, a slow smile creeping over my face as I stop in front of her and rest my hands on her hips. "You saying I get you all night?"

She looks at me with her big green eyes and bites her lip. "I mean, yeah. If you want a sleepover—I'm game if you are."

I sweep her into my arms, laughing at her squeak of surprise as I carry her inside and close the door with my foot.

"Rhodes, my bag. I need to—"

"I'll get it later." I grab her underneath the ass as she hooks her legs around my hips and I stride down the hallway.

"But what about Jak—"

I stop outside my bedroom door and press her back against the wall, dipping my head so we're nose to nose, her warm breath fanning over my lips as I lock eyes with hers. "Jake is out till eleven. He also knows that you're coming over, and apparently he *really* likes his dad and you too, because he said he's fine with you staying over."

Her mouth drops open, her surprise morphing into soft warmth.

"Dee, in a minute, I'm gonna take you to my bed, strip those fucking sexy jeans off that delectable ass of yours, and I'll devour your body until you tell me to stop or I exhaust myself with all the different ways I've imagined making you come. If either of those options don't gel with you, now would be the time to say so." My voice is rough with lust, visions of her laid out before me with hours to explore each other without any interruptions blowing any fantasy I've had about this woman in the past few weeks—okay, *months* since I first saw her videos—out of the water.

She doesn't even hesitate for a moment. Her hands grip my hair and tug my mouth to hers, her lips crushing against mine as she kisses me hard and deep and wet, her moans and my guttural groan echoing off the walls.

I guess that's a hell yes.

Still kissing her, I move us sideways and carry her across to my bed before putting a knee to the mattress and lowering her on to it and covering her with my body. Our lips don't separate as I clutch her head with one hand and drag my palm down her chest, cupping her breast in my hand and rubbing my thumb over her hard nipple.

Dee's back arches into my touch, her fingers tensing in my hair and pulling tight. I plunder her mouth as her tongue wrestles with mine, her body hot against me as I roll my straining erection against the seam of her jeans.

Her hands run down my back, scrambling to grab hold of the hem of my shirt and dragging the material up.

I tear my mouth away from hers just long enough to brace an arm on the bed and rip it off before throwing it away to a destination I don't care about. Knifing off the bed, I pull her with me and place my hands on the hem of her top. With the jerk of her chin giving me permission, I glide the shirt over her chest. She helps me remove it, then we're both stripping to our underwear.

Dee stretches out on the mattress in front of me again, and I near on dive on top of her with a groan—mine—and a moan—hers. Our lips lock, my cock throbbing and telling me it desperately wants more and it wants it now. But I ignore the need to bury myself deep and focus on stripping Dee naked so that I can start the journey of discovering every inch of her body. "Fuck, baby. You're a dream."

Her lips curve up wickedly. "I'll become a nightmare if you don't get back down here and kiss me again."

"Is that so?" I drag my gaze all over her exposed skin, cataloging every curve, every line, every freckle. I smooth my palms over her arms and to her shoulders before gently pulling her up to bring us chest to chest. My hands continue to move, gliding and touching as I lean my lips in so we're touching but not kissing. Her breath fans over my skin, driving me crazy as her body goads me into giving in and taking her mouth again. I undo her black bra and, tilting my head, brush my lips against her shoulder as I somehow find the patience to slowly glide it along her arms and onto the floor.

I glance between us, taking in this magnificent woman—the star of my dirtiest dreams and filthiest fantasies is in my bed and almost fully bared to me. I want to throw my head back and howl at the moon, but that would be a waste of precious time I *could* be using to make Dee scream my name over and over again.

But Dee proves she isn't a meek, shrinking violet when she growls in frustration, frames my jaw in her hands, and slams her mouth to mine. "Fast first, honey. Slow, later." As if to punctuate her point, she kisses me again, sucking on my tongue while her hands roam everywhere. Falling back onto the mattress, she pulls me onto her. Our bodies align, my hips rolling into hers as she thrusts up. The switch in speed makes my head swim and my cock throb.

I shift down the bed, straddling her thighs and wrapping my lips around her nipple. I roll the other between my fingers, loving the way she arches into my mouth. Her hands in my hair encourage me lower, and when I drag the tip of my tongue along the edge of her black satin underwear, any plan and self-control I had to take my time with Dee jumps out the window and runs down the road. I'm like a raging fire, and Dee is the fuel making me burn bright.

"Please, Rhodes. I want to feel you." Dee's voice is a rough, velvet whisper, and it unleashes something inside of me. I tear her panties away with her help before I splay my hands on her spread thighs, my gaze drifting from her flushed face to her exposed sex. And if I wasn't done for before, I am now. She braces herself on her elbows as I hook her legs over my shoulders and lay my chest on the bed before dragging my flattened tongue from her clit to her soaked core. Her taste explodes on my tongue, my senses jumping into overdrive. Then her fingers are gripping my hair, and I'm eating like a starving man who's never going to dine again. My own hands frame her hips and roll her against my mouth, wanting to reach every single inch of her, needing to drive her absolutely crazy with lust until she can't take anymore and begs for release. I want the memory of my name being torn from Dee's lips to haunt me every single time I'm in my bed without her near me.

I slowly push one finger inside her, vibrating my tongue against her clit, but it's not enough. I want to bury myself deep and make us fall off the edge together.

Surging over her body, I pull off my boxers and flick them away with my feet, leaving my bare cock sliding against her wet core.

"Rhodes . . . I need . . ."

"I just need to get a condom, yeah?" Then I'm kissing her hard and fast and pushing off her to stand beside the bed.

She frowns and scrunches her nose up, making me wonder why the fuck I don't have protection in my nightstand. It's not like I didn't *know* this could happen.

"Where are you going?"

Bending at the waist, I lean into my hand beside her head and touch my mouth to hers again, unable to get enough of her. "Since we promised to be honest . . . I don't have sleepovers. I don't bring women home, which means I *don't* have condoms within reach."

Her lips form an *O*, which of course I have to kiss with a grin on mine.

"So, as much as I don't want to break the mood, I'll be right back." I straighten and stride out of the room and along the hall to the main bathroom where I grab what I need from the vanity. I damn near run back to my bedroom before shutting the door and locking it behind me, grinning at a still puzzled Dee, who's now sitting up, leaning against my headboard, naked as the day she was born with absolutely no shame or embarrassment. My cock bobs in approval under her gaze. She looks me up and down, her smile widening when she spots the box of condoms in my hand.

She arches a brow. "Do I wanna know?"

"I'm a responsible parent of a sixteen-year-old, who I'm not going to talk about when I have plans for you. But I'll be replacing this box tomorrow—since, if I have my way, we'll be making a dent in this one in future."

"How about being responsible and putting one of those on and getting back into this bed with me?"

"Best fucking idea ever."

She nods at the box.

"How about you get on that before I have to take matters into my own hands . . .?"

My eyes jump to her arms as she lifts them to her breasts and palms over her nipples before dragging her fingers over her stomach toward her spread legs. She lies flat on her back in the bed as she does it and gives me the best view ever as she runs two fingers over her clit then lower... pushing them inside where my hands and tongue just were.

"*Fuck!*" I rip the box open and separate a foil packet from the strip, dropping all but the one condom onto the floor. I bring it to my mouth and tear the packaging with my teeth before spitting it out and moving to put the latex ring on.

"Wait!" Dee says, low and breathy. She crawls on her hands and knees to the edge of the bed, craning her neck to meet my eyes and crooking her finger to bring me closer. Her warm breath fans over the head of my cock before she licks around the tip and swallows me whole, her fingers wrapping around the base and working in tandem with her lips as she draws me deeper and deeper with every stroke.

My balls pull tight, and I grit my teeth, nowhere near ready to have this finish before I've lost myself inside her. Nothing less than that will do. I gently glide my fingers in her hair and pull her off me, loving her hooded, glazed eyes locking with mine as she moves sideways.

Dee lays herself out in front of me, legs spread, hands roaming over her skin as I hurriedly roll the condom down my length and move to the bed. I press every inch of me into every inch of her, clutching her head and tilting her face to slam my lips on hers right as I align myself at her entrance. Her expression morphs with plea-sure as I push my cock inside her. I clench my teeth at just how fucking good she feels—how right *this* feels—Dee kissing me, meeting me stroke for stroke, thrust for thrust, both of us speeding up, our desperation growing as the pressure inside gets stronger and stronger.

The tingling at the bottom of my spine is a sure-fire sign that this inferno is about to explode. I snake a hand between us, not breaking our kiss for even a second as I roll her clit with my thumb. Dee cries into my mouth and tears her lips from mine, sucking in breath. Her moans grow louder and rougher until she wraps her limbs tight around mine and screams out, "Rhodes. Fuck. Yes!" over and over again. She clamps around me, leaving me with no hope to control my own release. One more thrust as I plant myself deep, and my hips jerk as I come hard and long, biting the crook of her neck and growling her name. My vision turns white as I drop my weight against her and nuzzle her skin gently, my muscles twitching at her soft palms roaming slowly over my sensitized skin.

Dee brings her mouth to my ear before sucking the lobe between her lips and nipping me. "If I have a hickey, honey, you're gonna owe me big time."

I brace myself on one arm, meeting her amused gaze, her lips twitching. Arching a brow, I smirk at her. "Is that so?" My eyes drift to the red mark blooming on her throat, my inner caveman beating his chest with pride, my gentleman side wondering how something so fucking hot and good could ever be bad.

"You're good at the sex, Mr. Rhodes."

"Feel free to leave a yelp review, sweet cheeks."

She giggles, making my smile widen. Running her fingers over my lips and into my hair, she slowly brings my mouth against hers and we kiss lazy this time.

I press my lips to the tip of her nose and, reaching between us, hold the base of the condom tight as I pull out of her, loving her breathy whimper when I do. As I move to my feet, I reach out to pull the mussed-up covers over her to keep her warm.

"Rhodes?" she whispers, placing her hand on my forearm.

"Yeah, baby?"

"I really, *really* like you." She smiles, and I swear the entire room brightens.

It's then I realize I'm gone for this woman, and I'm far from complaining about it. It could've been a day, a week or four, and I wouldn't care if it was too much or too fast. I *know*, and the emotion in her gaze conveys the meaning of the words she's giving me.

"I really, *really* like you, too," I reply, my voice soft and gentle. "Let me clean up, and I'll be back."

Her eyes flash. "Good. Because you made big promises about wearing me out, and I hope you're a man of your word."

My rumbling growl fills the room, but it's soon drowned out with a better sound—that being my girlfriend's infectious giggle.

Game fucking on.

Chapter 14

Dee

Bang. Bang.

"Wakey, wakey. Rise and shine, people," a voice yells from the other side of the bedroom door.

I slowly open my heavy eyes to be met with Rhodes's naked chest, my body plastered against his from shoulders to feet.

Bang. Bang.

"C'mon, old folks. It's time to join the land of the living and get some fresh air into those lungs. I'll meet you downstairs. You've got forty minutes until we have to leave," Jake adds before giving the door one last friendly thump and walking away until all I hear is Rhodes's huffed laughter.

I turn my head to look up at him, my wide eyes meeting his lazy, hooded ones. He cups my cheek and runs the tip of his thumb over my lips. "Morning, sweet cheeks."

"Morning, honey," I say before lifting up and kissing him quickly. That was the intention anyway, but he's Rhodes and his voice is all raspy and rumbly, and when his tongue touches mine, I immediately want more. Which means I'm soon flat on my back with this delicious man spread out on top of me, and he's clutching me to him while *devouring* my mouth.

Lifting his head, he smiles down at me. "Definitely a good morning now, apart from the brat waking me up for the run I'd forgotten about."

"Wait, what?" I gasp in horror. Running . . . on a *Sunday? Surely he doesn't mean—*

His blue eyes fill with amusement. "Yes. We run on Sunday mornings. Well, at least one of the weekend days. We have a training schedule we've gotta keep to."

"Okay. Well that's alright. I can leave when you guys do and—"

He shakes his head. "No, baby. It's a family rule. If someone stays over, they have to come on the run too."

My words of protest are on the tip of my tongue when the best excuse ever hits me. "Wait. That's okay. I can't come because I don't have any running gear with me." I breathe a quiet sigh of relief, my inner Dee relaxing and snuggling back down to revel in her weekend laziness.

"That's okay. Renee keeps a spare set here for the days when we run straight after a twenty-four and before she goes to work. I'm sure she won't mind."

Dammit. I must huff out the frustrated little growl I *thought* I made in my head, because soon Rhodes has dropped his lips to mine and is laughing as he kisses me again.

Thankfully, another argument/stalling tactic comes to me. I gently push my hands on his chest and quirk a brow, eyeing my new boyfriend suspiciously. "Hang on. You said women don't stay here."

Rhodes is not even trying to hide his laughter. "They don't, but Jake's friends do, and it's one rule for all. Sorry." He shrugs, but he's not sorry at all. Maybe distraction might be the key to my escape from his crazy running idea. "Alright. But who the hell runs at . . ." I lift my head and glance at his alarm clock beside the bed before my gaze snaps back to glare at him. ". . . eight on a Sunday morning?"

"Jake, Marco, Gio, Luca, sometimes Renee, and me."

"Well there's obviously not enough room for all of us in one car, so maybe I'll stay here and cook you a hearty breakfast for afterwards?"

"Baby. You can do that *and* come with us. But if it's too far, we can stop early, and I can make it up later."

Make it up later? Who is this man? Miss a run and make it up, all day long you'll have good luck? No. Wrong. All day long you'll be unable to walk!

I pull out the big guns and pout, which doesn't succeed in any way other than to make Rhodes laugh as he kisses me happy again. *Damn this man. Does anything work on him?*

"Okay, I *suppose* I'll come. But I'm telling you—I'm only going to slow you down." I roll over onto my back and cross my arms over my chest.

Rhodes shifts to his side and smooths my hair away from my face. "That's okay, sweet cheeks. Haven't you realized by now that you're the one who sets the pace?"

All I can do is think about that hot-as-hell-carry-me-into-his-house move he pulled as soon as I told him I had an overnight bag. Note to self—sometimes straight to the point has *delightful* consequences.

"Okay. Well, we've got . . ." I glance at the clock again. ". . . probably thirty-five minutes left. Why don't you cuddle me and tell me why you all run on a schedule that means we *can't* stay in bed all day."

"Firstly, as much as I'd love to do that, my morning-alarm-clock brat is sixteen and impressionable, so he needs to see that you're *not* just here to ravage his father." His gleaming grin says he'd like nothing more than to be ravaged by me, which makes me snicker.

"And to answer the other question, we have our PT test coming up and, in three months' time, we've got our annual fundraising run for ovarian cancer research that we participate in every year to honor Lily.

I reach out and stroke my fingers over his face, loving the way his expression softens and he leans into my touch. "I'll go on the run with you," I whisper, my throat tight.

"Thank you, baby. It's important to me—you are too."

Well, fuck.

Narrowing my eyes, I point my finger at him. "Don't you make me cry now, Rhodes Anderson. That would *not* make me happy. It's *far* too early for that kind of nonsense."

"I agree. And we've got . . ." He looks to the clock this time. ". . . thirty-one minutes left before we have to leave. Maybe we should use that time to *not* talk."

"Yes." I lean in to smack my lips against his, but when he goes in for another, I roll away and get out of bed, grinning at him as I make my way to his bathroom.

Halfway there, I stop mid-step and slowly turn around, taking in the beautifully presented master. There's dark blue walls with half-height wainscoted panels lining the room. There's a built-in wardrobe along the far wall and plush carpet under my feet. This room has a woman's touch written all over it.

"Hey." Rhodes stands in front of me, rubbing my arm with one hand and resting the other on my hip, pulling me close. "What's wrong?"

"This is the master bedroom."

"Yeah . . ."

"And this is the house you bought with Lily, right?"

Rhodes's forehead bunches, his mind working overtime behind his eyes before they widen. "Dee, it's not—"

I shake my head. "Sorry. It's silly, and I shouldn't have said anything. It's not my place—"

He jerks back. "It sure as hell is your place—well, I hope it will be. Dee, this isn't the original master bedroom. After our year of grieving, Jake and I decided to renovate this place. His room now is what *was* our old master, and I knocked a wall out and added the ensuite to this one."

Biting my lip, I'm relieved but also confused. "Wait. Then are you interested in interior decorating or something?"

His eyes widen before he buries his face in my neck and bursts out laughing. "Fuck no. That's all Mom's doing. And maybe Skye and Mama Rossi too."

"It's nice." I try to sound upbeat and *not* the embarrassed mess I truly am. As always, something must give me away, because Rhodes straightens and stares into my eyes.

"We don't censor ourselves around each other, remember? You don't think I've thought about you living in the same room, maybe sleeping in the same bed as you and Flynn shared? But we talk about these things. Just like I talked to Jake before you came over last night, you no doubt had to tell Flynn you might not be home, right?"

"Yeah. I'm sorry. I just—"

"Stop apologizing, Dee. It's natural. It's *human*. Lily may no longer be with us, but her memory is everywhere in this house. I know that. I also understand your questions."

"You do?"

"Sweet cheeks, I'm a man who gets protective and territorial when I'm with a woman, and you just happen to *live* with your ex-husband and father of your child. A man who you spent years with. A man who I'd be worried about had I not met him and seen for myself that he's a good guy." He runs a line of kisses over my shoulder, pausing where he left a mark last night and soothing it with his tongue.

Thank god I have makeup in my bag to cover it.

"Don't hold back with me, because I like where this is going between us, and I don't care it's only been six weeks. Because six weeks with you feels the same as—"

"Six months."

He smiles and his eyes crinkle. "Exactly. But to add to what I said about this room. Just as I respect Lily enough not to bring another woman into our marital room and bed, I also respect you enough not to do that. Everything in this room was bought new about four years ago."

I swallow the lump in my throat and throw sass to mask my emotions, tilting my head and arching a brow. "Do you respect me enough *not* to make me run?"

"Nice try, baby. I'll give you an *A* for effort."

"Shit." I drop onto the bed as Rhodes's expression turns curious. "What?"

"My bag is in the car since *someone* held me hostage in this bed all night."

He quirks a brow. "A hostage is someone kept against their will. But since I did do a *very* thorough job of exhausting you, I went downstairs, grabbed your bag, locked your car, and put it in my closet."

My mouth drops open. Is this man honestly for real? "Just when I thought you couldn't get any better, Rhodes Anderson, you add thoughtfulness to the growing list of pros to dating you."

His voice drops low. "Growing list?" My eyes drift down and see my list isn't the only thing that's growing right now.

"Stop looking at my dick, Dee, otherwise we'll never get out of bed."

My lips curve into a wicked grin. "Well . . ." I say in a singsong voice, earning a growl.

Then I'm plucked off the mattress and planted on my feet in front of him. The only thing between us is the top sheet that I managed to bring with me. Rhodes's amused eyes shift between our bodies, his hands gripping my hips and pulling me hard against him. "We've gotta go do this run, sweet cheeks. There's plenty of time for looking and *touching* anything you want of mine *after* we get back."

I jut my chin. "I'm gonna hold you to that. Nobody makes me run in the morning and doesn't pay for it." I step around him and sway my hips as I walk to his bathroom, yelping when his palm taps my ass.

"I'll happily be in your debt forever, Dee."

"You'd like that too much," I call out as I turn the shower on before facing him again and dropping the sheet, not surprised when I find Rhodes's hungry gaze eating me up.

He closes the distance between us and slides his fingers into my hair as he kisses me soft and slow before nipping my bottom lip as he pulls back. "Fuck yeah, I would. Meet you downstairs?"

I nod and steal one more kiss. "Thank you for last night, Rhodes," I whisper, staring deep into his eyes.

"I should be thanking you, but you're welcome, baby. Best morning ever, waking up with you in my arms. Best way to set me up for the day." Then he kisses my nose, and I'm left standing there wondering how the fuck I lost the upper hand in that situation. But also, why I don't give a damn, because I meant what I said. I really, *really* like Rhodes Anderson.

I must if I'm willingly—albeit, begrudgingly--going on a *run* with him. *Jeez.*

IT'S AFTER OUR RUN—WELL, I ran two miles before I waved the white flag and walked the rest of the way— and the downside of being in the honeymoon phase of a new relationship as a single parent is the vanishing opportunity for spontaneous shower sex when there's a sixteen-year-old in the house.

Rhodes did make a point of personally bringing me a fresh towel, showing he's ever the responsible host. I repaid the favor by letting him watch me wash myself, following his directions about parts of my body that I might've missed and helpful suggestions as to where I could clean more thoroughly, and even then telling me of a very useful pulsing feature on his detachable shower head.

By the time I'd turned off the water and stepped into the towel he thoughtfully wrapped around my relaxed body, he'd kissed me deep and long and promised retribution as soon as we had adult alone time again.

"I'm gonna go downstairs and see if Jake wants to help me make us all some lunch," I say, looking into his languid gaze.

He quirks a brow. "You're leaving me here like *this?*" He punctuates his point with a roll of his hips, making me smile.

"I'm rather looking forward to seeing what kind of payback you might dish up." I quickly brush my mouth against his, earning a growl when I touch the tip of my tongue to the seam of his lips before stepping out of reach. I do pause at the door to watch him strip off his running shorts, enjoying the view of his tight, naked ass as he steps into the shower box and turns the water back on.

"Hey, Rhodes?"

"Yeah?" he looks over his shoulder at me, and I make a point of dragging my eyes slowly over his body, seeing the benefits of watching and delayed gratification. "More than two strokes and it's playing with yourself." I shoot him a wink then giggle as I close the door behind me.

Having dried off and dressed again—this time in loose-fitting lounge pants and a Blackhawks tee—I move along the hall to the kitchen where I find a fresh-faced Jake sitting at the dining table reading something on his phone.

He lifts his head and jerks his chin up. "Hey. I was beginning to think I needed to send out a search party." My eyes go wide and his lips twitch. "Nah. Just kidding."

A surprised giggle bursts out of me as I stand there and stare at this kid. "You're hard to get a read on, you know."

Jake shrugs. "Not really. I'm a growing young man who has his head screwed on straight and his eyes on the prize—and it *isn't* sleeping my way through my junior year. I also want to see Dad happy, and happiness seems to ooze out of his pores whenever you're around."

I bite my lip to somehow stop my heart from bursting all over the floor.

"But I *am* really fu—freaking hungry, so I was looking up some of the recipes on your website and seeing what we have in the kitchen."

"Okay. Show me what you've found."

His eyes flash before he pushes his chair back and walks over to me, putting his phone on the countertop in front of us. We scroll through a few of the light-lunch recipes in conjunction with the relevant demonstration videos I've done for them. A lot of them are already in Jake's favorites on the vlogging platform's website.

"What about my chicken pot pie? It may not be super healthy, but it'll fill you up."

His lips tug on one side, the beginnings of a dimple pop out. When I narrow my eyes at him, his grin gets bigger. "Dad tried to make it a few months ago and failed miserably. I swear the smell of burnt milk lingered for days after that."

"What are you two up to?" Rhodes says, coming up close

behind me. He wraps an arm around my waist and presses a kiss to the top of my head.

"I'm trying to persuade Dee to make the dish-that-shall-not-be-named."

Rhodes chuckles and points his finger at his son. "Hey, kid. Don't embarrass me in front of my favorite chef. I kind of like her. Besides, she can probably make that meal with her eyes closed."

I look up at him and scrunch my nose, waving my hand in front of us in a 'maybe/maybe not' gesture, making them both laugh. "Cutting the vegetables can get a bit dicey with your eyes closed, even with *my* knife skills."

"Okay, little master. How about you wow us with your *skills*, and Jake and I can be your sous-chefs?"

"*Or* . . . you could pour a coffee, sit over there and read the paper, while Dee and I cook for you." I don't miss the way his eyes are begging his dad to do that exact thing.

I turn in Rhodes arms and tip my face to his. "Yeah, *Dad*. Why don't you go take a load off and let us cook for you? Besides, an old man like yourself must need to recuperate after such an energetic morning . . ."

Rhodes's lips twitch and his eyes fill with amusement just as Jake starts making gagging sounds from behind us. I gasp when it clicks what I've said. "Oh my god, no. *No*. I didn't mean," I splutter before whirling around and pointing at the laughing teen. "You have a dirty mind, young man."

Jake holds his hands in the air. "Hey. I said I'm focusing on my future, not that I'm blind, deaf, and dumb. I am my father's son, after all."

Rhodes buries his face in my neck and laughs before straightening and giving me a discreet tap on the ass. "Feed me, beautiful. Make my son's day by letting him cook with his idol."

And damn if that doesn't melt my heart too.

I shouldn't have been surprised, but every step of the way, Jake is an avid participant. He asks questions, he checks if he's chopping the vegetables the right size, and when I correct his cutting technique to make it smoother and easier, he shows he has natural talent.

"So what do you wanna do after you finish school?" I ask while I'm greasing the pie dish.

"I kind of sway between medical school or something like a cop or a firefighter." He nods toward the living room where Rhodes is sitting on the couch watching a football game on TV. "I see Dad go to work, and even knowing he could get hurt or worse, but he's trained to make the best decisions and follow protocol to ensure he gets to come home at the end of every shift. It's honorable, and I like the idea of serving the community and helping people."

I blink rapidly, wishing I had an onion to blame for my wet eyes. "And med school? Do you want to be a doctor for the same reason?"

He looks up from the chicken he's browning on the stovetop and studies me for a second before he nods. "Yes and no. You know about Mom, right?"

"Yeah, Jake," I say softly.

"Right. So, I've always thought that if I could ever do something to help families and kids who were in the same situation, then I would do it."

"That's very thoughtful."

He shrugs like it's no big deal, even though we both know it is. "So research then?"

"Yeah. I like the idea of helping in any way I can so that other people don't have to go through what Mom went through."

I pause for a moment before I move beside him and wrap an arm around his shoulders, giving him a gentle squeeze. "You're a good kid, Jake Anderson. Your mom would be very proud of the man you've become."

"I hope so. I've got a good Dad, that helps too."

Glancing over at his father, I sigh and—not for the first time—thank the universe for making our paths cross, and for giving him and Jake each other too.

Jake turns my way and snickers, having caught me gawking at Rhodes. "She'd have liked you, you know?"

My body jerks at this unexpected revelation. "I hope so."

"I may have only been ten, but Dad has made sure I remember her. She was all about being positive and shining her bright light on those who need it. It helps that you're hot and you make him laugh, and you don't let anyone get away with shit."

"Stop before you make me cry," I say with a sniffle.

"What, you mean *again*?" he teases. When I meet his eyes, he pulls out the same charming 'butter wouldn't melt' grin his father has shot me a few times. "Am I good enough for lava cake?"

"I dunno. You didn't say you wanted to become a chef. That would've earned *huge* brownie points."

He smirks. "Oh, I do this for fun. I figure if I learn how to cook, then the chicks will dig it. Hey, maybe you should do a video called 'Food Men Can Make to Impress Their Dates.'"

Bumping him with my shoulder, I shake my head, trying hard not to laugh but ending up doing it anyway as we get back to the task of finishing lunch.

No kitchens or food items were harmed in the making of the meal, and not only did I get to watch Jake have a blast cooking with me, but it also gave me a new video idea—maybe even a whole new business idea—which I make a mental note of to brainstorm later: online cooking lessons for kids. Maybe a home economics course aimed at teaching the basics and working up to making things like pie and lava cake.

To make a good afternoon an even better one, Jake further proved just how great he is when he not only cleared the dishes away, but also announced he was walking to his grandparents' house three blocks over and wouldn't be back for a few hours, giving us even more unexpected adult alone time.

Something Rhodes did *not* waste any time on making the most of.

Chapter 15

Rhodes

I keep checking the clock all shift, which is never a good thing to do on a twenty-four. But today's a little different, because in a few hours, Jake is going to be taking his driving test at the DMV.

He's been working toward it for months. He's studied and practiced, and if anyone deserves to pass with flying colors and get his permit, it's my son.

Unfortunately, his appointment clashed with my shift, but my dad, Don, and Lily's dad, Connor, are taking him together, and Jake promised to call me as soon as he gets out, whatever the outcome.

Little does he know, we've got something planned for him. Dad and Connor are acting as wingmen in our endeavor, because if we're on a callout when he finishes, they're going to bring him to the firehouse. And if we're not, Marco and I have arranged with our Captain to run an errand that just happens to take us past the DMV office. Because nothing short of saving lives and property will stop me from being there for this next important milestone in Jake's life.

Marco, our friend and colleague, Zach, and I are all sitting in the big open space living/dining/kitchen area of the firehouse when Scotty walks into the room, four big white bags in his hands, and a bunch of giant blue balloons trailing behind him with the strings tied around his wrist. "Scotty, what's with the balloons?" I ask.

After dumping the bags on the dining table, he shifts the strings from his wrist to a chair then grins at me. "You only get your license once, right?"

"That's if you get it the first time, yes . . ."

"Well, Jake's a hell of a lot smarter than me."

"That's a given," Marco calls out, earning the middle finger from Scotty, who rolls his eyes at his lieutenant and turns back to me.

"Therefore, if we're gonna congratulate him, it's gotta be big. Most of us have watched him grow up. You've gotta let us all celebrate this too."

He's not wrong. I was already working here when Jake was born. Marco and I met at the academy, and Scotty wasn't that far behind us, joining the CFD a few years later. Zach has been here about eight years, but all of us at the station are like family. And our partners, girlfriends, wives, and kids are all part of that family just as much as our blood relatives are. When you put your lives in each other's hands every single call we attend, you get close. Even Scotty.

I get up and cross the room before reaching out and opening one of the bags. My mouth drops open at the sheer amount of streamers and party horns and hats, and a shiny foil sign that says it's fifteen feet long on the label. Quirking a brow at him, I nod at the bags. "I said a few things, not the whole shop, dude."

"Hey. Some of us don't have sixteen-year-old sons, and we're living vicariously through you. This is a big moment in a teenager's life. First you get facial hair, then your voice breaks, and then you get your license and then you can get laid."

I groan, Marco whistles through his teeth, and Zach throws his head back and laughs.

"Stop right there, Scotty. I thought we'd kept Jake away from you so he *wouldn't* be corrupted," Marco says, joining my side.

"Hey. I resent that," he mutters as he spreads all the different party supplies over the dining table. "I actually learned a lot of things at the shop yesterday."

"You did go to the *party* shop, right? Not the sex shop next door?" Zach muses, walking over to join us, taking in the loot, and shaking his head. "Dude, you got a piñata. This is a celebration, not a five-year old's birthday party."

Scotty grins and holds up a papier-mâché Tiki. "Now hear me out. Nothing says congratulations like hitting a cardboard vessel full of candy with a stick more than this."

"That piñata is a tiki. This isn't a luau."

"Not my fault they were out of unicorns."

My eyes are nearly bugging out of my head, but I let *that* little nugget of goodness go and move on. "Again, I appreciate you helping me out with all this, Scotty, but don't you think you got a bit too much?"

He waves me off and pulls out a cardboard party hat before reaching up to place it on top of Zach's head. "Look! It's perfect, right?" The hat is in the shape of a red, black, and white racing car helmet with the words 'Vroom vroom' on it.

"It's *something*, alright." Zach's lips twitch as he pulls it off and studies it.

"Scotty . . . just wondering, was the sales assistant female by any chance?" Marco asks, and suddenly realization hits.

"*Now* it all makes sense."

To his credit, Scotty shrugs, his lips curling into a guilty smirk as he lifts his hands in the air. "Look, can I help it if an attractive female wants to talk me into buying a bunch of stuff for my 'son's party?'"

I can't stop the chuckle that bubbles in my chest. Only Scotty would get conned by a woman into dropping a ton of coin at a party store. "Please tell me you didn't invite said attractive female to your *imaginary* son's birthday party."

"Hey. If she calls, I'll fess up. If she doesn't, she got a good sale out of me."

"Or me, since I gave you a fifty for all of this. Usually, the only person I give money to and don't get change from is Jake himself."

"This is for Jake. It's an investment in his future as a stud who gets all the chicks when he's driving around like the coolest kid at school."

"*Or*, you know, he's already a good kid *and* a cool kid, and he probably doesn't need a car to get laid," Marco says.

"Hey! Enough of that. I'm far too young for grandchildren."

"Why are you worried? Didn't you tell me you had to raid the emergency-condom stash last weekend when you—"

That earns my best friend an elbow in the ribs, which makes him grunt and shoot me a 'what the fuck' look. Zach's eyes bug out of his head before he chuckles under his breath.

Friends, who'd have 'em?

"Wait, you got laid, Rhodes? Who's the lucky girl?" Scotty asks, the party-supply-girl discussion all but forgotten.

I level him with a pointed stare. "She's not a *girl*. She's my girl-friend, and *no*, I'm not going to talk about my sex life at work."

"You told Marco," he retorts.

"He's also been with me for close to twenty years, and Jake's my god son. That gives me certain need-to-know privileges."

Scotty tilts his head, his mind working overtime. "But wait, you have an emergency condom box? My parents would never have done that."

"Your parents probably didn't think you'd need them," Luca strolls into the kitchen with a workout towel wrapped around his shoulders, his hair wet.

"Hey. I'll have you know I went through *more* than my fair share of condoms when I was in high school."

Luca smirks. "Was that third-year senior, or fourth?"

"Fuck you, Rossi," Scotty retorts with a laugh, sobering when he catches the quirked brow of Marco.

"What have I told you about telling your lieutenant to fuck off, firefighter?" he asks.

Scotty blanches but narrows his eyes when Marco can't keep up the act any longer.

"Jeez, Scotty. Breathe. I'm screwing with ya."

My phone vibrates in my pocket with a text.

"Oh, and if you ever need a pick up line at a party, just pull out a party blower like this. It'll *definitely* get you a laugh—or a phone number," Scotty says as I open my messages and smile at Dee's name on screen.

Dee: Any news yet? I was thinking I could arrange dinner for Jake tonight and send it to the house.

Rhodes: No news yet, and how come my son gets takeout to his door and I don't? Have I not earned that privilege yet?

Dee: You earn it every time we've had adult alone time in the past two weeks. But it's only once you get your driving permit for the first time, and I know that Jake likes my lava cake, so . . .

Rhodes: Wait . . . how do you know that?

Dee: 'Cause he stole your phone that night I gave you a doggy bag to take home to him.

I bark out a laugh, realizing the room has gone quiet. I turn to find four sets of eyes watching me like I've grown two heads or something. I ignore them and return to my phone.

Rhodes: That kid. Swear to god, he's going to turn me gray.

Dee: Oh, I dunno, I think you'd look good with a few more grays. You could be my sexy, silver fox.

Rhodes: You'd like that, would you?

Dee: Yep. It's truly unfair how guys can look hot with that salt-n-pepper look, yet women still color their hair until they can't anymore.

Rhodes: I think you'd look sexy whatever color hair you had.

Dee: Smooth, honey. Real smooth. You already know I'm a sure thing. No need to sweet-talk me.

Rhodes: I've never sweet-talked you. I only speak the truth. Honesty policy, remember?

Dee: Damn. Can you stop being so perfect? You're gonna give me a complex

Rhodes: Hey. You cook like a dream, you run with us even though you hate it, and never before have I seen a woman wear a pair of jeans that makes me jealous of the damn denim. Do you need me to go on? Because I'm barely scratching the surface when it comes to you, and I can't wait to burrow deeper and stay there.

I don't even hesitate to press send, because when it comes to Dee, she may say she's a sure thing, but I mean every single word. The more time I spend with her, the more things I learn about her, the more I want to know. She's a slow riser in the morning, but the minute I kiss her and roam my hands over her skin, she sparks alight like a freshly lit fuse. She's a dream with Jake, she's the best mom to Harvey, and the fact she and Flynn put their own lives and interests aside to keep a steady ship for their son after they split up is more than I think most other adults would ever consider.

Scotty is still proudly showing off his party shop wares when my phone vibrates in my hand.

Expecting it to be Dee, I freeze when dad's name appears on the screen.

Dad: You better get your butt here, son. Because our boy just passed with flying colors, and I know you're the one person he's going to want to see when we walk out of this office.

"Fuck yeah!" I yell, earning the attention of the entire crew now gathered around the dining table. "Luc tell the Cap we're offline for twenty minutes. I'll have my handheld on if he needs us."

"On it," Luca says, running out of the room and toward the Captain's office. As he goes to leave, the captain's daughter London happens to be in the hallway and the two of them crash into each other. There's no mistaking the blush that covers the young woman's cheeks as Luca says something I cannot hear before rushing away. *What was that about I wonder?*

While we wait for Luc to come back, I bring up my conversation with Dee and type another message.

Rhodes: He passed! On route to see him now.

Dee: That's awesome. Tell him congrats for me and that he's earned lava cake on demand for a month.

Rhodes: And what do I get?

Dee: You get me on demand for as long as you want. If you wanna swap that for dessert . . .

Rhodes: Saving this text as evidence. Talk soon, sweet cheeks.

A minute later, party supplies loaded, the guys and I are headed to the DMV office, my chest swelling with pride and my heart full.

We're only in the parking lot for five minutes before Dad, Connor, and a beaming Jake step out onto the sidewalk. 'Drive My Car' by The Beatles is blasting from Zach's cellphone, and all of us are looking a sight in cardboard race car helmet hats, party blowers in our mouths, and a huge 'Congratulations' sign hanging from the side of the truck. As soon as we see him, the guys start cheering and clapping as I move forward and shake hands with Dad and Connor, both of them seemingly just as proud as I am. I lock eyes with my son and pull him in for a huge bear hug, lifting him off the ground as I do it.

"Thanks, Dad. One more tick off the list," he says for my ears only.

"Your mom would be crying right about now."

He laughs, and we pull apart, my hand hooked around his neck and pressing our foreheads together. "Got something for you."

Jake looks over my shoulder at the guys, grinning from ear to ear. "You mean my own personal CFD cheer squad? Wait . . . is that a tiki piñata?"

I snort. "One guess who was in charge of decorations."

"God, Scotty is something else." He turns back to me. "Right. If it's not this—which is fucking cool—what is it? Dee's lava cake?" Jake's expression is so hopeful I throw my head back and laugh.

"She sends her congrats, and apparently you have dessert on demand for a month."

He actually does a fist pump at that. "Awesome."

Crossing my arms over my chest, I shake my head at him.

Connor comes over and nods at me. A silent conversation passes between us before he cups Jake's shoulder. "Don, Rhodes, and I, along with your grandmothers, decided to band together and get you something to show you just how proud we are of the man you've become and the man we know you'll continue to be. So close your eyes and give me your hand . . ."

Jake closes his eyes, and I don't miss his breath catching as Lily's dad drops something into his outstretched palm. Slowly, he opens his eyes, his mouth dropping wide at the blue Ford key ring with the car key attached for the 2005 Red Ford Ranger XLT truck we bought for him.

"No way," he rasps, his voice thick with wonder. He jerks his gaze to me first, then his grandfathers before he looks to the parking lot where Connor left it after arriving 'late' for Jake's appointment.

"No fucking way! Yes!" He hugs Don and then Connor, then turns to me and shakes his head in disbelief. "You said I'd have to save up five grand for you to match my savings. You totally lied,' he says with a laugh before tackle-hugging me then near on *running* toward his new truck.

Dad comes up beside me and hooks an arm around my shoulders. "You did good, son."

"Thanks," I say gruffly. It's hitting me that this is another step toward Jake growing up and getting closer to being an adult.

"Proud of you. And I know if Lils was here, she'd be crying buckets already," Dad adds.

I snort, because he's not wrong. "She'd have also insisted we install GPS to track him in it."

"You mean you haven't?" Connor chuckles.

"First thing I did. I'm not an idiot. He's a good kid, but I was a sixteen-year-old boy with a car too."

"Yep. Know that, 'cause it was around that time Lily started talking about the cute football player at school with the cool old mustang."

Don soon joins us laughing. "That car. I swear it was off the road more times than it was on."

"At least we got him something reliable."

"He's a credit to you, Rhodes."

I look between my two dads, the men who've always had my back before, with, and after Lily. Not once did I ever feel alone, and in the hard times—moments like this when there's a milestone in my son's life that Lily and I always wondered about—I've known Lily is right here with us, cheering him on, blowing her own party whistle, and beaming from ear to ear with tears streaming down her face, because that's just the kind of woman she was.

And ironically, she'd also be the kind of woman who'd be texting me to see if he'd passed yet and promising his favorite meals on demand for a month when he did.

I pull out my phone and bring up my text string with Dee,

smiling as I type out a message for her and counting down the hours until I can see her again.

Rhodes: I can't work out whether my son liked the lava cake boon or his new truck more, but I do know that his dad likes you a hell of a lot and is looking forward to crawling into my bed to find you in it in the morning. Get some sleep, sweet cheeks, because I'm in the mood to show you my appreciation.

Not even thirty seconds later, I receive her reply.

Dee: See what I mean, honey? You're perfect.

Rhodes: If you think I'm perfect, then that must mean you're perfect for me.

Dee: Stop being swoony when I'm not there to jump you.

That makes me smile.

"Now that's a good look on you, son. Wanna tell me what has you smiling like a loon?" Connor asks from beside me.

I slide my phone into my back pocket and glance between my father-in-law and my dad, who's also now watching me closely with a curious expression on his face.

"The *woman* who put this smile on my face is called Dee."

Connor's slow-growing grin hits me right in the middle of my chest. He cups my shoulder and gives me a squeeze. "Well, I hope to meet her at your birthday party in a few weeks then." *In other words, bring her along.*

"What birthday party is that?" I ask, playing dumb, because I'd already overhead Jake on the phone with Dad double-checking my shift schedule.

To his credit, Connor doesn't even try and cover his slip of the tongue. "You know your mother wasn't going to let you turn forty without a celebration. But I'm serious, Rhodes, bring Dee. I haven't seen you smile like that in years, which means she's special, and if she's special to you, we want to welcome her into the family."

I find nothing but absolute sincerity in his gaze. Lily's parents are the gift that keep giving, even six years later. "Okay. I'll bring her."

"Good. But let's not tell the moms," Dad adds with a wicked grin. "Maybe the surprise can be on *them* this year, instead. If anything, it'll give Connor and I some entertainment besides Scotty trying to be funny."

Laughing, we walk over to join the guys and Jake who are all still surrounding his new truck

Chapter 16

Dee

It's been situation-normal for the last few weeks. I film, edit, and upload two videos a week. I work at the restaurant during school hours, deferring to my restaurant manager and head chef the rest of the time, and for just one night a week, I run the kitchen like I used to. I find this keeps my finger on the pulse with my staff and also helps with morale and camaraderie, as well as giving them the opportunity to show their boss—me—how good they really are.

The afternoons and nights are spent with Harvey and Flynn when he's home. There has also been a lot of adult alone time with Rhodes, but as far as actual sleepovers go, we give ourselves one weekend night a week. Harvey knows where I am and that I'll be back after his time with his dad. Otherwise it's been stolen moments during the day or going over for a few hours after Harvey has gone to bed for the night. Once, Rhodes and I *planned* to go see a movie, but somehow got waylaid and ended up eating polish sausage sandwiches from Jim's Original on the side of the road, then making out like teenagers in the front seat of his car.

Life is good, and the more time that passes, the deeper I fall for the guy and Jake and the promise of what a future with our combined families could look like—the more I want to dive in head-first and get on with it already. I've never been surer about my feelings before, which doesn't say a lot for my first marriage. A lot of it has to do with the stage of my life I was in when Flynn and I first met and how well I know myself and what I want now that I'm closer to forty than thirty.

There's a lot to be said for maturity when dating after a divorce —albeit an amicable and mutual one. You know what you don't want, and what your must haves and must *not* haves are. You also know that when you find a rare diamond with a heart of gold, who is thoughtful, kind, sexy, charming, a great dad, and an incredible man, lover, and friend—you hold on tight. And as a divorced thirty-seven-year-old woman, I knew I might find another partner to spend time with, I just never anticipated I'd meet a man quite like Rhodes.

Now it's a Saturday afternoon, and I'm snuggling on the couch with Harvey as he reads me a book about ocean animals that his Aunty Faith gave him while I wait for Rhodes to pick me up.

Skye and Cohen had a beautiful baby boy a few weeks ago, and remembering what it was like to have a newborn, Rhodes and I decided we'd wait until they'd settled in at home and at least got into some sort of routine before visiting. Rhodes worked yesterday, so after sleeping this morning, we're on our way to meet the baby.

My phone vibrates against the coffee table with a text message.

I pick it up, expecting it to be Rhodes. Instead, it's Skye texting in our girls group chat. Recently, it's become a bit of a parenting forum with all of us moms—except Renee, who isn't there yet—

giving Faith advice about teething babies who never sleep and Skye about everything new-mom related.

Skye: I never thought I'd ever send a text like this but, Dee, can you PLEASE bring some cabbage with you and maybe a mouth guard for my vampire baby?

Dee: Cabbage, check. I'm guessing those milk makers are working overtime. And mouth guard, that's probably frowned upon until at least six months . . .

Skye: What about numbing cream then? Is that a thing? Like maybe the stuff that is supposed to prolong orgasm. Would that work?

Dee: On your nipples? Um . . . NO.

Faith: God I don't envy you. Those first six weeks of nursing were SO much fun. I swear my nips are permanently deformed after my two milk demons

Dee: It's also probably frowned upon to call your children demons.

Gilly: Oh no, demons definitely works.

Renee: Just saying, you ladies are TOTALLY making motherhood sound fantastic.

Skye: It's all good until you squirt your husband in the eye and almost blind him.

Gilly: Hey, some men like that. Breast milk, I mean. Or being squirted on. Wait . . .that doesn't sound right.

Faith: Eww. That's our brother you're talking about.

Dee: We're close, but not THAT close. Haha.

Gilly: Skye, lanolin cream and nipple shields. Maybe Dee can get you some on the way over.

Dee: Now THAT I can do. Any other requests?

Skye: My brain back? This morning I put the laundry in the dishwasher and poured my freshly brewed decaf down the sink before I'd even had a sip. Then I cried about it.

Faith: I shouldn't laugh, but that's funny.

Skye: Cohen laughed too until I threatened a home vasectomy and suddenly he was my perfect husband again.

Dee: If it helps, it does get better.

Skye: I hear you make a pretty mean lava cake. That would make me feel better.

I laugh, earning a puzzled look from Harvey.

Dee: I'll see what I can do. See you soon.

Gilly: If you're delivering desserts, your favorite sister-in-law is also a fan.

Dee: You're my only sister-in-law

Gilly: Therefore I'm your favorite.

Faith: Sisters rank higher, and I have a three-year-old who loves to see her Aunty Dee.

Dee: Let's see if I can sweet-talk Rhodes into making a few pit stops.

Skye: Do what you have to do, Dee. Take one from Rhodes for the team.

Faith: Not sure Dee sees that as a hardship.

Renee: Rhodes does seem to be very 'happy' these days.

Dee: Not talking about it with my kid next to me.

Gilly: It's okay. We'll wait till Rhodes's birthday party to get the details.

Wait . . . what?

Dee: Please tell me I've missed a memo somewhere. Rhodes is having a birthday party? How do I not know this?

Renee: Oh shit.

Gilly: I'm sure he'll tell you.

Faith: It's supposed to be a surprise. Maybe he doesn't know about it?

Renee: He knows. His father-in-law let it slip a few weeks back.

A few weeks? Father-in-law? Then it clicks. Lily's dad. Lily's parents will be there. Maybe that's why. I mean, I get it. I can't imagine inviting Rhodes to an event with Flynn's parents. Although, I also can't imagine *not* at least *mentioning* it.

"Mom? You just went stiff." Harvey sits upright and looks at me.

I school my confused frown and smile at my son. "I was surprised, that's all."

"Ooh. I like surprises. Well, except if they're for me. Then I wanna know what it is."

"I know that 'cause you always try to peek at Christmas presents, don't you?" I lean and tickle him, laughing as his squeals fill the air.

"Now, Mom has to call the restaurant and put in a few dessert orders for Aunty Faith and Gilly. Do you wanna run to your room and make sure you have everything packed for when Rhodes and I drop you off at Nana and Pop's place?"

"Yep." He jumps to his feet and kisses me before running away.

I turn back to my phone.

Renee: Dee, I know he'll invite you. That man is in so deep I doubt he'll ever wanna come up for air.

Gilly: Seriously, Dee.

Dee: I didn't even know it was his birthday soon.

Skye: Probably 'cause you don't show each other your birthday certificates before jumping into bed.

Dee: I should've known though. What kind of girlfriend doesn't know when her man's birthday is . . . and it's FORTY. That's a big one.

Faith: Ask him when you see him. He probably had a man moment and assumed you'd be there anyway.

Okay. That I can do. Honesty policy rules apply. Just ask, communicate, clear up any confusion, and then go from there. Yes, that's exactly what I'll do.

Skye: And if he makes you sad, tell him he gets no more cooking—or cookie—from you.

Skye: Sorry. Ignore me. I'm hormonal, horny, and helplessly leaking breast milk everywhere. I'm a hot mess of a dairy farm.

Faith: Oh my god, Skye. Now all I can imagine is you turning into a fembot and squirting milk out of your norks like a lethal weapon.

Gilly: Thanks for that visual, now Ez is looking at me strangely.

Dee: Tell him to be nice to his wife, otherwise Faith and I will beat him up like we used to do. Okay, ladies. Thanks for the entertainment. See you soon, Skye.

Skye: Don't forget the cake!

"THOSE TWO ARE NATURALS," Rhodes says as we pull out of Cohen and Skye's street after a short visit. By the time we'd run all our errands and got there, baby Austin had just woken up.

"Yeah. I remember being freaked the fuck out when I first brought Harvey home. *And* Flynn was starting his internship, so he knew stuff but not the stuff you need to know."

Rhodes laughs. "Yep. The hands-on stuff you can never learn beforehand, because babies don't come with instruction manuals."

In the comfortable silence that falls between us, I contemplate whether I'd actually want to go through the newborn stage again. There comes a point where you pass the constant dependency age and it seems like there's a sliver of light at the end of the parenting tunnel.

Rhodes reaches over and squeezes my hand. "You're thinking really hard about something over there. Wanna share with the class?"

I turn my body toward his as much as my seat belt will allow and study him. "Would you ever want more kids?" I blurt out. Rhodes's head jerks, his eyes widening.

"Shit. That's the last thing I expected to come out of your mouth."

Grinning at him, I shrug. "Well, I guess seeing our friends starting their families, and remembering what it was like when we were younger and going through it all with our own kids, it makes you wonder."

"Okay. That makes sense."

"And I like this thing we're building."

His lips curve up, his fingers flexing against mine. "We're already built, sweet cheeks. Now we're driving those foundations deep so nothing can shake us."

I squeeze his hand too tight at his words that he grunts.

"You like that."

"I like *you*."

"Thank fuck for that, otherwise I *would* have to stalk you," he says, making us both laugh. "But to answer your other question, if this thing with us continues the way it's going and you had your heart set on having another baby—and you wanted to have that baby with me—"

"Um . . . I'm not thinking about *practicing* making babies with anyone else, honey," I say in a 'duh' voice.

"Good," he growls, his voice gruff and rumbly and all kinds of sexy. "What I mean is, if you wanted to have that baby with me, then I couldn't think of anything more beautiful than creating a life with you. We make damn cool kids by ourselves. Combine our DNA and we'd have a genius."

"You didn't say *you* wanted another one, though."

"Because I have Jake, and you've given me Harvey, and together,

I think those two will keep us on our toes for a while. I think we have two amazing kids between us, and that's enough for me."

"I like that."

"You do?" he asks, tilting his head and glancing sideways at me while keeping his eyes on the road.

"You sound surprised. I'm a thirty-seven-year-old single mom with a kid and a restaurant that I may not run day-to-day, but I am still the face of the business and have to do all the important stuff behind the scenes. And I also have this sexy boyfriend who works hard, and when he has time off, I enjoy being with him. So none of that is conducive to starting all over again and having a baby."

"Really?" He actually sounds surprised.

I reach over and rest my hand on his head. "Yes, really. Especially that last part."

"I *did* like that bit."

My lips twitch. "Oh you did, did you?"

"Yep. and the bit about spending time with me."

I scrunch my nose up, and he growls when he catches me doing it. "Don't do that when I can't kiss that look off your face."

I twist my mouth to the side. "What look is that?"

"A look that has me grateful we're almost home. At least then I can bury myself inside you when you're turning me on."

I remember that there's still something I haven't asked about, and I must wear my nervousness on my face.

Rhodes turns to me, his brows bunched together in a frown. "Okay. Now *that's* a look I don't like."

"Before we get home and get distracted by each other, can I ask you something under the terms of our honesty policy?"

"You can ask me anything at any time, Dee. If it's mine to tell, then it's mine to give you."

"Stop being swoony," I mutter, making him chuckle and his lips quirk.

"Nope." His eyes turn soft and gentle. "What do you wanna know?"

"Gilly let slip that you have a birthday party coming up . . ."

"*Fuck*," he splutters before he slows the car down and pulls over outside a random house about ten minutes from his place. He turns off the engine and faces me. "I'm so fucking sorry. I had every intention to invite you, but then life got in the way and I forgot. The entire *party* slipped my mind, because I'm not exactly jumping for joy at hitting the big four-oh. That's no excuse, I know, but I truly meant "

"I thought—"

In the blink of an eye, he's reached over, undone my seat belt and hauled me to his side, his hands tangling in my hair and holding me there ensuring he has my complete attention. "You thought that because it's my birthday and both my parents *and* Lily's parents were going to be there, that I *wouldn't* want to introduce them all to the woman who has entranced me, who makes me laugh after a bad day, smile at just the thought of her, and has my kid eating out of the palm of her hand?"

"Well, when you put it like that . . ." I murmur, biting my lip and looking away, but Rhodes's flexed fingers in my hair bring my gaze back to his.

"I've already told Connor, Lily's dad, and my dad about you and that I want them to meet you. That's when they let it slip about the moms' surprise party plans. I'm sorry that I forgot to mention it."

"I might forgive you . . ."

He brings his face close to mine. "If . . .?"

"If you tell me when and where, I can make sure Harvs is taken care of and Suzy is fine to cover me at the restaurant should any emergencies crop up and—"

"Firstly, Harvs can come too."

My mouth drops open.

"And second, it's three weeks from today, and I've taken the entire weekend off, so if you and Harvey want to stay with us for those nights, I'd love that. Jake has even been asking about seeing Harvey again."

My head jerks back, my mind spinning like a Ferris wheel on overdrive as I try to catch up.

Instead, I lean my forehead to his and breathe through it until my heart stops racing. Because it may have only been ten weeks since I first laid eyes on this man, but I've fallen head over heels in love with him.

"Dee?" he whispers, his voice thick. "Is this a good moment or a 'shit, he really screwed up' moment? Because I really wanna kiss the hell out of you, and we've gotta get home to my kid."

"It's an 'I can't believe you're real and you're here and that you're mine'."

"Dammit. Now I wanna fuck you, and we can't do that in the car on the side of the road. It would be just our luck for Gio to be on patrol and catch us."

A giggle escapes my lips at that prospect.

"You're mine too, Dee. I'm yours and you're mine. That's how this works. We'll take it slow with the kids, but I can't stop how I feel about you."

"And how's that?" I whisper, my heart pounding against my chest.

"You know I love you," he says, like it's a foregone conclusion.

The side of my mouth quirks up. "Well, considering I just worked out that I'm in love with you, too, that's news to m—"

Rhodes shuts me up by slamming his mouth on mine and thrusting his tongue between my lips. I grip his shoulders, his jaw, and do everything possible to get as close as I can to him.

When we pull apart, I stare at him with wonder, my breaths coming hard and fast as I try to slow my heart rate.

Rhodes's blue eyes roam my face as his perfectly parted lips suck in much-needed air. "I'm the luckiest bastard in the world."

I shoot him my most wicked grin. "How about we go home and test out just how *lucky* you can get."

Chapter 17

Rhodes

"I'm impressed that Dee is still sticking to the running," Marco says as he drives the rig toward the elementary school we're on our way to visit. "She's not up to our distance, but considering we're training for something specific and Ezra told me she's not a running kind of girl, it's surprising."

My lips quirk up. "Maybe I give her good incentive to come with us."

"Like?" Scotty pops his head between the two front seats.

"Your ears flapping?" I ask.

"Nope. Just looking out for my favorite lieutenant," he says with a shit-eating grin.

Marco snorts and shakes his head. "Stop kissing ass just because Rhodes doesn't give you as much crap as I do."

Scotty shrugs, making me chuckle. "Maybe. Or maybe you're already hooked up and happy, and I like seeing Anderson smile. He's a bit easier on us when he's not so . . . *tense* . . ."

"Damn, Scotty. Them's fighting words," Luca calls out from behind us. "He'll have you on muck-out duty for weeks if you keep this up."

"Nah," Scotty replies, slapping my arm. "Rhodes has always looked out for me."

"I could look out for you a lot better if you weren't poking the Rossi bear over here and sat your ass back in your seat."

"Damn, Lieutenant. That's cold. I was being nice too."

I roll my eyes and smirk at Marco.

"By the way, does Dee have a sister? I watched one of her videos, and da—*fuck*." Scotty rubs the back of his head, and I turn my head to find him glaring at Luca. "Luc, what the hell was that—ouch. Quit it." This time it's Zach on the end of Scotty's none-too-impressed glare. "Stop whacking my head."

"Was seeing if I could knock some brain cells loose. You forget we *know* you, Jones. I'm not sure we'd willingly let you loose on any single woman."

"Thanks for the vote of confidence," he grumbles. "Must be good at something if Hayley came back for more."

Marco growls and spears Scotty a death stare in the rearview. Hayley is Renee's sister. She and Scotty had a one-time thing earlier in the year, but as far as we all know, it was once and done. *Apparently not . . .*

I glance at Scotty to find his hands up in the air in surrender, his eyes locked on Marco's in the mirror. "Okay. Okay. No talking about that."

"Smart man," I snort before facing the front again.

Soon enough, Marco is pulling into a no-parking zone outside the front of the school. "Right," he says turning round in his seat. "Cap says this is a straight demo and show-n-tell. Nothing flashy. Just take a group and give them a tour of the truck, let them turn the sirens on if they want, and then the teacher will get some photos of them in the driver's seat."

"How old are these kids?" Zach asks. "Seems a bit pre-K."

"Nine and ten. This is a part of their careers-week curriculum I'm told. They each signed up for things they were interested in. This is the first-responder group."

"All good. We all know how much Jake liked to hang around the firehouse when he was younger," Luc says, bringing a smile to my face.

"Yeah. And now I barely see him 'cause he's always out *driving*," I mutter.

"That boy has goals. He's not gonna fuck it up by doing anything dumb, and if he does, he's got three firefighters and a cop to ride his ass. And that's *before* Connor and Don even get involved," Marco says with a smirk. "Anyway, he's a good kid. He has to be— he takes after his godfather."

"*Say hello to my little friend*," Luc says in a terrible Al Pacino impression, holding up one hand and then two, and then making a show of slapping Scotty around the ears.

"Hey! Quit it," the man screeches, making us all laugh, which we're still doing when the front doors to the administration building open and a middle-aged woman appears, followed by two lines of kids, many of whom are almost pushing each other out of the way to look our way.

"Rhodes!" A familiar, excited voice says. I search the group and sure enough, there's a wide-eyed and amazed Harvey waving then pointing my way and talking to the guys around him.

"You're so gonna make his fucking day, aren't you?" Marco murmurs.

I nod. "You're right about that." Then I step forward to greet the teacher and introduce us to the group.

Forty minutes later, all the kids have looked around the rig, asked a million questions, and taken turns at trying gear on. This is part of the job that never sucks.

"Harvey Duncan, can you come up to the front and help me with a little demonstration?" I ask, watching Harv's eyes go wide and his friends' expressions turn to shock, wonder, and envy.

He stands and walks over to where Marco, Luca, and I are waiting in front of the group of sitting kids.

"Hey," I say when he reaches us. "This okay?"

"Um . . . *yeah.*" I can tell he's trying to temper his excitement, but there's no missing the way he's holding his shoulders back and his little chest is puffed out.

"Okay," I reply with a nod before turning my attention back to the group. "So, when there's an emergency, and a fire engine is needed, the dispatcher—that's the person who takes the call when you call nine-one-one—will give the call a priority depending on whether it's urgent or not. Then the bells at the firehouse will ring out. That's when we have to jump into action, and we have about a minute to get our gear on and hop into the fire engine and hit the road. So, I decided we should make a bit of a competition out of this." I turn to Marco and Luca and wave my arm at them. "Marco and Luca here are brothers, and they're always wanting to beat each other—at *everything.*" I reach into my pocket and pull out the stopwatch I stashed there for this very moment and hold it up for everyone to see. "Harvey is going to be in charge of the timer, and when he says 'go,' the guys are going to race each other to see who can get geared up the fastest. So, with a show of hands, who here thinks Marco—the oldest brother—is going to win?" About two thirds of the kids put up their hands. "And what about Luca? Who thinks he can beat his big brother?" The rest of the children signal their support.

I turn toward Harvey and hold out the stopwatch. "Okay. So, in a moment, I want you to yell 'go' and then stop the clock whenever the first person has finished putting their helmet on. Sound good?" I say, earning a beaming grin and an unmistakable nod.

"Right." I check that Marco and Luca are set with their gear in front of them.

The rest of the guys standing in a line at the side watching with amusement as the brothers nudge each other with elbows and gesture to the kids to make some noise.

"Okay, everyone, be quiet so the guys don't miss Harvey's signal." I nod down at Dee's son, and grin at him. "Ready bud?"

"Yep."

"It's all up to you now. You start them off whenever you're ready."

"On your marks, get ready, and *go!*" he yells, and the guys jump into action while I give a running commentary as the Rossi boys do what they do best—work as fast as possible while joking and jonesing around with each other.

They're putting on their turnout gear and suspenders, then head cover and jackets. When they're neck and neck, Luca quickly slips his helmet onto his head and raises his hands over his head in victory with a big "Done!"

Harvey's eyes widen as he quickly stops the timer and lifts it up my way.

I make a show of widening my eyes like it's the fastest time I've seen. "Wow! That was done in fifty-five seconds flat! Let's give Marco, Luca, and my helper Harvey here a big round of applause," I announce, joining Harvey's classmates as they clap and cheer. I give Harvey's shoulder a squeeze. "Thanks, Harvs. You can help me anytime."

"That was *awesome!*" he whispers. "Best day ever!" Then he gives me a hug around my waist and runs back to his friends.

"Now *that* makes it all worthwhile, man," Marco says, bumping my shoulder.

What can I say? The man isn't wrong.

DEE: You certainly made my boy's day today. He called me as soon as he got home and raved about you. I think you're his hero.

Rhodes: He's an awesome kid.

Dee: And you're a good man who made my son feel like the king of the world and most popular kid in the class today.

Dee: Which means now I'm feeling kinda grateful.

Rhodes: Is that so . . .?

Dee: Such a shame you're working until tomorrow and I have a private breakfast event I'm catering for in the morning.

Damn.

Rhodes: You do know that this is torture, right?

Dee: Have you eaten yet?"

Rhodes: Not yet. Scotty and the new candidate, Kyle, are on cooking duty, and Scotty tries to put that shit off for as long as possible, usually until someone gets sick of waiting and just cooks instead.

Dee: Can you hold them off for an hour . . .?

Rhodes: Yeah. Why . . .?

Dee: Tell them dinner is being delivered in an hour and the wait will be worth it.

Rhodes: Sweet cheeks, what are you up to?

Dee: That's for me to know and you to find out.

Dee: But I promise you . . . it's not only going to be worth it for the guys . . . See you soon.

I turn around from where Luc, Marco, and I are chilling on the couch and let out a high-pitched whistle. "Dinner's being delivered in an hour, so, Scotty and Kyle, you better go make sure the rig is squeaky fucking clean and ready to roll out for our next call."

"What's on the menu?" Scotty asks, looking like a kid on Christmas morning who got everything he asked for.

"Don't know. Don't care. Whatever it is, it'll be fucking delicious. So you better get to work, otherwise I'm sure the guys and I can sit back and make sure no food is wasted."

"I thought you were my friend," Scotty says with a pout.

I snicker and shake my head at him. "I am. But if my woman is feeding you lot, you can bet your ass I'm making you work for it."

"Dee's bringing us food?" Luc asks, suddenly all on board with this conversation. When I nod, he gets to his feet. "Then I'm gonna help them with the rig, because I remember how good her food was at the BBQ, and that's all the incentive I need to get the chores done before she gets here." Then he's rounding up Scotty and Kyle, and the three of them walk out toward the garage.

"Food deliveries. Someone scored brownie points today, didn't he?"

"Harvey? He *definitely* did. Dee is just *grateful* . . ."

Marco smirks knowingly and shakes his head. "Yeah. *Sure.* That's exactly why Dee is bringing food for the crew halfway during a shift." He leans in close. "And 'cause I'm your best friend, I'll keep the guys distracted so you can give her a *tour* of the firehouse."

"You *are* a good friend."

"Indeed. But don't worry," he says, straightening and shooting me a wink. "I'll cash in the favor you now owe me some other time."

Shaking my head at him, I can't help but chuckle. "Of course you will. What else are friends for?"

Just over an hour later, Dee walks in, her arms laden with four big catering trays as she comes through the door. Luca and Scotty rush to her side before I can even get there.

"Damn that smells good, Dee. What did you bring us?" Scotty asks, taking two of the trays off her hands.

"There's lasagna, green salad, those buffalo chicken wings you all loved at the BBQ, and then my specialty Greek orzo dish. And in that one . . ." She points to tray Luca has just placed on the dining table. ". . . there's dessert for now or later. All of it will keep in case you get a callout too," she says before turning her body toward mine. "Hey, honey."

"Hey," I say, wrapping an arm around her waist and kissing her lightly on the lips. "You've probably just become Firehouse 101's favorite person."

Tilting her head, she smirks at me with amused eyes. "Is that such a bad thing? Especially if it means I can visit you occasionally."

I dip my chin to bring my mouth to her ear. "You can visit me whenever you want, baby. My day was already good, but you've just made it even better."

She winks, her lips curving into a devilish grin as she lifts her hand to my chest and flexes her fingers against my shirt. "I'm sure there's still room for improvement."

Fuck yeah, there is.

I look over my shoulder and meet Marco's eyes, and with a jerk of his chin, I know I'm covered for at least a while—or until the bells ring.

After taking her hand in mine, we walk out of the living area and along the corridor, toward the back of the station. "So, do you want a tour?" I ask.

"I want to know where your office is." There's absolutely no mistaking the low husky tone in her voice. My Dee is feeling grateful, and who am I to deny her—even though I'd never want to in a million years.

As soon as I've led her into my office and shut the door, she's pressing my back against it and crushing her lips to mine. With a groan, I grab her hips and hold her to me, letting her control the kiss for as long as I can stand it before I drag my arms up her back and into her hair. I chase her tongue with mine and deepen the connection, swallowing her moans as we attack each other's mouths hungrily.

She tears her lips from mine, running them over my stubbled jaw and down to my throat as my hands roam over her back and ass, grinding my hard cock against her, desperate to feel more of her. "How long have we got?" she whispers, dragging her teeth over my neck.

"Not fucking long enough," I grind out, loving the feel of her but wishing I could lay her out on my desk and bury myself inside her. The memory would definitely improve my mood when doing paperwork later.

She straightens and brushes her lips against mine, pinning me in place with her heated gaze. "Guess I'd better get to work." She drops to her knees and works my belt open before I can even utter a single word. Quick as a flash, she reaches inside my pants and pulls me out before locking eyes with mine. She wraps her lips around the tip and swallows me whole.

"*Fuck, baby,*" I groan just as the head of my cock hits the back of her throat.

I rest my hand on top of her hair in the way she likes me to do, watching as she takes me down deep, humming against the sensitive skin and sending jolts of pleasure through my entire body. When she adds her hand to the mix and strokes me tightly in rhythm with the searing hot heat of her mouth, there's no way in hell I'll last long.

Still jerking her hand up and down, she moves to my balls before laving them with her tongue and humming. The vibrations make it hard to hold on to any self-control I'm fighting to keep. The whole time, her eyes stay aimed at me. "I'm going to take your cock in my mouth, and you're going to take what you want. I want the *boss* to take what I'm offering him," she says before she does exactly that, lifting her lips to the head and swirling her tongue around the sensitive skin before taking me deep again, lightly running her teeth against my aching shaft as she pulls out and does it all over again. Then she moans and reaches around, grabbing the globes of my ass in her palms and pushing me deeper, until I can't stop rocking my hips.

The erotic sight of my cock disappearing between her lips drives me closer to the knife's edge. "That mouth . . . *damn*," I grunt.

When she smiles victoriously, her lips stretched tight around my cock, I snap, thrusting in and out. Her moans and whimpers fill my ears as I push deeper and deeper. The sight of her own hand diving between her legs and knowing she's getting off on this is all it takes for me to shove between her lips again and again.

As soon as Dee's throat tightens around the head of my cock, I lose the fight. And with a flex of my fingers against her hair as my only warning, my vision turns white as I growl out my release, my hips jerking as she swallows me down, only stopping when I gently ease her off me.

With her hand still working between her legs, I'm already moving before she knows what I'm doing. I carry her over to the bed lining one side of my office and lower her onto it, jerking her shorts down her legs before diving in face first. Her back arches off the mattress as she quickly buries her face in my pillow, and I suck her swollen clit between my lips at the same time that I push two fingers inside her. I go at her hard, wanting to give back just as good as she gave me, ignoring my reinvigorated cock in the meantime. This is all for Dee, and the entire world could catch fire and it would not stop me from making her come right now.

Thank fuck it doesn't take my girl long—she's so turned on and on a hair's trigger already—I thrust my fingers deep and curl them up as roll my tongue over her clit, and then the sweet, muffled sound of her climax wracking through her fills my ears.

When she finally comes back to earth, I'm kneeling on the floor beside her head. Dropping my lips to hers, we taste each other as we kiss, lazy and slow.

A satisfied smile transform her face. "Best. Day. Ever."

"Love you, Dee."

"Love you too, honey. Also, *really* loved *that*."

"Me too. It was worth missing out on the food."

"Well you *did* eat . . ." she says with wicked grin.

My lips twitch. "So did you."

"Touché."

"Indeed. Now let's get cleaned up, and *maybe* Marco did me a solid and saved me a plate."

She shrugs and holds out her hands for me. I pull her to her feet, then we quickly set out to right out clothes again. "If he didn't, there's plenty where that came from. I have an in with the chef, you know . . .?"

"Hmm." I lean in and take one last, long, slow and deep kiss. "I think I have an *in* with her too."

She laughs against my mouth, and I enjoy every second of it. "Good. Because you can be *in* her, whenever you want."

"Or just with her. Because sometimes, seeing her is just as good."

"Dammit. I have to kiss you again. You can't say sweet, swoony stuff like that and *not* expect me to kiss you.

I can't help grinning at her and leaning in so she's all I can see. "Have at it, sweet cheeks. Never gonna stop you doing that."

Chapter 18

Dee

"Why are you looking peaky?"

"I'm not. I'm fine. *Perfectly* fine."

"Sure you are. That's why you're pacing a path into the rug," Flynn says, looking amused from his stretched-out perch on our couch. "Why are you nervous? You weren't worried when you met my parents for the first time."

"Because you were raised by Mr. and Mrs. Cleaver. I just had to play the nice, respectable girl, who their son wanted to sleep with—I mean *date*—and charm them with my perceived innocence."

Flynn arches a single brow. "Nice . . . respectable . . . *innocent?* Dee, we'd been banging for about three months at that stage."

"Yes. But *they* didn't know," I snap.

Flynn rolls his eyes at me. "Well, they sure as shit guessed when we got caught making out in the back seat of my dad's Buick."

The memory of that night makes me gasp. "Oh my god. I'd forgotten about that."

He tilts his head and looks up at me. "Bet you're not nervous now."

I bite my lip and shake my head. "Thank you."

"Honestly, you're an easy sell, but if I was in Rhodes's shoes—a widow, a single father, and not dating for how long did you say?"

"Six years."

His eyes widen. "There you go—*six* years—then the decision to introduce the woman I've been seeing for the past three months is not one I'd make lightly. Which *means . . .*"

"Which means he *wants* me to meet them and for them to meet me." I study him for a moment. "And how are *you* with me and Harvs meeting the parents and going to this party tonight?"

Flynn swings his legs over the side of the couch and leans his elbows onto his legs. "Honestly, I'm happy for you. I wondered how it would feel, you know—you dating, putting yourself out there, but Rhodes kind of . . ."

"Fell into my lap?"

Flynn chuckles and shakes his head. "The way I heard it, it was *you* that needed saving, and there was no falling-into-laps involved."

"Okay, two things. Stop talking to my brother, or mother, or whoever is giving you the goss."

"Father. But carry on," he muses.

My mouth drops open. "I never thought *Dad* would be the one to rat me out." Flynn, Dad, and Ezra play golf every now and then. Flynn does it a lot for networking, as does Ezra, and Dad is just a retired old man who wants a reason to get out of the house occasionally to have time to himself without Mom giving him a honey-do list.

"Hey," Flynn replies, holding his hands in the air. "I do kind of know what's been going on. You've been giving me the friendly cliff-notes version—which I appreciate by the way. You've gotta ease me into this whole 'the mother of my kid is dating another man' situation."

"Yeah, unlike you, I've had a bit of time to get used to you and Sophie."

He points at me. "See. Exactly. It's not easy, but—"

"Life never is."

"Nope." He pushes to his feet, crosses the room, and puts his hand on my shoulder. "Now, to end this little TED Talk—stop pacing, stop being nervous, and go powder your nose or something. Not that you need it, because you're beautiful, and you're going to impress every single person you meet tonight. But the fact you *are* nervous tells me that Rhodes is a good man and must be worth it, because *you've* cooked for celebrities and didn't even break a sweat."

"I love him, Flynn," I murmur.

He leans down so his eyes are on my level, his lips curved into a wry smile. "I know you do. This is a good thing, sweetheart?" He straightens, kisses the top of my head, then steps back. "When are you going to realize that men like Rhodes and I will do absolutely anything to earn the love of a good woman like you."

"And Sophie," I add, watching as Flynn's expression softens.

"And Soph."

"And we're set for you to pick up Harvs from Rhodes's place in the morning?"

"Yep. It's all sorted. Harvs has packed all his stuff for tonight, and he made me promise I'll be there at nine a.m. sharp, because—"

"You pinky promised you'd take me indoor rock climbing this weekend, and a Duncan man never goes back on a pinky promise," Harvs announces, walking into the room looking cute as hell and far too grown up in a bright blue button-down shirt and black jeans paired with his favorite—and thankfully clean—pair of white sneakers.

"Son . . . did you maybe spray some of my body spray on?" Flynn asks. He bites his lip and tries hard not to laugh and also gag, because as soon as Harvey entered the living room, it's like we've been transported smack bang into the toiletries aisle at Walmart.

The boy at least has the decency to look a little guilty. "Um . . ."

A snort escapes my lips before I can cover it with a cough, and I don't miss the twitch of both Duncan males' lips.

"At least let me rinse *some* of it off, Harvs. You don't wanna clear everyone's nostrils at the party."

"What do you mean?" Harvey lifts his arms and smells under them. "I think I smell awesome."

"You smell like your dad, but also like you've *bathed* in it, baby. It's the same as with chocolate, less is more."

That seems to make sense to him. Flynn winks at me and leads our son to the main bathroom .

About five minutes later, I'm upstairs checking myself in the mirror one last time and grabbing my overnight bag when Flynn calls out from downstairs. "Dee, Rhodes is here."

I grab my bag, give myself a spritz of my Coco Mademoiselle perfume, and make my way down the stairs, remembering the first time Rhodes picked me up and Flynn answered the door and how nervous I'd been. Ironically, now I'm excited every time I see the man I love get along with my best friend and father of my child.

My past and hopefully my future intermingling—it's more than I could've ever hoped for.

"Hey," I say as walk down the stairs. Rhodes tips his gaze my way, and going by the flash of heat in his eyes, he approves whole-heartedly. I'm wearing a bronze-colored silk cami underneath a relaxed linen blazer, my favorite skinny black jeans, and leather knee-high boots. It's smart, sexy, and I knew it would grab Rhodes's attention and keep him distracted if *he* was nervous too.

He takes my bag out of my hand when I reach him and wraps

an arm around me, brushing his lips gently against my cheek. When I look over at Flynn, he nods approvingly at me. Harvey is standing beside Jake talking his ear off and oblivious to anything except him.

"We'd better get going. If I'm going to pretend I have no idea that this party is happening, then I need to arrive on time or else my mom will have a conniption."

"Good to see you again, Rhodes. Don't be a stranger on my account," Flynn says as the two men in my life shake hands before he turns to Harvey and ruffles his hair. "Bye, kid. Be good, and I'll pick you up tomorrow morning. Rhodes said he'll make sure you're ready by nine."

My head jerks to Rhodes then Flynn, and I begin to wonder how much I missed. "Um . . ." I say, a little freaked out.

Flynn smirks and leans in, dropping his voice to a stage whisper. "You be good too, Dee. And don't be nervous."

My mouth drops open as Rhodes chuckles beside me and squeezes me tightly.

"Let's go, guys. We don't want Grandma Anderson blowing up my phone." Jake laughs, Harvey smiles, looking adorably confused but joining in on Jake's amusement.

We're at the bottom of the front stairs when Flynn calls out to us. "Rhodes, look after them for me."

"Always, Flynn."

"Yep," my ex-husband replies, looking between us with an intense, warm gaze. "I know you will."

This is not just a goodbye . . . This is a *moment*—a passing of the torch. My tear-filled eyes meet Flynn's soft ones, and it's clear that was Flynn giving Rhodes his seal of approval, and that means more to me than I ever thought possible.

Rhodes didn't miss it either. He pulls me into his side and presses his lips to my temple and holds me there. "C'mon, sweet cheeks. Parties to be surprised with, kids to feed, parents to introduce you to."

Nodding, because I can't trust myself to speak, I blow a kiss to a smirking Flynn and let Rhodes lead me to his truck.

I wonder what I could call a video where I'm so deliriously happy that all I want to eat is candy. Maybe 'Foods to Make when Life is Good.'

———————

"SURPRISE!"

"Happy Birthday!"

"Woo-hoo! Party time!" Both Scotty and Harvey yell. *Heaven help me.*

I try to step away from Rhodes to give people the opportunity to greet and hug him, but his fingers tighten in mine and keep me there.

"There's my boy," says a short, sprightly woman with curly brown hair and a huge, warm smile as she embraces Jake. "As handsome as his father."

"Ugh, Mom. I'm right here. You know, your *actual* son?" Rhodes teases, earning narrowed eyes from his mom.

"I *suppose* you're alright," she adds with a smirk before she wraps him up in a hug. Then she turns that bright smile my way, and I'm suddenly being released by Rhodes and pulled in for my own big welcome. "And you, Dee, you're as beautiful as Rhodes says. I'm Nora—Rhodes's mom if you hadn't guessed."

My head jerks to my smiling boyfriend. "You talked about me?" I mouth.

His brows bunch together and he tilts his head. "Why wouldn't I?" he mouths back.

"Don, my husband, told me you made videos on the internet, so when Jake came over, I got him to show me some." She leans in close. "I hope it's not weird, but I made a couple of your recipes for tonight."

My heart swells and this time it's me pulling her in for another hug. "I love that. It's very sweet."

"Would you believe that Jake made some not-so-subtle suggestions about *which* dishes we should do for the party, then got Don involved, and before I knew it, the two of them had planned the entire menu *and* written the grocery list for ingredients."

"You've trained them well," I say with a wink.

Nora turns to Rhodes with a beaming wide grin. "Ah, yes, I totally like her already."

Her son claims me once again, reaching out to tip my face up to meet his. "That's good, because I do too," he murmurs before laying a hard and fast kiss on my lips right there in front of his *mom.*

"Happy birthday, son," A deep voice announces. Turning my head, I'm met by identical blue eyes on a handsome, older version of Rhodes. And when he smiles, I swear I've fast forwarded into the future and I'm getting a glimpse into what Rhodes will look like in twenty to thirty years. Going by his dad, the future is looking bright for me if we go the distance.

"Damn, son. You do have all the luck, don't you?" Rhodes's dad teases, holding his hand out my way. When I slide my palm against his, he leans in and winks. "I'm Don, and I've taught my son every-thing he knows."

"Grandad, stop," Jake groans.

"What's he doing?" Harvey asks.

I press my lips together as my body shakes with silent laughter. Rhodes claims me back. "Stay away, old man. She's mine."

"I'll win her over. You know I will."

Resting my head against Rhodes's shoulder, I give up the fight and giggle at him. "He's totally just like you."

"Except I'm much more charming and handsome, right?" he asks, quirking a brow.

I nod overenthusiastically. "Oh yes. For sure. Absolutely."

Nora laughs, the sound as endearing as tinkling bells. She's totally the kind of mom I imagined would have raised Rhodes. She's all soft and sweet and full of joy, but you can tell she's the boss of the family. *Just like my mom, and just like me.*

There's another older couple standing off to the side, hand in hand, their curious gazes on us.

"Nana!" Jake calls out, walking toward them hugging them both affectionately.

Rhodes slides his hand into mine and puts his mouth close to my ear. "That's Connor and Celeste, Lily's parents. Do you still want to meet them?" He lifts his head, his gaze focused on my face as he waits for my answer.

Therefore, there was never a question for me, not about this. I nod and give his hand a squeeze, lifting up on my toes and lightly kissing his cheek. "No time like the present."

By the time we reach them, Harvey is beside Jake and telling Lily's parents all about the firefighter visit to his school and how awesome it was. They both listen to his every word, and it's only when Harvey looks across the yard and spots Marco that his attention is diverted. And after waving a quick 'bye,' he's tugging Jake's arm to go join the fire crew. That leaves Rhodes and I standing in front of Connor and Celeste, silence stretching between us.

I smile at Lily's mom first, then her dad. "Hi. I'm Dee. It's an honor to meet you."

Celeste's mouth drops open before it transforms into the most beautiful smile—the same one I've seen in the photos of Lily back at the house. "It's nice to meet you too. I'm Celeste, and this is my husband, Connor."

"Hi, Connor."

"Hey, there yourself, Dee. I must tell you, we went to your restaurant last year. The food was amazing."

My smile brightens. "Thank you. I must not have been working that night, but I'm glad you enjoyed it."

Celeste leans in. "Connor is a little bit obsessed with your desserts. When Rhodes told him who he was bringing to meet us, he made me watch your lava cake video and make it for him."

Upon hearing that, Rhodes throws his head back and bursts out laughing, earning puzzled looks from his in-laws. "Everyone is in love with Dee's lava cake. Jake even stole my phone before Dee cooked for me for the very first time and requested it in a doggy bag."

Celeste giggles, and the sound is so mom-like it warms my heart.

"I might have to get some cooking tips off you."

"You don't need any help, lovely. You've always kept me well fed. I mean, look at this belly." Connor rubs his stomach and grins over at me. "This is not the body of a man whose wife doesn't know how to cook."

While Celeste blushes and moves closer to her husband, Rhodes presses his lips to my temple. "See, what did I tell you? Nothing to worry about. I love you, so they love you."

He's right. I don't even know why I was nervous. Actually, I do, but having met Nora and Don, and now Connor and Celeste, I had nothing to worry about. And with that knowledge, I finally relax completely.

"MOM? Can I sleep in Jake's room?" Harvey asks once we're back at Rhodes's house.

We stayed at the party for almost four hours—enough time for everyone to devour Celeste and Nora's amazing food, sing 'Happy

Birthday' to Rhodes—with Jake and Harvey helping to blow out the forty candles on the cake—and for Don to give a heartwarming speech about how proud he was of his son. He also welcomed Harvey and me to their crazy family.

IT WAS A FUN NIGHT, and now I have an amped up ten-year-old boy who is excited to spend his first sleepover with his new teenage idol.

"I dunno, baby. You've got this awesome big bed in here, and Jake's probably not tired yet. Maybe you can just see him in the—"

"Hey, Harvs. I was thinking," Jake says, popping his head through the guest-bedroom door. "Do you wanna come bunk in with me tonight? You know, just in case I wake up scared in the middle of the night or something. It'd be good to know I've got a friend there. I've even set up a mattress on my floor for you."

Not for the first time tonight, I have to push my tongue against the roof of my mouth and blink rapidly to stop myself from crying like a mushy girl.

"Mom, can I?" Harvey asks hopefully.

"Sure, baby. Jake might need you."

Harvey rolls his eyes, not so clueless after all. "Okay. Yeah sure." His tone totally suggests he thinks *I'm* the clueless one, and it makes me smile.

Having settled the boys in and making sure Harvey is okay, we say goodnight, and Rhodes leads me by the hand along the hall to his room before shutting the door behind us. "I love you. Do you know that?"

"Yeah."

"You were spectacular tonight. I would never have thought you were nervous at all."

"I wasn't—" I narrow my eyes. "Flynn told you, didn't he?"

"Yep."

"Not sure I'm over the moon about my ex and my boyfriend colluding together," I mutter, looking away.

Rhodes cups my jaw and turns my eyes to his. "And I'm not sure of the last time I've felt this happy, and it's all because of you."

I tilt my head, my chest tight and my heart fit to burst. "I haven't even given you your birthday present yet either."

"Hmmm," he says, pulling me close and dipping his mouth to my neck. "I was planning on unwrapping *you* as my gift. What is it?"

I try to hold back my giggle. "Axe-throwing lessons."

He slowly lifts his head, the sight of his wide eyes and parted lips has me laughing.

"Really?"

I shake my head, still snickering. "No, but the look on your face was priceless. I've actually booked us a weekend away in Boston for some time later this year." His expression turns from surprise to smoldering.

"You planning on putting up with me for that long, sweet cheeks?"

"Maybe I was hoping you'd stick by *me* till then."

"For a dirty weekend away?"

"Mmm hmm . . ."

"With you naked the *entire* time . . ."

"That could . . . be arranged . . ." I moan.

"Uninterrupted adult alone time?"

"Absolutely."

"Fuck yes. Best birthday ever," he says before he puts a shoulder to my belly and picks me up, carrying me into his bathroom.

"What are you doing?" I shriek, wrapping my arms around his waist as I hang backward.

"Birthday rules apply, which means whatever the birthday boy wants, he gets." He ever so slowly drags my body down against his hard-in-all-the-right-places one.

"And what *do* you want?" He reaches out to turn the water on in his big walk-in shower before gripping my hips again.

"I want you naked and wet and rubbing up against me."

I bite my lip. "Is that *all* you want?"

"We'll start there and see what pops up."

Looking between us, I quirk a brow at his tented pants. "Doesn't seem to be a problem in that department yet, old man . . ."

"Fuck it," he mutters, then I'm up in the air again and he's carrying me fully clothed into the shower, getting the both of us dripping wet and distracting me with his mouth and other body parts until the water ran cold.

It seems Rhodes *is* right again. Best. Birthday. Ever.

Chapter 19

Rhodes

"I'm off, Dad," Jake says, popping his head through the living-room door.

I turn my gaze toward him from where I'm sitting on the couch with Dee's head in my lap as we watch a movie. "What's the plan?"

"Driving to Linc's place to hang out. Might go get some food, otherwise, I'll just stay there and come home by eleven."

"You need money for gas?" Dee asks, making me smile. I love how she treats Jake as if he's her own.

My son's eyes soften at the woman in my arms. "Nah, I'm good. Thanks though."

"Just don't eat crap food. If you're gonna do takeout, at least make sure it's *good* crap food."

His lips twitch at that.

I snort and glance down at her. "Good crap food?"

"Yep." She grins up at me.

Shaking my head, I meet her eyes. "You're such a food snob. I should've known."

"No, I'm a crap food connoisseur."

"Who would've thought? My top chef is a takeout puritan."

Her eyes darken.

"Hello? Kid here," Jake says, his voice full of humor. "Yes, Dee. I think the plan was pizza. So probably Lou's. Not as good as *yours*, of course, but it'll do in a pinch."

Dee nods. "I'll allow it."

Glad you approve," Jake mutters. "See you when I get home."

"Drive carefully and no funny business."

"Yeah, Dad." He turns toward the front door.

"I'm serious, kid," I say, gently easing myself off the couch and following him.

"I promise, Dad. Not gonna screw up, especially not when I've got my sweet ride to look after."

"Trucks can be replaced. You can't."

"I know," he murmurs. "I've got my phone tracking on. Feel free to stalk me as much as you need to. Engage the parents collective. Whatever makes you feel better. Got nothing to hide and nothing to lie about."

I hook my hand behind his neck and bring my forehead to rest against his. "Sorry. I trust you. It's other people I don't."

He snorts and cups my shoulder, giving it a squeeze before straightening. "I know. I'll be good. See you at eleven. Love you, Dad. Bye, Dee," he calls out before he grabs his keys from the rack and leaves the house.

I rejoin Dee and get settled again, lying behind her and wrapping my arm round her waist as she restarts the movie.

We did good with our kid, Lils.

I imagine if she *could* talk to me, she'd be rolling her eyes right now and saying '*Stop talking to me and enjoy your night.*'

"You okay?" Dee asks, snuggling in deeper.

I nuzzle my lips into her neck, my hands starting to roam her front. "Mmm hmm . . ." I try to ignore the niggling bad feeling in my gut and focus on Dee.

"Are we gonna make out like teenagers on the couch?" There's no missing the humor in her voice.

When I push myself up and brace myself over her, she rolls onto her back and pulls me on top of her. My eyes roam her face, and again I'm hit with just how lucky I am to love and be loved by this woman. "Yep."

Her lips curve into a salacious grin. "Excellent. 'Cause Dad won't be home for *hours*."

And that's how I end up laughing and kissing her at the same time . . . and missing the rest of the movie, because with Dee in my arms and an empty house, there was no fucking chance I was ever gonna *concentrate*.

WE MUST'VE DOZED off on the couch, because the next thing I know my phone is buzzing on the floor.

Dee stirs and burrows deeper into my chest. "What time is it?" she mumbles.

"Dunno. Could be Jake calling though. Haven't heard him come home."

"Hmm," she hums as I reach over her and pick up my cell, frowning when I realize it's nearly midnight and Cohen is calling.

"Hey, Co," I say, my voice still thick with sleep.

"Rhodes. It's Jake. He's been in a MVA. He got clipped by a car running a red."

My entire body goes still, and Dee must feel it 'cause she quickly sits up, her hand resting on my chest as she watches me.

"Is he okay?"

"Yeah. I'm here for the other driver, but I checked with the other crew when I recognized Jake's truck. He's bashed around and probably has broken ribs from the impact and seat belt, but he's fucking lucky, man. They're cutting him out 'cause his door was smashed shut."

I can barely breathe as my heart thumps against my chest like a battering ram trying to crush me. "Where are they taking him?"

"Northwestern. ETA twenty once they get him out."

"I . . . shit, man. I can't . . ." I can't speak. I can't think other than to go straight to the worst-case scenario.

Dee eases the phone from my hand and puts it to her ear. "Co? It's Dee. I've got him. We'll meet you there. And hey, can you give Marco a heads up." She looks my way as I stand, my body finally reacting. *Jake. My boy. Fucking late for curfew and some asshole crashes into him. I wanna throttle him and lock him in the house till he's thirty all at once.*

"Yep. We're leaving now. And thanks, Co. See you soon." Dee immediately takes control—grabbing our coats, getting me into the car, and driving us toward the hospital. The whole time she's taking calls and making them. She calls my Dad on my phone and asks him to call Connor to let him know.

All I can do is sit there and stare out the window, struggling to even comprehend that my boy was hurt and I wasn't there for him.

Dee reaches over and squeezes my knee. "It's gonna be alright, honey. Cohen said Jake was conscious and coherent, just a bit shaken and scared. As soon as he sees you, he'll be fine. Don is coming too, and Marco and Renee have already left."

I nod and cover her hand with mine, but I can't talk. The words won't come. Until Jake's in front of me and I can see with my own eyes that he's in one piece, I won't be able to breathe easy.

Look after our boy till I get there, Lils.

WE'RE unable to see Jake when we arrive, and although they say he's stable, I'm told I won't be able to see him while they're checking him over. I even tried to pull some strings with some of the ER staff I recognize, but rules are rules. Co comes and sees me before he has to leave as he's still on duty and explains they're sending Jake for a CT to check for internal bleeding and clear him of anything serious. As far as I'm concerned, they can give him the works as long as it means he's okay.

Mom and Dad arrive about fifteen minutes after we do, and we all sit in the family waiting room for what seems like hours.

Marco, Renee, and Gio come too, G updating me on the details of the accident that he's learned so far. Apparently the other driver failed a field sobriety test on the scene and walked away with scrapes and bruises. He's been checked out by a doctor and was discharged into police custody. Jake's truck, however, is wrecked.

Dee has not left my side except to get us coffee refills. She's been my anchor in the storm, and I'm not even sure I would've gotten here without her taking charge.

We've been here for three hours, and it's after three in the morning. I hold Dee in my arms and she rests her eyes on my shoulder.

"You okay?" Marco asks, having sent Renee home with Gio.

"No," I reply honestly. "Shouldn't have let him go out tonight."

"You can't keep him locked up. He's a good kid. What happened tonight wasn't his fault."

I nod once. "Yeah. But I could've taken note of the bad feeling I had in my gut. Something felt off, and I ignored it."

"You gotta admit, as far as teenage shenanigans go, Jake's been an angel."

"Compared to some of the stuff you got up to, boy, my grandson is a fucking saint," my dad adds with a small smirk. "Marco's right though. You can't wrap him in cotton wool and protect him from everything."

"I can damn well try!" I say, a little louder than I meant to. "He's all I've got left of her." This time, my voice is barely a whisper.

Dad's eyes soften. "He is, but he's not. You've had a good woman, and it broke all of our hearts when she had to leave us. But now you've got a son who's almost grown, a fine, strong woman sleeping in your arms, and your memories. Jake is almost a man. He's going to make mistakes like missing curfew and being in the wrong place at the wrong time. We all did it, and we all know he'll probably do it again. You can't stop it. All you can do is make sure he learns from it. Show him he scared you, tell him it shaved twenty years off your life expectancy getting that phone call, but remember what it must've felt like to be a sixteen-year-old kid, on your way home, and then having your life literally crashed into."

"Fuck. I just need to see him."

"Mr. Anderson?" the doctor says from the waiting room door.

Dee stirs, and I dip my head to kiss her hair. "Gotta go talk to the doc, sweet cheeks. Stay here, and I'll find out when we can see him. Yeah?"

She nods and tips her face up. I brush my lips against hers and make my way toward the door, taking one step and one breath at a time.

STANDING THERE at the edge of the room, my entire body shakes with anger and fear and relief—all of which are fighting for supremacy. Finally having him in front of me, I check every single body part is intact from his toes to the hair on his head.

His eyes slowly open, and his head turns. "I guess that's my NBA career over, Dad. Better call the scouts." But the smirk on his lips is strained.

His eyes are glassy, and from the splint on his arm and the gash above his right eye, I'm guessing he's in a bit of pain. Before I came in, the doctor gave me a full run down: two broken ribs from the seat belt, broken wrist from the steering wheel, a gash on his forehead from hitting the side pillar instead of bulls-eyeing the glass, and whiplash. He's fucking lucky he didn't get more injuries but I'm also thankful as hell that I'd taken him driving in all kinds of weather conditions so he knew how to react.

I cross the room and lean over the bed, bracing myself against the mattress as I hold my head to his temple. "Fucking scared the shit out of me, kid."

"I'm . . . sorry, Dad. So fucking sorry."

I lift up and meet his eyes, finding them filling with tears, and my heart stutters, because the last time I saw my kid cry was five and a half years ago. He had a nightmare and came running into my bedroom calling out for Lily. Right now, having just had another version of a nightmare, it's written all over his face that he's been waiting for is to see me. My heart splinters at the thought of him being scared and alone.

He throws his good arm behind my shoulder and clings to me. He buries his face in my chest and lets it all go. Knowing my boy, he's been holding this in since the crash. Sobs escape him, his entire body shaking with them. "So . . . rry. I was. . . and then . . . out of nowhere . . . scared I wouldn't see you."

"It's gonna be okay, Jake. I swear. You can break bones, and they can heal. But you, I can't lose you." My own eyes sting, but I don't fucking care. Seeing my only son in this hospital bed has brought everything back to me.

I straighten and gently lay my hand on his shoulder, staring into his bloodshot eyes and swallowing the giant lump in my throat.

"Don't you *ever* scare me like that again. I lost your mom, and it destroyed me. I can't lose you too. I wouldn't survive that."

He nods and pulls me in for a hug again.

A throat clears behind us. Standing up, I turn to find Dee's big green eyes shining our way. "Hi. Um . . . the nurse said I could bring your dad through."

I nod, turning back to Jake as Mom, Dad, and Dee walk over. I expect Dee to come straight to my side, but instead she stands at the foot of the bed, all her attention on my son.

Again, there's something weird niggling at me, but I dismiss it because I'm tired. I'm relieved. As dad said, I had years shaved off my life tonight, and everyone I love is in this room, safe and sound —albeit a little battered and bruised.

At least one thing is for sure, Jake will be homebound for a good few weeks after this, which means I'll have time to calm my nerves about letting him out of my sight again.

Hopefully.

Until then, I'm sure Dee will keep him well fed with all the lava cake and comfort food he could ever want, and Harvey can play games and entertain him.

Our family—by blood and by choice—will rally around us like they have tonight and coddle him until he's one hundred percent again. Then life will be back to normal.

Chapter 20

Dee

A week later

Monday

Rhodes: Hey, sweet cheeks. Do you wanna come over tonight?

Dee: Hey. I'm not sure when I'm gonna be able to leave the restaurant. Then I want to spend some time with Harvs.

Rhodes: Okay. I missed you last night.

Dee: While you were working and saving lives?

Rhodes: I miss you whenever you're not here.

Fuck, he's killing me.

Dee: We'll catch up soon. Maybe I'll pop round tomorrow and see Jake.

Rhodes: Not me?

Dee: Well, you'll be there too.

Rhodes: Okay. Text me later when you're home.

Dee: Will do.

Wednesday

Rhodes: Sitting in my office doing paperwork and remembering the last time you were here.

Dee: You mean when you cleared your desk and had your way with me on it?

Rhodes: Yeah. That particular memory is distracting as hell.

Dee: Does Jake need anything? I can call by there on my way home later.

Rhodes: He's staying at Connor and Celeste's tonight. No way will they not spoil him.

Dee: Okay. That's good.

Rhodes: Everything alright?

Dee: Yeah.

Rhodes: You seem a bit . . . distant. That's all.

Dee: Everything is fine, honey.

FRIDAY

Jake: Hey, Dee. Thanks for the lunch delivery. Thanks for letting me be your lemon lava cake guinea pig. I volunteer to be your food test dummy at any time.

Dee: Hey. You're welcome. Hope you're feeling better.

Jake: Yeah, I am. You should've delivered it personally. I wanted to say thank you.

Dee: You just did.

Jake: I mean for coming to the hospital and being there for Dad. I know it can't have been easy for him. I'm glad he has you.

Shot to the fucking heart, kid.

After seeing Rhodes and Jake a few times this week, I can now admit that things definitely aren't fine. And the fact I've been blowing off Rhodes all week—not sleeping over there, barely spending more than an hour here and there with them—I can sense he's now realizing it too.

But I can't help it. I'm a girl, and sometimes we overthink and twist things in our heads and can't get past it. That's where I'm at now.

Things have been so easy, so fast, so intense with Rhodes that I fell into a comfortable lull where I went with the flow and didn't stop to think about anything else. I love the man. There's no question in my mind that he'd ever do me wrong. If things keep going the way they're going, I can see us having a long and happy life together.

The problem is with me. I let a seed of doubt settle in my brain and allowed it to take hold, to burrow in and grow, digging in roots and making itself at home. And try as I might, it's been at the back of my mind ever since I saw Jake and Rhodes together in that hospital room and the words they shared, ever since I heard Rhodes, Marco, and Don talk in the waiting room.

And it all comes down to one big, formidable force that I don't feel I can ever equal. Lily.

I lost your mom. I can't lose you too.

He *lost* his wife. He didn't *choose* to leave her. There was no *choice*. The decision was taken out of his hands. Fate had other plans. And now he has me, and I love him more than I loved Flynn—my *husband*—yet I'll never be able to truly know if it'll ever be the same way for Rhodes when it comes to me.

I've been questioning that and struggling with it ever since the night of Jake's accident, and with it comes guilt, sadness, disbelief that I could even fathom being jealous of a dead woman—a wonderful, amazing, spectacular woman at that. I've been asking myself if I can live the rest of my life feeling this way, always wondering, never relaxing, feeling I have to prove myself, not fully trusting whether his feelings for me will be enough. It's a *me* issue, not a Rhodes or Jake issue or even a Flynn issue. It's all me, and until I can sort it out in my own head, I know I won't be able to explain it to anyone else, let alone Rhodes.

SATURDAY

Rhodes: Saw your latest video.

My breath catches, and I struggle with what to reply. Stuck for ideas for a new vlog, I decided to do a video about food to make you smile when you're feeling down. I figured it would be cathartic, maybe help anyone out there struggling with much bigger problems than the one I'm wrestling.

Dee: Did you like it?

Rhodes: I always do. But you weren't yourself, baby.

Dee: I'm okay.

Rhodes: Honesty policy, sweet cheeks. You're either lying to me or lying to yourself.

Dee: I'll be okay.

Rhodes: Wouldn't mind seeing that for myself. Why don't I come pick you up and I can make sure you're alright?

Dee: I can't tonight. Flynn has plans, so Harvey and I are having a mom/son movie marathon.

Rhodes: Maybe Jake and I could come over and join you then?

Dee: You won't wanna watch these ones. We kind of have a weakness for old-school Disney.

He doesn't reply for a while. And when he does, my heart aches.

Rhodes: Okay. Well, let me know when you want to do something? We haven't had much time alone since the accident, and I know I've been focused on helping the kid, but that doesn't mean I can't see you as well. You're important to me, Dee. I hope you know that. I love you.

Dee: I know. Say hi to Jake for me.

Rhodes: Will do. Call me later?

Dee: Yeah, if I don't fall into a junk-food coma.

Rhodes: You're a takeout snob, remember? No way you'd let anything bad pass those lips.

Dee: True, but everyone needs popcorn and cheap, greasy pizza now and then.

His next message doesn't come through for a few minutes.

Rhodes: I know something is wrong, Dee. I hope you know you can talk to me. You can tell me if things have changed . . .

"Why do you look like someone just ran over your puppy?" Flynn asks, startling me.

I jerk my head his way to find him studying me. "I'm fine."

"Yeah," he says, pushing off the doorframe and walking over to the one-seater chair next to the couch. "And you forget that I can read you like a damn book. So quit the bullshit and talk to me."

"I'm fine."

He arches a brow. "You said that already."

"Well, I am."

"Then why have you been here for the past two weeks and not stayed with Rhodes at all? Did something happen?"

"No . . ."

"Dee . . ."

"What?" I snap.

Flynn's eyes soften. "Talk. To. Me."

"I can't. Harvey will come in soon, and—"

"Our son is in the shower. So, you've got a good ten minutes until I have to drag him out to save all the hot water. What's wrong? You've been . . . not yourself."

"It's dumb."

"Nothing's dumb if it's bothering you."

"Okay. *You'll* think it's dumb."

"Try me."

I tilt my head. "Aren't you going out tonight?"

"Nope. So, you're stuck with me. Now tell me what's wrong. Maybe I can help untangle whatever it is that's tying you up in knots."

"I'm just being a silly girl who can't stop thinking that sometimes things are too good to be true."

"You mean Rhodes?"

"Yeah."

"Why?"

I scrunch my nose up. "What do you mean why?"

"I mean exactly that. Why are things too good to be true?"

"You wanna know?"

"Wouldn't have asked otherwise, sweetheart," he says matter-of-factly.

"I can't explain it."

He huffs out a breath. "Then don't explain it. Tell me. Break it down. Does he make you happy?"

"Yes."

"Did something happen that made you *un*happy?"

"Well, no, not really . . . Maybe?"

Flynn shakes his head and reaches out to touch my arm. "Now *that* you have to explain."

"I'm just struggling with the idea that our situations are different."

"Us?"

"Well, no. Mine and Rhodes."

"You've lost me. You're both single with kids. You like each other, you spend time together. Harvey loves seeing them and staying over. I'm not seeing the problem here."

"Isn't it strange for you, seeing me move on?"

"It was, but I've been waiting for you to get out there and go after what you want for a while. When we spilt up, it was because we loved each other enough to want the best out of life, and we knew that it wasn't going to happen by staying married. Now, I've moved on, but you've been in limbo."

"But—"

"Then you met Rhodes, and I started to see that old Dee that you'd lost over the years. The one who lights up a room whenever she walks into it. The one who smiles at a man and makes his day. You had a new spring in your step, and you seemed like you'd finally found your happy."

"Flynn . . ."

He shakes his head. "No. You're missing my point. This isn't about knowing I couldn't give you that anymore. That ship has sailed. Rhodes helped you find yourself. He was the kind of happiness you've been looking for. And don't say he's not, because I know that man loves you. It's clear as day whenever I see him look at you. So I have one question, and I'm invoking the honesty policy, because we've never lied to each other and we're sure as shit not gonna start now."

"Okay . . ." I hold my breath as I wait for the proverbial axe to fall.

"Why are you not letting yourself have that? What's changed?"

I look down at my hands, my mouth suddenly dry as I try to breathe through the tightness in my chest.

"You and I *chose* to separate. We *chose* to not be together anymore."

"And . . ." Then his eyes flash as realization dawns. "You're shitting me?" he says in disbelief.

"I told you it was dumb."

"It's not." He leans forward and places his finger under my chin, lifting my eyes to meet his. "What's dumb is that you're sitting here talking to *me* when you should be talking to the man in question."

"I can't," I whisper.

"Why?"

"Because what if I'm right? What if he tells me he could never love me as much as he loved Lily? What if—as much as he wants to, as much as he tries—I could never be *that* woman for him?"

"You'll never know unless you talk to him, and avoiding the issue is just making it worse because it's going to fester and turn bad. Don't let that happen, Dee."

"I'm trying not to."

He glances at my phone then back to me. "By making excuses not to see him?"

My eyes jump wide. "How do you—?"

His lips curve into a knowing smile. "'Cause I know you, Dee. You don't spend over a decade with someone and not know everything about them. Rhodes has had four months. He's still learning about all the little nuances that make up Delilah Baker, and unless you stop avoiding him and start *talking*, that man has no idea what's going on in that cute little head of yours. Right now, he's probably just as confused as you are and wondering what he's done to push you away."

"But he hasn't done anything."

Flynn leans in, eyes still locked to mine. "*Exactly*," he says before moving to his feet. "Now. I'm going to save our water-heating bill from further damage, and you can think about the fact that maybe —this time—your issue, while valid, is also all in your mind. You can't work through it without talking to the man himself. Believe me, putting your head in the sand doesn't solve anything. We both know that. We did it for the whole last year of our marriage when we knew things had changed but couldn't admit it. Don't make the same mistake twice, Dee. Rhodes is everything I could've ever wanted for you. Let him be the one to fix this."

"You mean fix me?"

"Whatever it takes, sweetheart. But this time, I can't do it. It's down to you. Any answers you need, he's the only one who can give them to you. Not to freak you out even more, but I'm starting to think he's the only man who can give you everything you've ever wanted. And, Dee?"

"Yeah?"

"That's the only thing I've ever wanted for you."

Chapter 21

Rhodes

Enough is enough. I've tried to give Dee space. I've tried to be understanding. But after almost two weeks of Dee not being herself, it's time to call her out on it. I'll use our damn honesty policy if I have to, but all I know is that when she comes to see me tomorrow night, she's not leaving until she tells me the truth. Because there's nothing worse than having all of someone and knowing without a shred of doubt that they're the person you see a long-lasting future with, than having them pull away without any obvious reason or explanation.

Even Jake has sensed something is up. That's why I gave him Dee's phone number, so he could text her the other day. I figured if it was something I'd done, at least she wouldn't brush my son off. And I was right. She didn't. Ever since the accident, she's been present, but just . . . different. Well, whatever caused the change is about to be fixed or I'll go down fighting.

Rhodes: Can you come over tomorrow night? I think we should talk.

Dee: Okay.

And that's all I get. No 'What do we need to talk about?' or 'Is everything alright?'.

Fast forward twenty-four hours, and Dee's car is pulling into my driveway. I arranged for Jake to stay at my mom and dad's tonight, and I was honest with him about the fact that I thought something was up with Dee and I needed time to talk it out with her and make sure everything would be okay. He was wholeheartedly in favor of it and even had the cheek to ask, "What took you so long?"

I already have the front door open when she moves up the front path toward me. Her body language is tense, almost defensive, as if she thinks she's approaching battle.

Surely she knows by now that I'm all for 'making love, not war.' I'm also not about to let her walk away without a damn good reason why. We didn't fight, I didn't lie to her or stand her up, or do anything else that could warrant her version of 'silent treatment.' It hasn't even been silence, she's been distant, which is decidedly worse. "Hey," I say, leaning into the doorframe.

"Hey." She stops in front of me like she doesn't know what to do.

I step forward and run my fingers through the hair at her temple until my hand is cradling the back of her head and I have her eyes on mine. I relax a little when she leans into my touch. "You're a sight for sore eyes, sweet cheeks."

"I was here a few days ago."

"Yeah. You *were* here." I step in, bringing our bodies in close. "But you weren't *here*." Then I lower my mouth to hers and kiss her soft and slow, my fingers flexing in her hair as she melts into me, chasing my tongue with hers.

When I pull back, her lips are swollen and her eyes are a hell of a lot more relaxed than when she first arrived.

"Feeling better yet?"

Her teeth dig into her lip, but she doesn't answer me. Taking that as at least *some* progress, I reach out and grab her hand and walk inside before closing the door behind us and leading her into the living room.

She places her purse on the coffee table and looks around. "Where's Jake? I thought he'd be here."

"He's at Don and Nora's. I told him you and I needed time alone to talk."

Dee's mouth drops open. "You what? Rhodes! He's still recovering. You didn't need to kick him out of his own house."

I pin her in place with a pointed stare. "Yeah, I did. But no, I didn't kick him out. Mom and Dad love having him there, especially Mom. She can fuss and fawn over him and make him all his favorite foods while Dad has a buddy to watch all the sports he wants with. It's a win-win situation for everyone."

"But—"

"*And* I wasn't lying to my kid about why I wanted the house to ourselves. We need to sort this out, Dee, and we need to do it without any distractions." I give her a moment to collect herself and walk past her and through to the kitchen. "Would you like a drink?"

Her head spins around and she shoots me an adorably confused look. "Um . . . sure. A wine?"

"Well, look at that, I have your favorite white right here in the fridge waiting for you." I pour her drink and grab myself a beer before handing her the half-full glass.

"Rhodes . . .?" she asks as she takes it from me.

"Yeah?"

"What are we doing?"

"We're about to sit down, have a drink, and then talk."

She nods jerkily before following me to the couch and taking a seat. Her posture anything but relaxed.

I wait for her to say something—anything—but she's too busy gripping her wine glass in both hands. *Fuck it.* I need to know what the hell is wrong so that I can start working toward making it better again.

"Dee?" She turns her head my way and takes a deep breath, slowly closing her eyes before reopening them. "Baby, you've gotta talk to me. Tell me what's wrong. If I don't know, I can't make it right, and there's no fucking way I'm letting you hold me at arm's length, not anymore. Not when you gave me all of you and I made a promise to myself that as long as I could, I'd never let you go. What we've got is too good, too special, too important . . ."

"I know," she whispers. "I've just been trying to work through some stuff in my head."

I move over, ease the wineglass out of her hold, and place it on the table before covering her hands in her lap with mine. "Tell me, Dee."

She shakes her head and squeezes her eyes shut. "I can't."

"You can't what?"

"I can't talk about it."

I rub my palms over the back of her clasped hands. "We can't get past this if I don't know what I'm up against." Searching her eyes for clues, there's worry and concern there as she bites her lip and averts her gaze.

"Look. We don't have to talk about this now. It's been a long day, and I bet you're tired too. Why don't we just go to bed, and we can discuss this in the morning," she says, trying to delay our conversation.

It's only eight o'clock, and that's early even for us. When I narrow my eyes, she releases a resigned sigh as if hoping I'd let this go for tonight. *Wishful thinking sweetheart.* "I'll have absolutely no problem taking you to bed once you tell me what the hell is wrong," I say.

"Please, Rhodes. I want to talk. I do. It's just . . ."

"I think it needs to be now. Because to lay it all out there, I didn't find you after six years of *not* finding you, to give up without a fight. You've been different ever since Jake's accident. Was it that? Did that scare you? 'Cause I swear to god I get that. I was fucking terrified."

"I know, and I hated that for you. For all of you."

"So it *was* that? Baby, that's not something you work through by yourself. You do it with people who are going through it with you. Is that why you've been putting space between us?" I ask, my heart easing a little because this is something I can deal with.

Her head jerks from side to side, and my heart jumps in my chest at the wide-eyed look of worry covering her face. "I can't. It's stupid. It's something I just have to get through. I'm sorry I haven't been here. I never meant to . . . I mean . . . I was just trying to process stuff on my own, and I couldn't do it when I was with you."

I frown, because that makes absolutely no sense to me. "Sweet cheeks, we promised to be honest with each other, remember?"

She grabs her glass, downs the rest in one go, and leaves it on the table before walking over to the doors leading out into the back-yard. She stands there looking more beautiful than ever, gazing outside as if coming to a decision in her mind. She's quiet for a long time before she lets out a breath and breaks the silence filling the room. "Please don't hate me for what I'm about to say."

"Okay. I promise. Just tell me, baby. Please. This is killing me." I say, and yet she still can't look at me.

"These past few weeks, I've been wondering whether I can live the rest of my life being second best."

My head jerks back like I've been slapped. "Why would you ever think that?" I hold my muscles tight. Every part of me itches to jump up and go to her. But she needs to get this all out before that happens. "Dee, please look at me." Her body stills, and she slowly turns her eyes to mine. "You are not a woman who should ever be second best, and you have not—and never will be—with me. This is not our first rodeo, and we both have baggage, but never—not once —have I ever thought of you as runner-up."

"When we started this, I was a single, divorced mom. I made a *choice* to end my marriage with Flynn. It was a decision we made together, because we both knew that we were only holding each other back from future happiness."

I nod since this isn't news to me.

"But you *lost* the love of your life. You didn't *choose* to separate from her. She was taken from you, and that's something you can never get back."

My brows furrow. "I'm not sure where you're going with this. None of this is anything that we both don't already know."

She swallows hard, her eyes wet with unshed tears. "This is where I've gotten things twisted up in my head. I fully admit that."

"I love you, Dee. That's something I've only ever said to one other woman in my life. I don't take it lightly, and I mean it every single time I say it." There's a force behind my words, and I hope to hell she's hearing it, feeling it, and letting it sink in.

"I know," she replies quietly. "But I heard what you said at the hospital . . ."

I go completely still. *I* can't even remember what I said at the hospital. I was so worried about Jake and what his injuries might be that I was running on autopilot. "What did you hear?"

"That losing Lily destroyed you," she says, her voice breaking.

"It did. But I had Jake, and my parents, and the guys to help me through. And when Jake was hurt and in hospital, I had *you* by my side." Her head snaps my way and I push to my feet before slowly approaching her. "And it was *you* that got me to the hospital and stayed strong by my side until I could see him."

"Anyone would do that."

"I didn't need anyone to do that. I needed *you*." I stop in front of her. I reach out and cup her shoulders, turning her body my way, needing her full attention so that what I'm about to lay on her sinks in once and for all.

"Six months ago, a beautiful, sassy, enigmatic woman made my dead heart beat again, and she's continued to breathe life into me ever since."

Dee's mouth drops open with a soft gasp.

I smile down at her as I place my thumb under her chin and push it closed again. "Lily may have shown me I could love. *You* were proof I could love and let myself be loved like that again."

She stares at me with those big blue eyes of hers, and I know I'm getting in there.

"Did I choose to lose my wife? Fuck no. Would I want that to happen again? Absolutely not. But does that mean I should put my life on hold and never have the chance to fall head over heels in love with you?" I step closer, eliminating the last remaining space between us. "Should I have ignored everything I was feeling just from *looking* at you, before I'd even *met* you? Or do I tell you that it taught me life is too fucking short to lose one love of my life, let alone two? Especially when the love I feel for both is completely different, completely separate, and cannot be compared."

The well of tears in Dee's eyes finally break and fall onto her cheeks. I cradle her face in my hands and try to swipe them away with my thumbs.

"The one who taught me how to love was taken from me far too soon, and the one who changed my entire life and taught me to love again is standing in front of me telling me she thinks she can't be enough, when all she's ever been is too much. I love you, Dee. I love you in a way I've never loved anyone before, and that's because of Lily, not despite her. She's my history; you're my future. "

"Oh my god. I'm *such* an idiot," she whispers tearfully.

"No, you're not. You had a moment—we're all allowed those. But I'm not going to let *you* get in the way of *us*, and that's something I will never apologize for."

Her lips part, but she doesn't say anything.

"She would've wanted you for me."

Dee jerks at that statement before shaking her head. "No, she wouldn't. Because there's nowhere else in the world she'd want to be than by your side."

She trembles as I pull her body close to mine and I'm standing so close I'm all she can see. "You're right, but when she knew she wouldn't get the chance to be with us any longer, she made me promise I'd find someone who made me feel alive again, and loved, and like I'm one of the most important people in their world." I cradle Dee's face, tipping her chin so my eyes can lock with her wet ones. "The first time I saw you, something told me that would be you," I say, resting my forehead on hers. "And, baby, I wasn't fucking wrong."

Dee kisses *me* this time, and it makes me want to beat my chest and growl in victory. Her tongue spearing between my lips, seeking mine and tasting deep and long, both of us pouring all of our passion and fears into this kiss, as if we've spent years apart, not mere weeks.

When we pull apart, we heave in much-needed air, her nose scrunches up and she's glaring at me. "Don't call me, *baby*. 'Cause when you do, I swoon, and we can't have a serious, adult, potentially life-altering conversation if I'm weak at the knees and thinking about jumping you."

My eyes soften as my lips curve into a slow-growing, shit eating grin. "If it gets a reaction like *that*, there's no fucking way I'm going to stop calling you baby . . . *baby*." My voice is rough and low. "Besides, I know the look you get when you *want* to jump me."

Dee's eyes flash. "What look?" She tries to wriggle loose from my arms, but I tighten my grip and keep her right where she is.

I pin her with a stare and shake my head, my gaze never once looking away. "Oh, no you don't."

"This is important, Rhodes. We're talking."

"Not anymore we're not. We're done talking. You love me. I love you. We've untwisted whatever it was that had you doubting us, and *now* . . ." I lower my mouth to her ear. "I'm going to spend the rest of the night making sure you know it deep down to your fucking bones."

"Well, um . . ."

An amused grunt escapes my lips as I run my hands up her back and tug her body flush against my hard one. "You were saying?" I rumble.

"Maybe we should . . . Ah, fuck it." She jumps into my arms and her lips collide with mine. I turn around and push her back against the living room wall, caging her in as I plunder her mouth.

"I agree," I murmur as I run my lips along her jaw. "We should. Actually, we need to. I *definitely* need to. And from the way you're squirming against me, you do too."

She drags her hands through my hair and tugs my head up, touching her mouth to mine again.

"I love you, Dee, and I know I always will."

A sob escapes her and she crushes her mouth to mine before pulling away and burying her face in my neck.

"Hey. What's wrong?" I say, rubbing my hand over the back of her hair.

"Nothing. I'm just happy."

"Okay . . . so why the tears?"

"'First you were being sweet. Now it's because I'm ugly snot crying, and you'll never want to sleep with me again if you see me like this."

I chuckle, which earns a cute little growl akin to a baby lion cub. "I'll never not want to look at you, sweet cheeks, ugly snot crying or not."

She lifts her head and narrows her red-rimmed eyes at me, all brimstone and fire but still absolutely irresistible. "Prove it."

"With pleasure."

And that's all the talking we do for the next few hours other than 'yes,' 'more,' 'fuck,' and my favorite, '*please.*'

LYING in bed later that night with Dee draped over my side, her fingers drawing lazy circles on my naked chest, the only thing on my mind is how happy I am to have Dee back here where she belongs.

She lifts her head to look at me. "So, I think we need to expand on our honesty policy and maybe set some ground rules," she says, her voice soft and husky.

"Okay . . . hit me with them. There's a rule of my own I wouldn't mind implementing."

"Whatever happens, don't let me ruin this."

"I promise you, I won't ever let happen."

"So what's your rule then?"

I roll her to her back and lean over, holding her head in one of my hands. Locking my gaze to hers, I love how bright and clear her eyes are, gone is the doubt and fear I saw when she arrived earlier. Now I have my Dee back, I want more nights like this. In fact, I want all of them. "My proposed rule is that you think about spending every single night in my bed . . ." Her expression goes from relaxed to shocked to one of contemplation. Then, to my surprise, a slow-growing smile stretches wide over her face.

"I wholeheartedly agree."

"What?" I whisper with a laugh. "You will?"

"I mean, unless you weren't serious, then I—"

I shut her up by kissing her speechless, then that leads to another kind of celebration, which ends with us *both* yelling yes in far more satisfying ways.

"I love you, Dee. Best thing I ever did was accidentally stalk you," I murmur against her lips, earning a giggle.

"Maybe we should go thank that kid Pete. After all, if he hadn't run off with my purse, who knows if you'd have said hello."

"Oh, I would've. It might've taken you publishing a video called 'Food to Feed Stalkers You Want to Date,' but we would've crossed paths eventually. Nothing this good could be anything other than meant to be."

"Maybe I *should* film that video. Might see what other stalkers I have out there."

"Don't you fucking dare, sweet cheeks."

"Or what?"

"Or I'll tie you to this bed so that you can never leave."

Then she's laughing against my lips. "Don't make promises you can't keep, Rhodes Anderson."

"Believe me, Dee Duncan. That's one you can count on."

Epilogue

Rhodes

With Harvey and Dee walking hand in hand behind us, Jake and I make our way to the group of familiar faces already waiting for us. All of the crew are here including Zach, Scotty, Marco and Luca, along with Gio. There's also Cohen, Ezra, Bryant, and the other two Cook brothers, Jamie and Jax, along with their wives and children.

Gio makes a point of checking his watch. "You guys are cutting it close. Who's fault was it? Did ya take too much time doing your hair, Jake?"

Jake shakes his head and laughs. "Nah. Blame the parentals."

Everyone turns their attention to me. Dee's giggle gives us away. I hold my hands in the air. "Hey. Don't lay this all on me. Dee is just as complicit."

Ezra groans. "Dude, that's my sister."

"And mine!" Faith adds.

"And my mom!" Harvey joins in even though he has no clue what the joke is.

"What can I say? It's a Sunday morning, and for once, I didn't get dragged out to run."

"Decide to warm up another way, huh?" Scotty flashes a shit-eating grin, making the entire group groan and Marco whack the back of his head. He rubs his scalp and glares at my best friend. "What was that for?"

"There are kids present, idiot," Marco replies with a 'duh' voice.

"Jake's not a kid."

"No, but Harvey is." Marco jerks his chin our way.

"Oh, shi—shoot. Sorry, bud."

"It's okay. Mom and Rhodes said they were sleeping. It's important to rest before a big run. Right, Jake?" He stares up at my son, who grins at me then Harvey.

"That's right. How about we go and see my grandparents? They've all just arrived, and I *bet* Nana Nora brought us snacks for the walk."

Due to the accident, Jake hasn't been able to keep up his training with the rest of us. And when Dee and Harvey told us they wanted to walk the race as a show of support, Jake volunteered to do it with them, which lead to all the wives putting their hands up. Now what is usually a Firehouse 101 and Jake tradition has grown into a *rather* large event all in Lily's memory, making it all the more meaningful.

"Should we go register and start stretching?" I turn to face Dee, who's moved beside me. "You gonna help me stretch, sweet cheeks?"

Her lips tip up into a salacious smile. "I thought I did that a few hours ago."

"You did. That's probably why I'm feeling so lax and limber."

Her eyes dance with amusement. "Would've been hard to explain if you'd overexerted yourself though."

I lean in and rest my forehead on hers. "Would've totally been worth it." Then I kiss her gently. "I'm also thinking it's time we try and get Gio a girlfriend. Then he might have other things to keep him busy rather than watching the clock like a fucking hawk."

Renee sidles next to Dee and hooks her arm over her shoulder. "Funny you should say that. He told us at lunch yesterday he's advertised for a roommate. Says he's going to buy Marco out of his half of the house and take over the mortgage himself."

My brows lift at the news. It makes sense, of course, but Gio has always been a lone wolf and a bit of a homebody, much preferring to stay home than go out looking to get laid with Luca and Scotty. The fact he's willingly going to invite someone to share his house with him is an interesting development. "I wonder if Marco and I will get vetting privileges," I ponder, earning a snort from Dee and approval from Renee.

"We should volunteer our services," Renee says. "And make sure the roommate is female. If anyone deserves to live with a woman who'll keep him in check, it's Gio. He's always giving the rest of us shit. Maybe it's time for him to get a taste of his own medicine."

Dee laughs. "You're so mean."

"Hey. Do you remember who gave me shit right in front of you when we first met?" I say with a smirk.

Both of the girls snicker. "*And* called Marco to tell him what happened?" Renee nods.

"Well you *did* stalk me," Dee adds.

My mouth drops open. "I did no such thing, and I'll deny it until my dying days."

Renee winks at me "Yeah, yeah. We believe you."

I shake my head. "Anyway. I'm gonna go over with the guys. See you at the start line?"

"I'll be wherever you are," Dee says softly, lifting on her toes and giving me one last kiss.

"Move in with me?" I hold her to me and smile against her mouth.

"Considering I'm doing that *tomorrow*, I'd say you already know the answer to that."

"Just checking." I touch the tip of my tongue to her lips briefly before letting her go.

"Take care of my girl, Jake?" I meet my son's eyes over her shoulder.

"Done deal, Dad." Don and Connor walk beside him while Harvey is being doted on by my mom and Celeste behind them. To say Harvey has been wholeheartedly adopted by all of the grandparents would be an understatement, and he loves every single minute of it.

I meet Don and Connor's eyes and lift my chin. "You old men ready for today?"

"We were born ready, and even if we weren't, we'd still run anyway."

"Yeah, I know." My voice thickens with emotion. Dee reaches out and squeezes my hand, drawing my eyes to hers. "See you at the finish line, sweet cheeks."

She smiles and shines that bright light of hers my way. "I'll be waiting for you, honey. Go get ready. We've got a wonderful woman to remember today."

"That we do."

She's wonderful too, Rhodes, Lily says in my head. *Dee's exactly who I wanted for you and Jake. She's perfect in every way.*

So were you, baby. So were you. Then together with Don on one side and Connor on the other, we walk over to my other family and get ready to run for Lily.

Dee

"Moooom, do you know where my soccer ball is?" Harvey calls out from down the hall.

"It's in a box!" I yell back.

"Didn't we pack it in the box with *stuff* written on the side?" Jake shouts from the kitchen.

"I can't find it," Jake continues.

I snort and shake my head. "Why do we suddenly sound like *The Waltons*?"

"Who are the Waltons? Are they our neighbors?" Harvey asks, making me laugh out loud.

"Isn't that an old person TV program?" Jake bellows.

"Good night, John Boy. Good night, Elizabeth. Good night, Daddy. Good night, son. Good night, Mary Ellen . . ." I murmur to myself with a smile.

"I can't see any boxes with *stuff* on it. Maybe Dad is bringing it with him," Harvs hollers.

"I'll come and help you find it, Harvs. Gimme a minute," Jake offers. For an almost seventeen-year-old guy, he's really taken to the little brother concept like a duck to water."

Out of interest, I check the label on the box *I'm* unpacking and giggle when I see *'bedroom stuff'* written on the side.

"They all have *stuff* written on them," Rhodes replies, appearing in his—now our—bedroom doorway with two more boxes labeled *'Dee stuff'* on the side.

Looking up from where I'm sitting cross-legged on the floor, my lips twitching. "The word *stuff* has a lot of uses."

He pushes off and slowly stalks toward me—and it's totally a stalk, there's no other word to describe the long, measured strides and the hunger in his eyes. "It does, does it?" His voice is low and rough, and all kinds of hot.

I lick my lips and crane my neck as he stops in front of me. It takes everything I have not to squirm as he gazes down at me. "How about 'Honey, all the *stuff* you wanna do to me will have to wait till the kids are asleep?'"

"*Or*..." He bends and hooks his arms under mine, hoisting me up so I'm plastered to the front of him. "Maybe you can give me a taste of the *stuff* you want me to do to you later . . . hmmm?" His arched brow and sly smirk are my undoing.

I slide my arms around Rhodes's neck, and standing there, in the middle of our bedroom, with our sons still yelling a conversation back and forth, I lift on my toes and press my lips to those of the man who says I changed his life. What I realized six weeks ago when Rhodes asked Harvey and I to move in with him, is that before Rhodes ran to my rescue, I'd been treading water—and had been for at least two years. It's only since then I've felt myself moving forward and doing it while falling head over heels for the man who just makes everything feel so damn easy.

"Do you think we could lock the door. I'm craving a taste of *you*?" I murmur against his lips.

He groans and grips my ponytail, tilting my head to the side before spearing his tongue in my mouth and rendering me speechless. The hungry, carnal, desperate kiss drives all thoughts of *stuff* from my brain.

It's one of the ones where Rhodes is frustrated he can't lay me out and take me like he wants to, and I'm right there with him, meeting his tongue stroke for stroke, my hands roaming wherever I can reach until we're pretty much screwing with our clothes on.

When he finally pulls back, his pupils are huge, his gaze still promising to devour me. "I promise to make it up to you later. Then we can *both* taste each other," he mutters, his attention dropping to my mouth again.

Brushing my lips against his jaw, I step away and try to cool my jets. "I'll hold you to that."

"Fucking hope so. By the way, Flynn called, and they were about ten minutes away with the final load from the house."

"Okay," I say quietly, my throat tightening.

Rhodes's eyes soften before he wraps an arm around my shoulders and pulls me into his chest, his chin resting against my temple. "Hey. It's alright. This is a big day for everyone."

"It's just . . ."

"The end of an era?"

"Yeah. Kind of. It's not like we won't see him ever again."

"Considering Harvey is gonna be there half the time, and then there are holidays, events, parties. . ."

"I know. But it's different."

Rhodes puts enough space between us to reach out and cup my face, his gaze locking with mine. There's no jealousy or worry there —just understanding and so much love I can barely stand it.

"You'll never know how fucking happy I am that you're taking this chance with me, Dee. This is a huge step—for all of us—but whatever you need, whenever you need it, I'm here. Okay?"

"I love you."

"Thank fuck for that. Otherwise sharing a bed for the next fifty years could've been rather awkward," he replies with a smirk.

I tilt my head and scrunch my nose. "Fifty years?"

"Yeah. I figure if I can keep you till I'm ninety, then I might deserve you."

"Fuck," I whisper, placing my hands on his chest and leaning on him. "Now I really *do* want to lock that door. Stop turning me on when I can't do something about it."

As we're about to kiss again, the cross-house yelling match

resumes, and Rhodes chuckles against my lips, which might just be right up there with my favorite kisses.

"Flynn and Sophie are here," Jake calls out.

"Mommy, Dad's here," Harvey repeats.

"Coming!"

"You will be," Rhodes says before giving me a hard and fast kiss.

I giggle and step around him as I walk toward the bedroom door. "And *that* will have to tide you over until I do."

"I get you in my bed and in my life. Just knowing that is all I need."

I stop and look over my shoulder at him. "You say I changed your life, Rhodes Anderson, but while I was doing that, you restarted mine. And I'll love you forever for that reason alone." Then I move toward the front door to help my ex-husband and his girlfriend move the last of our stuff into the house my boyfriend and his son lived in with his late wife; the house that Rhodes and I are going to make our own.

Once again I'm stuck with how the most complicated situations on paper can turn out as if they were destiny in reality.

All I know is that I'm happy, my son is happy, and the man who caught my attention with 'Are you okay?' almost six months ago will never have a life without happiness again, because that's what we both deserve.

A few hours later, after Harvey's new bed has been successfully constructed under the watchful eye of project manager Jake, Rhodes and I walk onto the porch with Flynn and Sophie to see them off. "Thanks for your help today. We really appreciate it," I say to both of them.

"You're welcome. And we're all set for dinner at Delish next week?" Sophie asks.

I nod. "Yes ma'am. Table for six on Thursday, Rhodes's night off."

"Awesome. Well, have a good first night together in your new home, and we'll see you tomorrow." She turns to Flynn and kisses his cheek. "I'll just wait for you in the car, babe."

"I'll walk you out." Rhodes follows her and leaves Flynn and I standing on the porch alone.

"So," he says, facing me, his lips turned up on one side. "This is it, I guess."

"I don't know how to feel. Is that weird?"

Flynn chuckles and shakes his head. "Thank god. I was starting to get a complex that this was easy for you."

"It's not. It's . . . *different.* But it's good." I reach out and grab his hand. "It's the next step."

"It is. And I'm happy too because I can finally move on and not worry anymore."

My entire body jerks. "What?"

"Dee, all I've been waiting for is for you to find your happy. You've got a man who would move heaven and earth to see you smile, and that's all I ever wanted for you. Knowing you've got that . . ." He looks to where Sophie is getting into his car. ". . . I can enjoy my happy too."

I wrap my arms around him and hug him tight as he does the same to me. "We had a good run, but it's the right time."

"Yeah." He shifts back and presses his lips to my forehead. "And don't think you're getting rid of me that easily. I'm not going anywhere, sweetheart, and neither are you. We're still Dee and Flynn. You're still my best friend. We've just expanded our circle. And Harvs is gonna be fine."

"I know. You might even lose him to Jake at this rate. He idolizes him."

Flynn grins. "Maybe. But then again, I get a week of non-Jake time in between to win him back."

I laugh and shake my head. "True. So you're all set for tomorrow?" As part of our discussion about Harvey and I moving in with Rhodes, we decided that Flynn and Sophie would live in our old house and Harvey would switch between the houses

"Yep. We'll swing by tomorrow night and pick him up."

"Awesome."

"Okay. Time to go. I'll see you both tomorrow," Flynn meets Rhodes's eyes as he steps onto the porch, the two men sharing a look. Flynn holds out his hand to Rhodes. "Good luck with this one," he says, shooting me a wink.

"Thanks. Something tells me I'm gonna need it."

Oh my god. It's like I'm not even here.

Flynn laughs. "Have a good night."

Then he walks down the path to get into his car.

Rhodes wraps his arm around my shoulders and turns me into his side, dipping his chin and brushing his lips against my temple in that way that makes me melt. "Guess you're stuck with me now, sweet cheeks."

I tilt my face to his and smile. "Funny, I can't imagine ever feeling stuck when I'm with you. Just lucky."

Rhodes quirks a brow. "You offering to help me get lucky tonight?"

I snort and brush my lips against his. "Let's go get the boys, and we can talk more about how lucky you're gonna get once we're home from dinner."

Rhodes's eyes flash and suddenly my back is against the house and his body is pressed hard against mine. "Say it again."

"Lucky?" I whisper, earning a growl.

"Not that."

"*Home . . .*"

"Love hearing that from your lips. Home. Mine. Yours. The boys. *Ours.*"

To stop him being so damn sweet I might jump him, I kiss him instead, which is exactly how the boys find us five minutes later.

"Eww, gross," Harvey says.

"Don't worry, Harvs. You'll get used to it," Jake replies.

Rhodes and I stop kissing and start laughing.

Be happy, I hear in my head. Except this time it's not Flynn saying it.

It's what I imagine Lily Anderson would sound like.

The End

Gio and his new roommate will feature in Miracle Worker - Preorder HERE

Also, sign up to my mailing list to be alerted when the next book in the series releases.

Other Books by BJ Harvey

Romantic Comedy

Bliss Series

Temporary Bliss (Bliss #1)—Mac and Daniel

True Bliss (Bliss #2)—Kate and Zander

Blissful Surrender (Bliss #3)—Sean and Sam

Permanent Bliss (Bliss #4)—Mac & Daniel's Wedding

Finding Bliss (Bliss #5)—Noah and Zoe

Game Series (Bliss series spin-off)

Game Player (Game #1) —Matt and Mia

Game Maker (Game #2)—Zack and Danika

Game Saver (Game #3)—Cade and Abi

Game Ender (Game #4)—Thomas and Amy

Game Breaker (Game #5)—Cameron and Sarah

Game Planner (Game #6)—Jase and Natalie

Cook Brothers Series (Game series spin-off) - House Flipping Rom Coms

Work in Progress — Jamie and April

Work Violation — Jax and Ronnie

Working Back — Bryant and Faith

Hard Work — Cohen and Skye

Working For It — Ezra and Gilly

Chicago First Responders

(Cook Brothers spin-off)

Show Stopper — Marco and Renee

Life Changer — Rhodes and Delilah

Holiday Romance

Stranded (Christmas novella with Bliss connection)

Romance Suspense

Lost Series

Lost in Distraction (Lost #1)

Lost For You (Lost #2)

Lost Without You (Lost #3)

Standalone

Crave

Contemporary Romance

Chances Series

One Shot (Chances #1)

Second Chance (Chances #2)

Third Strike (Chances #3)

Sovereign Series

Touch (Sovereign Part One)

Taste (Sovereign Part Two)

Feel (Sovereign Part Three)

About BJ Harvey

BJ Harvey is the USA Today Bestselling Author of the Bliss Series. She also regards herself as a smut peddler, suspense conjurer and a funny romance thinker upper. An avid music fan, you will always find her singing some hit song badly but loving every minute of it. She's a wife, a mom to two beautiful girls, and hails from the best country in the world—New Zealand—but currently lives in Perth, Australia.